. . . and so the running dog

By the same author:

Trans-Africa Motoring
Trans-Asia Motoring
Trans-Africa (*in Italian*)
Trans-Asia (*in Italian*)

... and so the running dog

Colin McElduff

SERENDIPITY

First published in 2002 by
Serendipity
Suite 530
37 Store Street
London

ISBN 1 84394 020 5

Printed and bound by Bookcraft, Midsomer Norton

I dedicate this book to Gillian,
my wife and soul-mate
whose enthusiasm was an inspiration

Author's Note

Fact is often a basis for fiction and it may be synonymous of some of the stories told, for many of the incidents did occur in one way or another.

The characters, apart from those referred to in the historical sense, bear no resemblance to any persons living or dead, as also Alexander MacIntyre. Any resemblance is purely coincidental.

Colin McElduff
Dumfries 2002

Contents

List of Main Characters

Background

The Government of the Federation of Malaya in June 1948 were forced to declare a State of Emergency because of accelerating outbreaks of terrorism. The Pan-Malayan Federation of Trade Unions, a Communist organisation, instigated strikes throughout the country causing labour unrest, and armed bands began to roam the countryside forming estate workers into quasi military units. These units were drilled and armed with weapons recovered from caches made by the Malayan People's Anti-Japanese Army (MPAJA). At the end of the war it was difficult to ascertain exactly how many weapons were in their possession, and many firearms in pristine condition, ammunition, grenades and explosives, air-dropped during the occupation, were concealed together with surrendered Japanese arms.

The wartime guerrillas (the MPAJA) made hidden armouries throughout Malaya to ensure that they could take up arms again in the future. It transpired that their secret aim was to take over the Government when the time was right and replace it with a Malayan People's Republic backed by China. In north Johore the situation became grave; a rubber estate was seized and held for a month by armed Communist agitators.

At this time the newly established Federation of Malaya Police were far below strength and not fully trained, likewise the units of the Malay Regiment. The Brigade of Gurkhas (also not yet up to strength) and two battalions of British troops were the only other forces available for active service. The very nature of the attacks by the terrorists, and afterwards the ability of the groups to disappear at will into the dense jungle and swamp which covered four-fifths of the country, made it virtually impossible for these forces to cope.

The Government's only option therefore was to increase the size of its own services by recruiting from abroad Police and Army Officers with recent jungle warfare experience. They were needed to take charge of Police districts, and train and command jungle squads and the newly formed paramilitary Police Field Force, which was based on Army lines.

The latter enabled the Army to hand over to the Federal Police the military commitments of some areas.

The main terrorist targets were rubber and palm oil estates, mines, and the workers within, road and rail transportation, Police, Army, civilians, and vulnerable people such as Aborigines and timber-felling labourers who lived or worked in deep jungle. It was difficult to cover them completely, and the latter were intimidated into becoming a source of food supply for the Malayan Races Liberation Army (MRLA), which was more usually known by its Chinese title of Min Yuen. These timber felling groups, commonly called timber *Kongsis* were invariably Chinese and worked for contractors who operated under the control of the Forestry Department and were vital to the economy of the country; the nature of their work entailed large amounts of food being consumed which was always under threat of being stolen.

Lt. General Sir Harold Briggs, KCIE, CB, CBE, DSO, was appointed Director of Operations in April 1950. His task was solely the execution of the Emergency and to ensure that the maximum effort was effectively directed against the terrorists by the Security Forces and the Civil Administration. By this time it was realised there was no quick or easy way to end the Emergency, since the terrorists killed were quickly replaced by others. Consequently, he conceived an overall plan of action which became universally known as 'the Briggs Plan'. Basically, the objective was to break the Communists' morale and to remove or disrupt their sources of supply.

It was now clear that the thorn in the side of the Government was the Chinese squatters (market gardeners and casual labour), who had taken to living in clearings on the jungle edge, in odd corners of estates and on open ground near towns and villages. These squatters were defenceless against the terrorist who demanded food from them; it was easy for one with a hidden weapon to pass himself off as a squatter.

It was therefore vital that these sources of supplies and concealment for the terrorist should be eliminated and that the squatters should be brought into what was to become known as 'New Villages'. All Chinese farmers and squatters were therefore transported into these newly designated villages which were surrounded by wire and protected by Special Constables (SCs) and Home Guards. Similarly protected were the Malay *kampongs* and estate and mine workers' living quarters. All food supplies were brought in under armed guard and no-one was allowed to take food out under any circumstances.

The plan worked well despite the great upheaval of people, mostly Chinese, throughout the country. As Security Force operations continued in the years ahead the terrorists, deprived of their source of food, were driven deep into the jungle where they preyed upon the aboriginal dweller who, in turn, was brought under the influence of the forts built for their protection. These forts were manned by the Police Field Force who patrolled and protected the Aborigines' gardens, or *ladang*. The very presence of the forts denied the terrorists food from the jungle dwellers and the Communist Terrorists (CTs) were eventually starved out of their last place of retreat.

One of the most important aspects of the emergency was the dissemination of information received from enemy sources in the form of surrenders, arrested persons or captured documents which were often found from hurriedly evacuated camps. The public also played their part in providing verbal and written information which often had to be translated. It was essential that to achieve good results in the field a very high level of intelligence was required and this was supplied by the Police Special Branch which was expanded throughout the Force and would not have attained its goal without the co-operation and loyalty of its Straits born Chinese officers. Nevertheless, the long years of the emergency exacted their toll of casualties on the Security Forces; in the beginning it was easy for the terrorists to choose their targets without casualties to themselves since their actions were hit-and-run with the element of surprise always on their side.

Police casualties in particular were high, especially at the beginning of the emergency when European Police Sergeants were recruited. The rank was abolished and Police Lieutenants were introduced and bore the brunt of operating throughout the country without adequate armour and back up, working between the many vulnerable points, the mines, the rubber and palm oil estates, and all in single vehicles; the thin-skinned bodies of Land Rovers were death traps in an ambush. Many also lost their lives in jungle operations and leading Surrendered Enemy Personnel (SEP) squads. Terrorists were encouraged to surrender and many were found to be fully co-operative, both in actively leading the Security Forces in pursuit of the unit they had just deserted and in revealing all they knew, except that which would have incriminated themselves. Their immediate use was to guide Security Forces to their last camp and, if found empty, to proceed on to the likely route the unit may have taken. Other camps, vital food and arms dumps, and known routes their ex-comrades used, were all vitally important pieces of information.

Last but not least, there was the Marine Branch of the Police who operated in all weathers in converted naval Motor Torpedo Boats in which heavy machine-guns replaced torpedo-tubes. They worked with their Naval counterparts to combat gun-runners and the boats patrolled along the coastal reaches up the Straits of Malacca in the west to the Thai border and through the South China Sea to the east; they too suffered casualties, as did all branches of the Security Forces involved in the conflict. Their ultimate, valiant, sacrifice will always be remembered with gratitude in the annals of Malaya.

Colin McElduff
Dumfries 2002

Prologue

The long hot fingers of tropical sunlight shafted through the lush, dank undergrowth on the cutback jungle along the foot of Gunung Ledang (Mt. Ophir), causing misty spirals of air to crown its peak. High above, a kite hawk circled lazily on the noon day thermals and in the still oppressive air the bird at first appeared to hang motionless. After a while it began to soar in ever increasing circles, higher and higher, until it was directly over the last bend on the road to the summit of the pass.

The rain forest's elaborate, undulating pattern of thousands of crowns made a multicoloured carpet of green and blue, stretching unbroken into the distance, except for short glimpses of the road twisting beneath. The intense silence over the hillside was punctuated momentarily by the cooing of doves and screams of monkeys from high in the branches, orchestrated by the insistent noise of cicadas and chirping of crickets.

The kite hawk high above suddenly changed the pattern of its flight and with wings tipped it began a slow glide following the curves of the road. The bird's piercing eyes had spotted movement, the unfamiliar shape of humans.

Furtive figures clad in dingy green and khaki flitted to and fro across the road's dusty surface to disappear within the mantle of the secondary growth of the forest's perimeter. Communist terrorists were setting an ambush!

The bird soon lost interest, and drawn by a rapid thermal began to climb again, disappearing over the top of the pass.

Meanwhile, down in the valley a minute cloud appeared above the trees, its size increasing with every second. A lone car enveloped in swirling red laterite dust eventually emerged, carefully taking the winding curves of the road. Its European occupants, a man and woman were deep in conversation.

Slowly, round the last bend, the Morris tourer came into view. It had been driven fast over the intervening miles and the engine was beginning to labour in the hot humid air.

The auburn haired girl, clad in a silk dress of vivid hues, gently touched the arm of her companion and, turning her face to him, said,

'I'm so glad, darling, we had this week in Malacca ... it was heaven being on our own!'

'Yes, it was, sweetheart, we'll do it again, I promise.'

He smiled, trying hard not to look at her pretty face but to keep his eyes firmly ahead.

'I've always had a soft spot for the place ... now I have good reason!'

He reached across and took her hand in his, giving it a squeeze.

'Love you, sweetheart ... I've never been so happy ... I can't wait to tell everyone we're engaged.'

She smiled happily as the car began to huff and puff on the sharp ascent causing it to slow down.

In that split second, fate grasped her moment!

Suddenly all around them the air was rent with a long, rattling burst of Bren gun fire, followed by sporadic cracks of rifle.

The girl's face changed from one of happiness to that of abject horror ... she cried out,

'No! ... darling!' ... and threw her arms around her companion, causing the car to swerve to the left.

'Quick ... *down* ...!' he commanded.

Lines of dust kicked up by the machine-gun bullets ran across the road in the direction of the vehicle, ricocheting on stones, whining and screaming about them like banshees. Some ripped into the car's canvas roof and blew out the windscreen, others burst the front inside tyre causing the car to continue on its erratic course, and overturn with a crunch into the ditch.

Shots echoed and rebounded across the hills and jungle edge, awakening its inhabitants and causing flights of birds to rocket into the air. Guttural commands in Chinese echoed across the road controlling the attackers' fire towards the crashed vehicle.

At that same moment the car burst into flames and the firing ceased, the assailants holding back, gloating over the spectacle.

A minute or two later, fire from the engine compartment ran along the ground, sniffing its way towards the petrol leaking from the tank. It ignited, erupting like a furnace, black plumes of smoke billowing into the sky.

The onlookers waited, like vultures, for the eventual explosion which reverberated across the hills making small monkeys on the jungle peri-meter scream with fright.

Fragments of the car were strewn about the area so the perpetrators made no effort to hunt their quarry or look for booty, assuming there would be none!

On a bugle note they quickly regrouped, and in single file slunk back out of sight under cover of the jungle, with self congratulations on the achievement of their plan, without casualties to themselves ... 'and so the running dog.'

1

Outward Bound

He shifted impatiently, waiting for the queue to move, wrapped his coat tightly around to counter the chilly autumn air and stamped his feet. His breath swirled foggily over the heads in front, highlighting more vividly the crisp golds of the dying trees, as he took a last look before boarding the airport bus. October in England ... he felt nostalgic, homesick already, yet finding it hard to believe that in two and a half days' time he would be back in the lush, overblown humidity of the east.

It seemed no time at all since his return from Burma and he wondered how long it would be before he felt the cold again. Malaya was his destination; he was to take up an appointment with the Federation Police Force. The Malayan Government had asked for volunteers and Alexander MacIntyre, this tall, blue eyed man in his late twenties, was one of the many who had offered their services.

The bus wound its way through the teaming London suburbs and a wave of excitement enveloped him, his heart quickening, thoughts pondering on his decision to join the Malay Police. This was the longest journey he had undertaken by air and he wondered how it would go.

He was no stranger to serving with Colonial Forces, having done so in India and Burma during the war which ended five years ago. Sandy had said all his goodbyes the night before and Malaya would be a new challenge. It hadn't been easy to resign his commission in the Army; however it was now in the past and he needed to look to the future.

Gazing through the windows of the bus now speeding westwards, the slanting rays of the early morning sun provided an ever changing vista of the passing countryside. He was aware of everything standing out in sharp relief; the uniform rows of houses and shops in contrast to the orderly avenues of trees. Similar to soldiers on parade, smart and tidy, nothing out of place, as though awaiting the bugle call to send them marching forward to the duties of the day.

Gradually Sandy became mindful of his immediate surroundings and the trance that had overtaken him broke almost as quickly as it had begun. Reluctant to change his view, his attention shifted initially to the passengers sitting nearest to him, his leisurely gaze moving from one to another.

It was difficult to concentrate, there were so many, not all of them European. He perceived a mixture of Eastern races, Indians, Chinese, Malays, and others not so readily recognisable. There were men and women of all ages and modes of dress, from the simplest to the exotic; many of them presented a kaleidoscopic picture of the country they had originated from.

His gaze wandered, quickly losing interest in some whilst his eyes lingered on others, taking in more fully their attire and general appearance. He conjured up in his mind their occupations, reasons for travelling and ultimate destination.

On boarding the bus at Victoria Sandy had passed the time of day with the occupant in the seat next to him but, due to his preoccupation with the journey ahead, had not pursued a conversation.

He now began to make an appraisal of the person and a sidelong glance revealed a man about his own age with broad shoulders and dark tousled hair. His face, gaunt and tanned, appeared in need of some padding due to (as Sandy was later to learn) the lack of a full set of teeth, the absence of which exaggerated the hollowness of his face.

'Nice day for flying!' the man blurted.

Sandy, caught unawares, floundered.

'Yes ... yes indeed.'

'Are you going far?'

'Singapore ...' the man replied.

'No! Good heavens ... so am I ... I'm MacIntyre, by the way ... Alexander MacIntyre, Sandy for short.'

'Ted Bell ... better known as Dinger Bell, late of the Metropolitan Police ... I'm off to join the Singapore lot!'

'Talk about coincidence! ... I'm going to the Federation of Malaya Police!' Sandy responded.

They fell into silence, but with a common bond the short pause was soon broken, firstly by Bell as he quizzed Sandy.

'First time out?'

'Eh? yes ... to Singapore and Malaya that is, not the East ... I was in India and Burma during the war.'

'Interesting! I served in Italy ... in the Military Police ... got some good memories of the country ... even though we were busy after the capitulation trying to stamp out the black market.'

He laughed, as though some memory had flooded back.

'You married?' he said.

'No ... not much time to do anything about that, had to go back to Nigeria with our African troops when we left Burma after the war and served on for some time with a newly formed battalion of the Royal Nigerian Regiment.'

He glanced at Bell.

'Are you?'

'Yes ... and I've got two little girls, real poppets they are. I hope to get the wife and family out when I'm settled and have a suitable quarter.'

The bus juddered at the lights.

'What's your tour?'

'Three years ... what's yours?' Sandy queried.

'Same ... feels a long time.'

'Yes, but not when you're looking forward to your wife and family joining you, not to mention your own home!'

'I suppose you're right ... never thought of it like that. You'll have to come and visit us,' Bell said spontaneously as though he'd known Sandy for years.

Leaning over he delved into his inside jacket pocket, fumbled, then produced a wallet from which he selected a photograph. With an expectant look he handed it to Sandy.

'Pretty ... eh ...?' he said in a voice filled with pride.

Sandy studied the photo and saw two little girls who looked just as their father had described them.

'How old?' he asked.

'Nine and a half and seven ...'

Gazing at the smiling faces of the children ... Sandy's mind wandered back to the last days of the war in Burma, when his platoon was part of the Brigade HQ defence perimeter on the Sandoway Chaung, his sector embracing the village of Kinmaw in which he had set up his headquarters.

Ma Hla Shwe was about the same age as Bell's eldest girl. There was, however, no other resemblance, as Bell's girls were fair. It was only the innocence and trust in the small smiling faces that brought back the memory of his only real contact with children of that age.

The Japanese had not been long out of the village when Sandy set up his defences; in fact they were still in the vicinity across the Chaung, which was fordable at low tide.

The crossing point was identified by a long sand and pebble bar in the middle of the river, on which he enfiladed two heavy machine-guns and a mortar. The bar was a stepping stone for the enemy to cross over and also for the Burmese filtering back to the village carrying the few possessions they had managed to take away when they fled.

They now had very little food; all of their livestock, together with the harvest of rice from the paddy fields along the river bank, had been taken by the retreating Japanese.

The village headman, Ma Hla Shwe's father, and the few villagers who had survived the bitter fighting were adamant on their return that they should remain and try to rebuild their lives out of the debris. They simply refused to move back to a safer place. Sandy couldn't blame them, it was their village and where else could they go?

Kinmaw was deserted when he entered. Ma Hla Shwe and her little brother were the first people to make contact with him. He recollected that in those early days the smaller child appeared sexless and Sandy thought that the youngster might be another little girl. It was only later, during one of their brief visits, that all became clear. He had been trying to make conversation with Ma Hla Shwe who, in a moment of inspiration, lifted up the child's sarong to reveal all.

'A boy ...!' Sandy laughed, and thereafter she called her brother 'boy' when referring to him; consequently Sandy never discovered the youngster's real name.

Ma Hla Shwe was a pretty child, with long raven hair which tumbled around her shoulders and down her back. It framed an olive skinned, intelligent face, out of which quizzed beautiful brown, almond shaped eyes. He guessed her age to be about ten.

After surveying the village for the best vantage point overlooking the river he chose the old post office for his headquarters. It was whilst sitting on the wooden steps of the newly formed HQ, eating his midday meal of bully beef and tinned vegetables, that the little girl came up and sat down beside him. He had been in the village about a couple of hours, during which time he had seen no-one, though his patrols had reported movement of some Burmese.

The sudden appearance of the child was his first indication that the villagers were coming back from hiding in the bush. The little girl looked up at him appealingly, hardly able to take her eyes off the food in the mess tin.

Sandy, having already eaten some, handed her what remained. She grabbed the tin and bolted down some food, stopping when she had finished half, then lifted up her hand as if to say something, put down the tin, and disappeared around the corner of the wooden building. After a few moments she reappeared with a small child to whom she gave the remaining food, which was soon polished off.

Realising how hungry they were Sandy felt a deep sense of shock that little children such as these had become involved and thus deprived, so he resolved to help as much as he could. Later, he was to discover they were the only children left in the small community!

The children turned up daily around the same time. The smaller child was apparently Ma Hla Shwe's charge and, consequently, her constant companion. Sandy made sure there was always an extra mess tin of food waiting for them.

At first, the little Burmese children were shy, but as time went on their timidity left them and they called frequently throughout the day when he was about. Sandy looked forward to their visits and tried hard to teach the little girl a few simple words of English, so that they could have a means of communication. He began the lessons by saying,

'Name …' pointing his finger at her. She quickly understood him and answered,

'Ma Hla Shwe … you name …?' pointing in the same fashion at Sandy.

He found out later that the village postmaster, who was also the school-teacher, had been killed quite recently on his way back from the nearby town of Sandoway; he had been blown up when he stepped on a mine. The Japanese in their retreat had hastily laid mines along the verge of the road.

The postmaster had been a great friend of the headman and Ma Hla Shwe had learned from him a few words of English. Although their communication was good, conversation remained limited to the little that Ma Hla Shwe had been taught by the schoolteacher and her father.

One day in the late afternoon Sandy was invited to the house of his little friend. She ran up to him at the river jetty which he was inspecting for the forthcoming visit by the Divisional Commander to Brigade HQ.

'You come house!' she cried excitedly, insistently repeating it. 'You come house! My father like you come house!' Her face was alight with excitement.

He could hardly refuse such an urgent request!

'All right then … I'll come … I do need to speak to your father anyway … but you will have to wait a few minutes.'

He returned to the old post office to inform Sergeant Audu, his platoon Sergeant, where he was going and also to collect a haversack into which he carefully placed a number of items. He slung the bag over his shoulder and offered his hand to the little girl. Bashfully she took it and off they went, hand in hand, through the village, past the few remaining houses in whose shadowy doorways old ladies squatted amidst a blue haze of cigar smoke, the aroma of which wafted to him on the breeze as they walked by.

The house of her father was just off the main road at the other side of the village, down a winding, overgrown path. It was a small wooden building on stilts and surrounded by thick undergrowth.

U Aung Bo was obviously awaiting their arrival; he was sitting on the top step of the veranda. As Sandy approached he stood up, then cautiously made his way down the steps to greet him. The two men shook hands ceremoniously, silently measuring each other up.

The Burmese was slight of stature, in common with his race. His once good looking face appeared emaciated and belied his true age ... probably no more than forty. Sandy was the first to speak.

'I am sorry I have not been able to see you again since you brought your people out of the bush ... our defences and the daily patrols across the Chaung have kept me busy, I'm afraid.'

'I ... understand ... Sahib,' the Burmese answered softly in halting English, at the same time indicating with his hand the mat on the floor of the veranda upon which Sandy was to sit.

As he sat, Sandy became aware of the bustle of activity within the house – clinking of plates and glasses – excited whispers and muffled laughter. It was obvious that his visit was something of an occasion for the household. He had only just settled himself when the beaded curtain over the entrance door parted and a small, slim, good looking woman passed through carrying a tray upon which was placed a bottle and two tumblers.

Sandy gave her a swift sidelong glance as she set down the tray in front of them; in deference to his host he tried not to show too much interest. He guessed she must be the mother of Ma Hla Shwe; he was, however, never introduced and she retired, her eyes cast shyly down so that he could not see her face more fully.

U Aung Bo picked up the bottle and slowly poured the clear amber-coloured liquid into the tumblers, filling them about halfway. He handed one to Sandy, took the other himself and raised the glass in a silent salute, then drank half. Sandy followed suit and, to his delight, discovered it was a fine rice wine. He felt its pleasant warmth reach down into his stomach, and a feeling of contentment swept over him.

'Very good,' Sandy bowed his head courteously, breaking the silence and U Aung Bo replied,

'The time has come for ... celebration ... I have been keeping this for such an occasion ... it is my last bottle.'

He hesitated a second or two, as though trying to capture long forgotten words.

'When ... Japanese come ... I hide my wine ... you welcome to it, Sahib ... and ... my humble home.' Again, he paused.

'My little daughter tell me ... you are very kind to her and my son ... she like you and say you can be trusted.'

Sandy was deeply moved by his words.

'I am honoured to be invited to your home and share with you the last bottle of your excellent wine.'

Meanwhile, his little friend had seated herself beside him and was, at that moment, watching him closely with an unmistakable look of anticipation on her pretty face. She had watched him fill the haversack with some tins and, although she did not know what the contents were, she somehow sensed that they must be something special.

Sandy picked up the haversack which he had placed alongside him. He opened it and took out the tins one by one, giving them to his host. Condensed milk, mixed fruit, vegetables, bully beef.

Lastly, he produced a tin of boiled sweets, which only that morning he had received on his weekly airdrop of food and supplies. He opened it and gave it to the little girl. The child's eyes bulged at the colourful contents, the like of which she had never seen before.

As she stared mesmerised, it slowly dawned on him that she didn't know what they were, so to break the impasse he took one of the sweets and popped it into his mouth; immediately she copied him!

He was never to forget the radiance that lit up her little face ...

'Hey! ... you all right?'

Bell's voice broke into Sandy's thoughts as he stared intently at the photograph held tightly between his fingers.

'You all right?' he repeated.

'Yes, fine ... sorry! Seeing your little girls stirred my memory of some Burmese children I met during the war. You're a very fortunate man to have two such lovely daughters!'

Bell was visibly pleased.

'What's your rank in the Singapore Police, by the way?' Sandy asked.

'Cadet ASP ... I don't know much about the ranks in the Colonial Forces ... what are you?'

'The same ... the rank is an Assistant Superintendent of Police.'

He changed the subject.

'According to the flight plan I see we have an overnight stop in Cairo ... have you been there?'

'No ... do you think we'll have time to look around? I've always wanted to see a belly dancer! Are there any others going to the Police?'

Sandy shook his head.

'Well, so far you're the only one I've met.'

He looked round, his eyes wandering afresh over the occupants of the bus in the hope that he might spot someone who'd fit the bill. Most of the men were over the age of recruitment, or didn't appear the type.

The bus was now rapidly approaching its destination having left the main westbound traffic flow and turned into the airport approach road proceeding to the Departure Terminus building.

Everyone began collecting their hand-luggage and moved slowly towards the exit door where they alighted on the pavement and stood, like a gaggle of geese, waiting for the heavy bags to be unloaded from the belly of the bus.

Sandy and Bell were last to disembark and by that time most of the bags were out and they had little difficulty in finding their own.

They were met by an attractive hostess who bustled them into the main departure hall which, even at this early hour, was thronged with passengers. She ushered them to the BOAC reception desk and, in a clipped BBC voice, informed them that there was a delay caused by a pre-flight inspection.

'Please wait here ... you will be called to reception to weigh-in and deposit your bags and receive your boarding card ... after that you will go to emigration and customs.'

Sandy placed his bags alongside one of the nearby vacant seats and said to Bell,

'We might as well stick together since we're going to the same place; would you mind keeping an eye on these while I go and get a newspaper?'

Bell nodded his consent.

Sandy wended his way across the congested hall to the newspaper stand, gave the display a cursory inspection and bought a copy of the *Telegraph*, then retraced his steps and sat down.

'You don't mind me looking at this first? I want to read the weather forecast to see what's in store *en route* to Egypt.'

As he spoke he opened the paper and scanned the relevant page.

Engrossed though he was Sandy became aware that someone had stopped in front of him. Lowering his gaze to below the open pages his eyes focused on the scruffiest pair of brown shoes he'd ever seen!

They were not only dirty, but scuffed and scratched, almost beyond renovation; they hadn't seen polish in a very long time! Intrigued, his eyes wandered up the grey flannel trousers, which had also seen better days. He deduced that the wearer must have slept in them!

He now carefully lowered the paper and allowed his gaze to continue surreptitiously upwards until the person came into full view.

An old, light coloured, crumpled, mackintosh completed the stranger's outer attire. He was average height, thickset, about thirty-five, his swarthy, tanned complexion and piercing dark brown eyes tending to make him look older.

His face was broad and clean shaven, except for the small black moustache which adorned his upper lip; his hair, likewise black, gave him the appearance of a gipsy. There was an air of bewilderment about him, a *lost look* that led Sandy to think that the man might be ill, or possibly suffering from an enormous hangover!

He deliberated.

'Engineer? ... possibly! ... returning to the Middle East after a spot of leave ... must have made the most of his last night!!'

The 'Mystery man' hesitated as though to say something, changed his mind and moved on. Sandy went back to his newspaper.

At last the public address system sprang to life.

'Attention please ... all passengers for BOAC Flight number one, zero, two for Rome ... Cairo ... Damascus ... New Delhi ... Calcutta and Singapore ... please report to gate number three!'

Alerted, Sandy and Bell hastily joined the group already at the barrier. Sandy handed his passport to a blank-faced official who, scrutinising it, gave him a cursory glance, stamped it and handed it back without comment.

His air-ticket was checked and he was handed a boarding card which gave him authority to buy duty-free goods from the shop within the terminal.

The passengers, now silent, pushed forward with gathering momentum and since there was little time left for shopping Sandy and Bell shuffled forward with them, stopping at the departure gate to the tarmac.

The tannoy blared again, asking the passengers to follow the air hostess to the aircraft where a flight stewardess took over.

'This way, Sir ... your seat number and boarding card please!'

'Thirty-two ...' Sandy handed over his card.

Indicating Bell he asked,

'Is it possibly for this gentleman to take the adjoining seat – we're both bound for Singapore?'

'Seat number thirty two? Sorry Sir ... I can't do anything immediately. I'll see what can be done later when we're airborne.'

Sandy found his seat whilst Bell passed through to the rear.

Amidst the hubbub of voices he settled down. The total seating capacity was about sixty so it didn't take long for the aircraft to fill up.

The four Wright turbo-compound radial piston engines of the Lockheed Constellation started up, turning over one by one until the crescendo became a deafening roar. Up and down the central aisle each stewardess checked that seat belts were fastened properly and everyone was conversant with the safety procedures in case of emergency.

Pre-flight signs were displayed and eventually the plane began to roll its vast bulk slowly across the tarmac ready for take-off.

Sandy, now acutely aware of the throbbing of the engines, noted their change of pitch as the Captain increased or decreased engine revolutions. They arrived at the take-off runway then halted, the engines roared again and with a note of bravado the aircraft shuddered, lurched a little and began to move forward with an insistent thrust, gradually gathering momentum. The engines thundered, the ground sped past, faster and faster, then Sandy felt a bump followed by another and the ground began to recede rapidly out of sight. They were airborne!

He was at last '*Outward Bound*' and a feeling of detachment came over him.

The plane continued to climb, then banked steeply to port, before slowly straightening up. As they gained altitude and the atmospheric pressure increased Sandy's ears popped. He felt a thump beneath his feet, followed by a clank as the undercarriage retracted and locked into place. The note of the engines changed to a distinctive purr as they were throttled back and the propellers given a finer pitch in an effort to conserve fuel for the journey ahead.

The stewardess approached him.

'Mr MacIntyre ... no-one will be occupying the seat next to you ... Mr Bell may now come forward.'

Sandy thanked her and turned to catch Bell's attention, waving to him, indicating the empty seat. A couple of minutes later he plonked himself down.

'I've just been talking to a chap back there who tells me he's a Malay Police candidate ... I told him that we'd get together when we reached Cairo this evening.'

'OK ... we'll have more time then to make his acquaintance,' Sandy replied.

They read and dozed and from time to time requested drinks; only the voice of the Captain intimating their position and progress interrupted their thoughts.

Rome was only a short stop, allowing passengers to alight and new travellers to board. Once airborne again and on their final leg to Cairo a warning was given that turbulence could be expected over the North African coast and desert.

Their arrival in Egypt was heralded by the acute popping in Sandy's ears as they entered the approach corridor leading into Cairo Airport.

Looking out of his window he was rewarded with a magnificent panoramic view of the city, with the Nile river snaking its moonlit way through a sea of twinkling lights. As he gazed, the view constantly changed and he caught a breathtaking glimpse of the Giza pyramids and the Sphinx stretching up into the sky out of the moon-drenched desert; the colossus forming a spectacular back-drop.

The steady, assuring, purring of the engines suddenly changed and he felt the aircraft bank sharply and level out as it entered the glide path. Now almost silent, he heard the familiar whine of the undercarriage being released as it came down and, with a thump, lock into place.

The landing lights of the runway sped by and the aircraft touched down with a squeal of tyres, lurching a little, then like a lion rudely awakened, the engines roared their final note of defiance as the turboprops went into reverse pitch to act as a brake.

The noise decreased and they taxied towards the disembarkation point as the stewardess's voice droned over the intercom telling them to stay in their seats; she explained the outside temperature was 77 degrees Fahrenheit and the humidity negligible.

The main cabin door opened and a fat, swarthy little man entered, dressed in a tight-fitting khaki uniform with a red fez adorning his head and armed with a pump-action flit gun. With a broad grin he proceeded to squirt an evil smelling liquid into the air in an effort to kill any insects and bacteria the aircraft may have brought in.

Sandy quickly discovered it was preferable not to breathe!

Ten to fifteen minutes later they disembarked and, as Cairo was a night stop, they were told to take with them all their hand luggage.

Next was immigration control and customs, from whence they proceeded to the Helminya Palace Hotel in Heliopolis, a suburb of Cairo.

The bus started with a jerk then sped quickly through the airport gates. The dun-coloured, dusty countryside spread out into the distance and the skyline, lit by a full moon, appeared punctuated only by the palm trees along the roadside: motley green sentinels reaching up into the cloudless, starlit, sky. The warm evening air exuded a musty, earthy odour, which Sandy knew was prevalent everywhere in the Middle East.

People thronged the highway even at this late time in the day. Overladen donkeys and camels, with panniers full of bundles of vegetable produce, struggled with the combined weight of master and goods. They staggered along the road intermingling with carts of all shapes and sizes which, whether partly loaded or empty, were not so for long; someone would always jump on for a free ride.

Small, grubby, snotty faced urchins of indeterminate age, wearing long, dirty white shifts – like night shirts – their heads adorned with round, close-fitting hats, grinned at the occupants of the bus and made rude gestures with their fingers. Others lifted their long garments to expose thin upright shafts which they gleefully manipulated with permissive abandon; the final outcome only to be imagined by the bus passengers as they continued on their way!

In due course they turned off the main road and proceeded through a picturesque wrought-iron gateway, down a long drive leading through floodlit gardens to an impressive building set amidst a variety of tall palms, frangipani, hibiscus, and surrounded by lawns with coarse brown grass burnt the colour of amber. Herbaceous borders abounded everywhere, planted with tall canna lilies, their long, thick, pointed leaves supporting brilliant red flowers.

At last they arrived at their destination and the bus halted at the bottom of a flight of marble steps which led up to the main entrance.

A palace it was, by any standard, right out of the *Tales of the Arabian Nights*. A troop of bearers in highly coloured uniforms waited to take the luggage and within seconds they were whisked off to the reception desk in the spacious hall.

Sandy stood in awe at the palatial decor of the interior and a quick sidelong glance at the momentarily silent Bell confirmed that he too was more than a little impressed. He appeared rooted to the spot; only his eyes moved, revolving round and round, his mouth open as though he were a python about to swallow a rabbit.

The remainder of the passengers stood bunched up, chattering in their numerous tongues, waiting to be attended by the clerks standing behind the reception desk. Eventually, Sandy's and Bell's turn came and formalities were courteous and efficient. They were given adjoining rooms.

'Your room, Sir ... is number seven.' He turned to Bell. 'And yours, Sir, is number eight ... first floor!'

The bearers hovering in the background took note and beckoned them to follow. Together they moved off, slowly ascending the magnificent marble staircase leading to the open balconied first floor which overlooked the palm-festooned central hall through a series of Moorish mosaic tiled arches.

Sandy arrived first and turned to Bell.

'See you later, Dinger ... say, an hour ... what about a drink in the bar before dinner?'

'OK,' grinned Bell and Sandy, having given his key to his bearer, walked in.

To his astonishment the room was enormous, the high, ornate ceiling looking down on the beautiful marble floor of a double suite. The bearer set down the luggage.

'*Ya fandi* ... please ... I come again – five o'clock in morning ... for bag.'

Sandy thanked him and made a mental note to get some Egyptian money for *baksheesh*.

The warm water trickled over his tired body and he lazed in the shower wishing he didn't have to move.

Wrapping the voluminous, white bath sheet round his waist he slipped his feet into the straw mules and wandered round his suite. Firstly he lay on the king-sized bed, put his hands behind his head and stared at the ceiling, then he moved round the furniture, running his fingers over the elaborate woodwork.

'My hat, I could certainly get used to this.'

He spoke the words aloud as if to imprint indelibly on his mind the experience of such luxury. Then he picked up his watch.

'My God, drinks in the bar in fifteen minutes, I'll have to move,' and with that he towelled down and changed, emerging from his room with a minute to spare!

He walked swiftly along the corridor to the head of the staircase where he spied Bell passing through a huge archway in the hall below, the sign above indicating he was going in the right direction. Sandy followed and as he approached Bell turned to face him.

'What a room!' they both chorused simultaneously. The barman was alerted by their laughter and Dinger called for a round of drinks.

'Two large whiskies and sodas, please ... by the way, Sandy, I saw that chap I told you about earlier. I only had a few words with him ... he smelt like a brewery ... suffering from a prolonged hangover, but says he has a touch of malaria and wants to get off to bed!'

'Well ... I'm bound to meet him sometime!'

Sandy bought the next round and they carried their drinks through to the sumptuously decorated dining room where they were shown to a table. The mysterious Police candidate failed to materialise at dinner, so they were none the wiser.

As the meal came to an end Dinger turned the conversation round to belly dancers and repeated his fantasy of seeing one whilst in Egypt. Their ensuing enquiries at reception revealed that there was a resident, nightly show put on in the ballroom, which had been turned into a Bedouin tent. The show began at midnight and, as that time was fast approaching, they decided to investigate.

The throbbing beat of native drums and the high-pitched, warbling shrieks of Berber women drew them to the Bedouin tent.

They found the entrance swathed in yards of brilliant scarlet tulle, tied back with swags of heavy gold cord and flanked on each side by two burly Nubians dressed in white baggy pants encircled by wide scarlet sashes. Their broad, deep chests, barely covered by the ruby and gold waistcoats, glistened in the subdued light. A red fez completed their attire.

The pair were an awesome sight, standing on guard, immobile, legs apart, leaning on massive, curved scimitars. Out of coal-black faces their eyes focused straight ahead in pretence that they were oblivious to Sandy and Dinger's presence.

On passing through the doorway they were greeted by a sea of faces looking up from the floor of a huge tent. The room had been transformed beyond recognition, the walls and floor festooned with exotic carpets and rugs.

Ornate, exquisitely carved, low wooden coffee tables were dotted around the floor's perimeter and surrounded by equally low leather pouffes and highly coloured cushions. Hubbly-bubble pipes were strategically placed and the air was heavy with the smell of incense and Egyptian tobacco.

In the centre of the tent was a large clearing for the dancing girls who had not, as yet, put in an appearance. In one corner musicians sat cross-legged on the floor playing flutes, drums and other oriental instruments. A bevy of magnificently dressed, veiled Berber women sat apart shrieking their heads off and banging tambourines to the rhythm of the musicians. To Sandy it sounded like bedlam!

As they continued forward a gesticulating figure in the ornate robes of a Sheikh descended on them.

'*Ahlan wa sahlan ... leiltak saida ... ya fandi.*'

At the same time he bowed and touched his forehead, lips and heart in the customary salaam then, quite unexpectedly, said,

'This way Sir ... I will show you to a good table!'

He promptly escorted them to one opposite the musicians and explained to them that the entrance fee for the show could be paid in either Egyptian or English money and that it should be paid to him, now!

They had obtained some Egyptian currency from the money exchange in the reception hall so the required sum was quickly produced and, without further ado, the 'Sheikh' took their order for drinks.

Sandy and Dinger settled down into the soft cushions on the floor and waited in anticipation for the show to start. The wailing women stopped and there was a momentary hush, the atmosphere charged with expectation. The musicians began to play and a troop of Bedouin dancing girls appeared through an opening in the rear wall of the tent, gracefully gliding their way to the centre of the floor.

The music Sandy recognised; it was an old number, *Hizzi Hizzi* (The Handkerchief Dance). The girls revolved in a circle singing, their handkerchiefs swaying to and fro. A young man standing with the musicians accompanied them, singing in Arabic and describing the excellence with which his beloved could dance the Handkerchief Dance ...

Tune after tune was played and the dancing continued. They were taken, as it were, on a Caravan of musical rhythms and melodies, wending their way from city to city, over arid wastes and burning deserts and stopping at thirst-quenching oases; where, in the cool of the evening, to the haunting sound of native instruments, stories were told to conjure up vivid memories of bygone splendours of a '*Thousand and One Nights*'.

At last the moment they had been waiting for arrived!

A single, voluptuous girl appeared wearing the flimsiest of attire. With the sinuous grace of a cobra, she glided onto the floor to the melody *Banat Iskandaria* (the Girls of Alexandria) for whom men and love are just playthings.

She wore almost nothing, for her baggy silken pants were transparent, showing her tiny 'G' string below a prominent, rounded, naked belly, her navel embellished with a jewelled stone. Her large, firm, sensuous breasts were bare except for a red tassel which adorned each nipple. Her face was covered by a transparent veil.

From the centre of her belly she danced, her body revolving around her navel. Swinging her hips from side to side, round and round she danced to the rhythm. Her belly, ever gyrating as though it would never stop, appeared at times to be the only part of her body in motion. Eventually the movements changed, the upper part of her torso took over, and the tassels on the nipples of her breasts began to revolve, faster and faster, with the rise and fall of her unrestrained flesh. She danced as though possessed by a invisible lover, her movements becoming more and more sensual. With the change of beat in the music the lower part of her body became alive again, gyrating, until once more it was the only part of her that moved.

Once in a while Sandy quickly looked at Dinger and observed him, entranced by the spectacle. A memory to treasure!

It was late when it finished. The dancer was the last spot in a spectacular show of jugglers, acrobats and musicians, and they returned to their rooms relishing their experience. Now it was time for a couple of hours sleep before an early breakfast and the airport.

Dinger was first down and sat at the same table they had dined at the evening before. They had little time to discuss the previous night's entertainment and the mysterious Police candidate again failed to appear and board the bus for the airport. Before they knew it they were airborne and bound for New Delhi.

Conversation was minimal as they tried to make up for lost sleep. Bell, dozing with a smile playing at the corners of his mouth, led Sandy to wonder if the belly dancer was featuring somewhere!

The day passed more or less as before, landing briefly at Damascus without leaving the aircraft and they arrived and departed Palam Airport, New Delhi only to refuel. They saw little of this part of India and were grateful to be protected from the stifling heat by the air-conditioning.

They were, however, to experience a little of the discomfort of the climate when they arrived in the evening at Dum Dum Airport, Calcutta. Here, the aircraft changed crews and they had dinner in the airport restaurant whilst the aircraft was being refuelled. The walk across the tarmac was a welcome break only marred by the extreme heat to which they were not acclimatised.

India was only into its second year of independence and vestiges of the long British rule could still be recognised by the attire and courtesy of the officials. Everything went off without a hitch and after an excellent dinner they were airborne again on the overnight journey to Singapore.

The last leg of the route took them across the Bay of Bengal and the southern tip of Burma. Sandy felt a twinge of nostalgia. He found it difficult to sleep during the night, his mind active, thoughts dwelling on the day ahead and Singapore. He eventually dozed off, waking to a magnificent sunrise, one of hundreds he was to experience.

The approach to Changi airport was smooth and soon they were disembarking. Sandy was first out.

He had forgotten what the atmosphere was like. The humidity was a hundred per cent and he began to perspire freely as though someone had thrown a wet blanket over his head. Fortunately formalities were quick and a Federation Police Officer met them and helped with their luggage through customs.

They were taken to HMS *Terror*, a shore based establishment in the Naval Base on the north side of Singapore Island, where a Police transit mess had been set up. Sandy was told he would stay there until instructions were received as to where in the Federation he would be posted.

Bell, on the other hand, destined for the Singapore Police, stayed only the one night.

2

The Key

HMS *Terror*, the Far East shore establishment of the Royal Navy on Singapore Island, in the Johore Straits facing the Malayan peninsula, was a hive of industry for ships of the Far East Station who used its facilities constantly for routine maintenance, repairs and refitting.

It was an ideal location from which to process the appointment of new Police Officers prior to posting to Singapore or the Federation. Consequently a transit mess, mostly occupied by resident, unmarried, Naval Engineers, had been set up within the confines of the wardroom and Sandy and Bell joined the many officers who spent their first days in its environs.

Bell's stay was short and early next morning a Police Land Rover arrived to collect him. They exchanged temporary contact addresses, both promising to get in touch as soon as they were settled.

For Sandy the following few days passed slowly without the redoubtable Dinger, despite having numerous fittings for uniforms carried out by the Chinese tailor stationed at the base. He was issued with a handgun – a Browning 9mm automatic – and was instructed that, once in the Federation, he must carry it at all times.

Hours were spent on browsing through Force publications, regulations and Interpol notices. Lectures were attended on the duties of a Police Officer in a national emergency and a number of informal talks were held on the upcountry daily Situation Report (Sitrep), terrorist tactics, and the formation and organisation of the Malayan Communist Party (MCP), usually known by its Chinese title, *Min Yuen*. Classes were also held on *Instant Malay*, so that he could converse and understand a little of the language.

Nevertheless, Sandy's boredom continued and the weekend arrived without news of his posting. Five days had elapsed and he was impatient to see the outside world, so requested permission to visit the city of Singapore.

Deliberating, he planned to make Raffles Hotel his first stop. He'd heard so much about it and thought it would make a good place from which to start. A couple of days later another officer, Robert Carson by name, arrived in the transit mess. He was well spoken, in his mid twenties, clean-shaven with dark, straight hair and with sleepy brown eyes, which gave him an odd appearance.

They met during the normal day's activities and had a nodding acquaintance, but Sandy couldn't make up his mind about him. He wasn't forthcoming – always appeared to be in the background of events and when Carson approached him he was taken aback.

'How about taking a trip into Singapore tonight, you could share a taxi with me?' he said.

'Well, yes ... thanks, that's a good idea,' Sandy replied, 'we could visit Raffles and have a look round from there.'

Carson nodded his head, appearing interested. He offered to order the taxi which would pick them up outside the gates of the base.

At 19.30 hrs the two officers were met at the entrance by a grinning Chinese standing beside a brand new Ford Prefect saloon. He greeted them in Malay.

'*Selamat Tuan ...*' and then in stilted English, 'you want good time Singapore ... me know plitty clean gal ... velly cheap, bang bang ... velly good.'

He then began, at length, to describe the sordid details of the sensual delights of the Orient. Sandy politely declined this generous offer of a sexual feast.

'Tonight we only want to go to Raffles Hotel and return ... could you collect us later and bring us back here?'

The man grinned, knowingly.

'*Su'e Tuan* ... I do that ... cost twenty dolla' lound·tlip ... ten dolla' now ...!'

They agreed without hesitation to his terms, which appeared reasonable, and climbed into the back of the car. The Chinese set them on their way amidst a clash of gears and kangaroo hops!

The taxi followed a route which went through palm-oil and rubber plantations interspersed with tracks of virgin jungle. Eventually they passed through the military cantons of Woodlands and Nee Soon, which had interesting little wooden shops full of Chinese *objets d'art*, fakes for the unwary buyer. Continuing, they entered Thomson Road where the driver eagerly pointed out Government House.

At last they emerged into Orchard Road and drove down its length past the Cathy cinema building, a skyscraper festooned with coloured lights which dominated the city skyline.

Raffles Hotel was soon caught in the headlights of the taxi and they drove through the open, pillared gates into a gravelled courtyard and stopped between two spectacular fan palms which flanked the short steps leading up to the entrance. A Sikh doorman immediately came to attention as they alighted and saluted them in a military manner. From his bearing Sandy deduced he must be an old campaigner, one of those who went over to the Japanese during the occupation of the Island.

After confirming with the driver that, no matter what happened, he was to wait for them to turn up at the end of the evening, he screeched off to his next fare.

Sandy and Carson entered the cool, spacious hall with its high ceilings and marble colonnades built in the late colonial fashion. Their shoes clipped sharply on the tiled floor.

Sandy imagined its glorious past and wondered if the unseen eyes of its ghosts were observing them. Strangers, hesitant in manner, uncertain of their surroundings, blindly striding forward, loath to ask and give themselves away as newcomers.

With hardly a glance they passed the reception desk and continued down the corridor formed by the beautifully veined marble columns. A dance band could be heard playing a popular tune and through an archway Sandy could see an open doorway revealing a large room with a central dance floor. The tantalising notes of the music beckoned them, an irresistible invitation to two young officers at last free from the confines of duty. Thus they were drawn in.

They entered the ballroom, with its comfortable bamboo chairs placed beside tables set around the perimeter. Couples twirled to and fro to the distinct tempo of a fox-trot, their heads momentarily turning towards the two men as they entered.

Sandy, making a quick appraisal, chose a small table away from the band but near to the door they had come through. Sitting down he let his eyes wander about the room and caught the attention of a white-uniformed Chinese steward.

'*Dua Stengah,*' he said, in his newly acquired, stilted Malay.

'*Tabe Tuan,*' came the reply, and the steward returned to the bar to get their whiskies and sodas. Sandy continued to gaze about the room.

'*What on earth do these people do all day!*'

Europeans were in evidence everywhere, interspersed with a few young Chinese couples; the men all seemed to be wearing some sort of evening dress. His eyes stopped, subconsciously, just passed Carson's shoulder and alighted on a pretty, well dressed European woman sitting on her own at the table next to them. She was a real beauty, quite desirable in fact! He noticed there was only one glass on the table.

He couldn't resist taking a second look, this time observing her more fully. She was slim, and had wide-set, blue eyes and a pert nose. A generous red mouth completed her features, which were framed by a short, blonde bob. The blue dress was cut low, which enhanced her creamy, naked shoulders and sensuous, ample breasts.

Sandy sat back and focused on her.

'Around thirty? ... ring on her finger – married!'

Carson's voice invaded his thoughts.

'What do you make of this chap Winter?'

Charles Winter, the Superintendent of Police, met everyone on arrival at the airport and was in charge of the transit centre. He had responsibility also for the issue of sidearms and equipment and the briefing and posting of new recruits to the Federation.

He was a pleasant man about Sandy's age and had been badly wounded whilst visiting a rubber estate in Ipoh during a terrorist ambush; a burst of Bren gun fire resulted in a nasty wound to his left arm which left him nervy and accounted for his hesitancy of speech. He was reluctant to discuss the action which had killed two of his men and left him disabled and was, understandably, in need of a change from active service. Sandy never pursued the matter, respecting the other's silence, but the subject was never far from the lips of the officers in the mess and the information was readily passed on to newcomers.

'Quite honestly ... it's not a matter I've thought much about ... nor one I feel qualified to discuss,' Sandy said dryly.

Carson changed the subject.

'I'm glad the taxi driver agreed to pick us up here at midnight ... this is certainly the best place to do a recce from ... Excuse me a moment ... just want to see a man about a dog.'

Getting up, he winked and ambled towards the door.

With Carson out of the way Sandy had a clearer view of the lady at the table beyond and he quickly gave her his full attention. As his gaze reached her face their eyes met fleetingly, only to return again as a wisp of a smile flitted across her face.

'Hi ... say, you two guys seem to have a lot to talk about ... how about having a drink with me ...? I'm on my own.'

Her voice was husky with a slight American inflection.

The invitation took Sandy off guard; difficult to imagine she would speak first! His mind raced as he fumbled for words.

'Thank you ... that's very kind of you ... but how about having one with me first?'

As he spoke he rose to his feet and took the few steps to her table, looking down on her pretty, upturned face.

'May I ... have this dance?'

She gave him a broad smile and laughed.

'Sure ... why not ...' and stood up exposing a willowy figure.

'About five feet three – lovely shape!'

His arm encircled her slim waist and he drew her close. Her supple body melted into his and he was conscious of the full, rounded breasts with the hard, pointed nipples straining through the flimsy material. From the feel of her body under his hands she had very little on.

The tango swept them onto the floor, exciting, sensual, and left them oblivious to everyone in the room. Sandy held her tight and, from time to time, could feel her breasts on his chest and her flat, firm, stomach on his, as they executed the intricate, erotic steps of the dance. Her breath, hot and moist, caressed his neck and the intoxicating fragrance of her perfume made his head swim.

In harmony, they moved backwards and forwards, twirling and circling the floor, executing every step to perfection and, as the music drew to a close, Sandy tightened his grip on her waist, ending the dance with a flourish as she flipped backwards across his arm, her hair brushing the floor. Gently he brought her upright as she gave a little sigh, exclaiming.

'That was – divine, just divine. I don't often get the chance to tango ... I've really enjoyed it with you ... you're good.'

Sandy, flustered at the unexpected compliment, realised suddenly he didn't even know her name.

'I'm sorry, we haven't been introduced – I'm Alexander, Alexander MacIntyre ... known as Sandy. What's yours?'

She hesitated a second before replying, 'Blanche ... Skinner ... just call me Blanche!'

He escorted her back to the table where Carson was waiting for them.

'Blanche ... this is Carson ... a colleague of mine.'

Carson had risen to his feet as they approached and replied a trifle pompously,

'Robert Carson ... at your service!'

Sandy caught the attention of a passing steward.

'Now, drinks all round, what's yours, Blanche?'

'Whisky-mac, please,' she answered with ease.

Sandy repeated the previous order and added a whisky-mac for Blanche. She looked intently at Sandy.

'What are you two guys doing in Singapore?'

Giving nothing away that would endanger their position, Sandy knew just how to reply. He looked hard at Carson and answered,

'We're in the services ... living in the Naval Base waiting for a posting – we've only been here a few days. This is our first visit to the city.'

'Right ... I see ... I'll have to show you the sights – I know Singapore well ... I've been visiting the city for about three years now – to do my shopping – I live just outside Djakarta, Java.'

The steward placed the drinks on the table. Carson, who hadn't yet paid for a round, made a point of ordering another and, with a grandiose gesture meant to impress, ordered doubles.

The rhythm of the fox-trot floated over the conversation and Sandy once again asked Blanche to dance. Her face lit up, she smiled and nodded her head. With an uncanny familiarity, they put their arms about each other and glided across the floor, enjoying every moment of the intimacy of their bodies. They danced together as though they had done so all their lives – a perfect match, with effortless ease and grace.

She whispered, 'I like you ... I'm really enjoying myself tonight – generally Singapore's a bore – I never stay here long enough to get to know anyone – you're good company and I like the way you dance – you make me feel alive!'

Sandy, elated by her direct approach, replied, 'Me too ... I've enjoyed this evening Blanche ... you've certainly made my day ... thank you.'

She danced with them both and the time flew but, much to Sandy's delight, Carson could not command the same expertise which he possessed. Blanche insisted on ordering her share of drinks and paid for them from a large leather bag which, at the touch of a clasp, flicked open to reveal, to Sandy's utter amazement, bundles of tightly rolled, high denomination American dollar bills. She was in possession of a very large sum of money indeed. From what he could see, he calculated she must be in possession of many thousands of dollars.

They laughed and drank all evening and she seemed to carry hers well, like Sandy. Carson, however, not used to whisky, was the only one who became a little fuddled. Blanche and Sandy had danced again and again when, out of the blue, something happened which was to completely change the course of events.

On returning to the table and sitting down Sandy felt Blanche's hand on his knee, her fingers bending and stretching as they moved upwards to his thigh. With increasing pleasure he put his hand under the table and instinctively placed his over hers. He did not, however, expect to feel the hard object she was holding! Nevertheless, although caught unawares by the sudden gesture, he palmed, without a flicker of an eye, the key that had been offered to him and slowly put it into his jacket pocket!

His now shaking hand returned to hers which had not moved from where she had placed it. They looked into each other's eyes and a pensive smile passed over her face; at the same time she gave his hand a squeeze and her head gave a little nod.

She said quietly. 'Yeah ...?'

'Yes …' he replied huskily, hardly able to contain the stirring in his loins. Carson, now babbling, didn't appear to notice.

It had been a fun evening and it was late so they took the decision not to venture further afield. Blanche suggested sandwiches and beer in her suite.

As midnight struck Sandy excused himself to go and look for the taxi driver to ask him to wait a little longer for them. The Chinese was there as promised and agreed to wait till they were ready to go back to the base.

By this time Carson appeared half asleep, the unaccustomed whisky exerting its effect. Sandy and Blanche, with Carson bringing up the rear, climbed the wide, central, staircase from the entrance hall and made their way to her room which was on the first floor overlooking the Palm Court.

Sandy now realised that his imagined evening alone with her was going badly wrong; he hadn't reckoned on having Carson in tow! Nevertheless, he felt he'd better play it 'off the cuff' and was determined not to make a hash of things by rushing.

The suite, comfortable but not large, was entered through the veranda lounge overlooking the palm court. The double bedroom and *en suite* bathroom were entered from the back of the lounge; the occupant had to pass through one to get to the other.

As soon as they entered Carson made a beeline for the bathroom and, much to Sandy's relief, was not seen again. The sandwiches and beer had been set on the table in the lounge; Sandy poured two Tiger beers and he and Blanche, with occasional glances at each other, picked at the food. Nothing had been said of the key, which was now in its rightful place, on the inside of the door.

After a while, she excused herself to change into something more comfortable. Sandy picked nervously at the sandwiches – time passed – and as neither Blanche or Carson had returned he decided to investigate. He knocked and was just about to open the bedroom door when the crying, dishevelled figure of Blanche staggered out.

'What the hell …!'

He grasped her momentarily round the shoulders, then rushed into the room, where he found Carson partly dressed and lying on one of the single beds, ostensibly out for the count.

In a flash Sandy realised that Carson was not as intoxicated as he'd made out and discovered later that the blackguard had been aware of the key being passed by Blanche. All he'd done was bide his time then take advantage of the situation. Sandy returned to the lounge and the distraught Blanche threw herself into his arms, sobbing.

'I'm sorry Sandy … I wanted you all the time … I didn't mean to go to bed with him ... but he was there and made a pass at me ... I thought you'd lost interest.'

Her small frame shook as she continued to weep.

'You won't understand ... it's hard for me and I'm so unhappy – I've left my husband ... he ... he's a swine – I came home unexpectedly from a visit to my mother in America and caught him in bed with a native women ... I've left him for good ... don't go, Sandy – stay with me – I need you ... send Carson back to the base!'

The words came out in a torrent as deep sobs racked her body. She clung to him and he did his best to comfort her; it was all so embarrassing. There was little he could do now, Carson had spoiled everything and, from the look of him, he would certainly take some getting out of the hotel.

Holding her, he became aware that she was not wearing anything under the flimsy negligée; it had fallen open, revealing her voluptuous breasts. Steeling himself, he carefully drew the negligée about her, covering her nakedness, and said gently,

'Sorry Blanche ... I have to get back to the base ...' He continued, trying to ease his embarrassment, 'Maybe we could have dinner this evening ... the Royal Lancers are playing in the Palm Court and ... if you like ... we could listen to them from here.'

However, the vision of Carson on the bed next door plus Blanche's confession had already dampened his ardour; it had thrown a different light on what could have been a marvellous evening. He realised he was playing for time and needed space to sort things out.

Her tear-stained face nodded in agreement.

'You will come?'

'Yes ... I'll come ... I could be here by 6 o'clock ... OK?'

Again she nodded her head, appearing calmer. He sat her down.

'I've got to go now, Blanche ... it's late and the taxi's been waiting since midnight ... I'll get Carson out – you'd better wait here!'

He entered the bedroom, got hold of Carson and shook him. He came round with a grunt.

'What the ... where am I? What's happened?'

Looking at him in disgust, Sandy snarled.

'Get up, you bastard ...! it's time to get back to the base! – if you don't move NOW ...! I'll kick you all the way out of this bloody room!'

Sandy, itching to get his hands on him, could hardly restrain himself. Carson shook his head from side to side as though to clear it and got to his feet.

'... all right, all right ...! all *right* ... have it your own way – don't know what you're beefing about!' Carson whined, then grunted, 'Let's go!'

With that, he stumbled towards the door and, without so much as a glance at Blanche, staggered through, and down the corridor.

Sandy turned to her, she rushed into his arms, her hungry mouth finding his and for a few seconds he stood there, helplessly locked in a passionate embrace.

'Must go, Blanche ... must go ... that blighter is quite likely to go off and leave me without transport!'

Before he could stop himself, he kissed her mouth long and hard, wishing the evening had been different.

'Next time ... you won't have Carson pestering you!'

Leaving the little pathetic looking figure framed in the doorway he made his way out of the hotel to the waiting taxi.

Carson was already lolled across the seat and the journey passed without incident, taking only thirty minutes; he roused himself sufficiently to get out of the taxi and pay his share of the fare. Sandy hung back as the befuddled man weaved his way into the darkness.

The taxi driver's eyes sparkled as he agreed to pick up his fare again that evening and deposit him at Raffles. He grinned and bowed politely saying, 'Yes, *Tuan* ... you got my numba?'

His sleep was disturbed, images of the other two kept floating in front of him. The one he preferred was of Blanche and the negligée – but damnably, Carson kept darting in and out of his tangled thoughts.

He rose early, planning what he would do, and knew his duties must be completed by lunchtime, to allow him to concentrate on what was nagging his subconscious.

Terrorist activity made it essential the signals received from the mainland during the preceding twenty-four hours were read with infinite care. Sometimes there were only a few, but it was impossible to tell what the day would bring. In addition, the notices from Interpol had also to be studied, and since these covered the whole of south east Asia they took some time to digest.

Sunday was always a busy day; the reports tended to build up at the end of the week and this Sunday was no exception. Just before noon Sandy picked up the last Interpol report and his attention was drawn to details of an incident that had occurred during the earlier part of the week in Djarkarta, Java.

The manager of one of the largest offshore oil drilling rigs had been attacked in his bungalow, hit over the head with a blunt instrument and rendered unconscious, his keys taken and the safe opened. A large sum of money in American dollars was missing; money he was holding to pay the monthly wages of the locally employed staff. Police were looking for the man's wife to help them with their inquiries, but she'd disappeared.

The name of the manager was – *Skinner*!

'My God ...!' he muttered under his breath, 'so that's why she's carrying such a large sum of money.'

He sat back for a moment to think things through.

'*There's really only one course of action – confront Blanche on my own and question her ... after that I'll decide what action is deemed necessary.*'

His mind was in turmoil.

'*In a million years I couldn't have dreamt this up. Bloody hell, I hope Carson misses this and does his usual fast-track scan of reports ... be damnable if, just this once, he read them all! Still – he's a bloody lazy individual ...*'

The afternoon was interminable; he felt sick to the pit of his stomach and was tempted to ring Blanche, but drew back from the obvious.

'*Had the Singapore Police already traced her – or not? She could already be heading back to the States.*'

Five thirty arrived none too soon and the waiting taxi took him at lightning speed to the hotel. The traffic was easy and he arrived just before six o'clock. He'd made a tentative plan and arranged with the Chinese to collect him at eleven o'clock; that would be late enough, whatever transpired.

He presented himself to the clerk at the reception desk.

'Good evening, will you tell Mrs Skinner that I've arrived?'

Without hesitation the clerk cast his eyes towards the keys hanging on the rack behind him; the key was missing so he turned to consult the ledger.

'Sorry, Sir ... *Memsahib* closed her account and left this morning!'

'*Planned to the last ...!*'

Sandy didn't know what he felt – relief? ... regret? ... possibly both.

'*Still – at least I didn't have to make that vital decision concerning Blanche Skinner – one way or the other.*'

'Double Scotch, *terima kaseh.*'

Standing at the Planters' Bar Sandy took a sip before walking to the window and gazing out at the fan palms gently swaying in the breeze. He smiled, allowing his thoughts to dwell on the pleasurable side of the previous evening. The incident of '*The Key*' was closed, but he knew that in time this was going to make one helluva tale over dinner.

3

Posting and Initiation

At last Sandy received notification that he was to be posted to the State of Johore which stretched north across the straits adjacent to the Naval Base.

To get there it was necessary to cross the mile long causeway, a combined umbilical cord and carotid artery, a lifeline joining the island of Singapore to the Malayan peninsula. The causeway supplied not only the road, rail and a communications link, but was also the means of supporting the giant water pipes that fed fresh water from the hinterland to the reservoirs of the Island.

Standby instructions were received to proceed to the Johore Contingent Police Headquarters at Bukit Senyum, Johore Baharu, the state capital, where he would be interviewed by the Chief Police Officer (CPO) and instructed about his final appointment.

Sandy set about preparing his number-one dress uniform, the silver buttons of which depicted a Malayan Tiger running through *lalang*. The Police, sometimes called by their enemies the Min Yuen, *the Tigers of Malaya*, were generally referred to as '*the running dogs*'.

With a couple of minutes to spare, Sandy strapped on his loaded Browning automatic – Police Regulations dictating that all officers travelling within the Federation must be armed – and, on the stroke of 08.00 hrs a Police Land Rover driven by a Malay arrived to take Sandy to Johore Baharu. The journey to JB took only fifteen minutes to the border at the end of the causeway, which was crossed without formalities.

The Police HQ and Depot were situated at the back of the town, on the brow of a hill to the north, and commanded a wonderful view of the Straits and Singapore Island. The approach road traversed past the railway station along the banks of an old canal which was, in reality, a combination of both tidal-stream and large monsoon drain. Bordering it, over the edge of the water, sat little wooden huts on stilts. The area hummed with activity and smelt like an open fishmarket.

The Land Rover passed through the wide gates, which were flanked by two armed guards who came smartly to attention, presenting arms.

31

As they pulled up in front of the main building the Duty Officer emerged to escort Sandy to the office of the CPO. Sandy dismounted and saluted and the welcoming figure did likewise.

'Morning Mr MacIntyre! The CPO will see you right away ... follow me, Sir!'

Having climbed to the first floor they marched along a veranda corridor, stopping outside a room which had half swing doors. Sandy smiled inwardly at the vivid boyhood pictures they created – *westerns, cowboys and saloon bars!*

'Wait here, Sir ...!'

Seconds only elapsed and the Duty Officer returned, indicating to Sandy to enter. The room was big, running the full width of the building. He observed at the far end a large desk and the robust figure of the CPO. The senior officer smiled as Sandy walked forward, his red, genial face creasing to a broad grin. Sandy halted and saluted and the CPO stood up and shot a great horny hand across the desk at him.

'Pleased to meet you, MacIntyre!'

His voice was pleasant and deep.

'I've been going through your personal file ... we know a good deal about you and from what I've read we could do with more like you ... I hope with us you'll have a good tour and a safe one.'

Sandy, still at attention, was trying not to wince. His fingers, tingling from the big man's handshake, felt as though they'd been crushed.

'*My bloody trigger finger!*'

'Sit down, MacIntyre, make yourself comfortable. We're a mixed bunch ... no doubt you'll come across some old comrades. I won't keep you long ... you're going up-country to relieve an OCPD who's due leave ... his name's Alfred Cannon and he's just completed his first tour!'

The CPO then told Sandy he would be the Officer in Charge of the Police District of Labis which came under the jurisdiction of the Officer Superintending Police Circle (OSPC) of Segamat, situated in the northern part of the State. He would be responsible for the prevention and detection of crime and the recruiting and welfare of the Malay Special Constabulary. For the latter he would be allocated two Police Lieutenants whose duties would be to train the SCs and generally look after them. His primary job, however, was to eradicate the communist terrorists in the district.

The CPO went on to inform Sandy that on the journey out the second Lieutenant had gone down with malaria but would join him as soon as he arrived. His name was William Beaumont, an ex regular Army Warrant Officer.

He instructed Sandy to get ready to leave that night on the Singapore-

Kuala Lumpur train, which arrived in Johore Baharu at midnight to pick up its armed guard. All passenger and goods trains were preceded by an armoured pilot train to ensure the line remained clear of obstructions and to check the track hadn't been tampered with. Passenger trains had an engine at both ends to ensure mobility if they got into trouble. The whole operation then hinged on the guards who were backed up by the machine-guns of an armoured Scout car on an open wagon situated between the passenger coaches and the goods wagons.

Sandy liked and felt at ease with the friendly Colonial who had spent the greater part of his life in Malaya and had been a guiding hand in Force 136 during the Japanese occupation. He was straight to the point, informing Sandy it was not 'a bed of roses' and that he'd have to be careful when moving about.

'The district is an active one, straddling the main road and railway line north to the Federal Capital and therefore often a terrorist target. Any questions?' he asked.

'Not at the moment, Sir! I'll have some later, no doubt, but the OCPD will fill me in. I'll be ready for the train and ... I assume, Sir, that I'll be met on arrival at the other end?'

'Yes! A coded signal was sent this morning. Best of luck, MacIntyre, and keep your head down ... I'll see you again when I come up on my tour of inspection!'

With that he stood up, towering over Sandy like some big grisly bear, then shook his hand. Sandy, standing to attention, saluted; and felt as if he was waving a broken branch!

Outside the swing doors the Duty Officer was waiting for him.

'Follow me, Sir, I'll take you to the registry where you'll be given a travel warrant for the journey ahead.'

They retraced their steps to the ground floor and entered the main administration office where he was introduced to a Malay Police Inspector who had the warrant already made out.

'You'll find your warrant and posting instructions inside, Sir! have a safe journey, Sir!'

Sandy thanked him and left to return to the Land Rover with the Duty Officer.

'Sir ...! if the bandits attack tonight, keep your head down ... don't leave the train if it stops. We once had a chap who thought he'd be better off on the ground and the train went off without him ... never seen again!'

'Thanks for the advice ...! I'll certainly keep my head down ... now I know what the CPO meant!'

'I'll be at the station tonight, Sir, to see you off – Mr Winter has been instructed to provide transport. You'll be the only one going up the line from here ... on the train there'll be a Lieutenant commanding the guard, so you have nothing to worry about on that score ... see you later, Sir.'

He saluted Sandy and dashed off in the direction of the parade ground where a group of uniformed men were being drilled. Sandy called up the driver, who'd been waiting in the car park, and instructed him to drive back to the Naval Base.

The day passed quickly and Winter confirmed that he personally would take him to the station in his own car. Sandy was pleased to be going and glad that Carson kept out of his way; he never saw him again. Carson was killed in a terrorist ambush on the Perak border some five months later.

The train from Singapore came in on time and he was shown by Winter to the air-conditioned first class coach where a reserved seat was kept for officers travelling from JB.

The coach was furnished in the style of a saloon, with easy chairs and small side tables set on a fully carpeted floor. There was a small bar at one end and the usual offices at the other. The train wasn't busy but a number of service personnel in uniform were in evidence; everyone, including civilians, was armed to the teeth.

'Best of luck, MacIntyre, take care and don't rush into things ...!'

At that moment the Duty Officer came hurrying up; he was gasping for breath.

'Thought I was going to miss you Sir ...! got held up at the last minute ... there's terrorist activity around the Kluang area! ... Hello, Mr Winter! haven't seen you for ages ... how are you, Sir ...?'

And without giving the other a chance to reply he rattled on,

'I say ... Mr MacIntyre, you are a lucky devil ...! I've just heard that the Gurkhas are going on operations in your district ...! bloody good lot in the jungle they are ... should put the wind up the CTs ...! Take care, Sir ... don't do anything I wouldn't do ...! Must be off now ... got to get to the *Istana* and check the guard or the old Sultan will be after me ...!'

With that he was gone, disappearing through the cloud of steam pouring from the rear engine of the train. Winter chuckled quietly.

'Typical of Mallet ...! Harry is always in a rush ... he's one of the permanent Lieutenant Duty Officers at HQ where he's known as Blah Mallet ... By the way, give my kindest regards to Cannon when you get to Labis ... we came out together, he's a good type! I'm sure you'll get on with him. He's well liked as an OCPD!'

With this last piece of information ringing in his ears, Sandy heard the Station Master's whistle heralding his departure and turned to Winter.

'Thanks for all your kindness and advice ... Be seeing you one of these days ... Hope all goes well for you ...!'

The two shook hands and nodded to each other then Winter left, an isolated figure walking slowly down the platform and out of sight.

Whilst the two officers had been chatting the train stewards had pulled down the blinds and put up substantial shutters on the windows. The train would now travel through the night to its destination completely blacked out.

Sandy made himself as comfortable as possible; he felt sleepy after the day's business but dozed fitfully as the train continually stopped and started whilst awaiting clearance to travel over the line ahead. As they approached Labis the dawn was breaking.

'Excuse me, *Sahib* ...!'

The subdued voice of the Indian ticket inspector woke him.

'The train is stopping only for you, Sir! Could you please be ready to get off as soon as we arrive ...!'

He then inclined his body towards Sandy in a confidential fashion and murmured,

'The line ahead is clear and it is most important that we get started as quickly as possible!'

It was a very small station that Sandy found himself standing on. He glanced round then picked up his baggage and walked towards the waiting room. He opened the door and was engulfed immediately in the welcoming handshake of a tall, gangling Police Officer.

'Alexander MacIntyre? ... Cannon! Glad to see you're in one piece ... must have been a quiet night ... any nasty moments ...?'

'No ...! nothing to report – we stopped a lot but I suppose that's how it goes ... better that than a shoot-out! By the way ... Winter sends his kindest regards and hopes to see you in JB before you go on leave.'

'Great ...! how is old Charles these days? He'd a nasty experience y'know ... the buggers nearly shot him up for good!'

'He didn't say much but seems to be coping ...!'

Cannon stretched his hand out.

'Let's have that bag of yours ... I'll give it to Elias, he'll look after you ... he's a good honest chap.'

With that, he took the bag from Sandy and charged out of the doorway and down the steps to the Land Rover parked outside.

'Put the rest of your gear in the back and get in the front with me ...!' he said, climbing into the driver's seat.

Sandy did as he was instructed and with a crunch of gears they shot off down the road heading towards the small township of Labis, which consisted simply of an assortment of buildings built from wood and brick.

In the town centre they passed the Police Station on the corner of the crossroads and proceeded up to the top of a small hill where Cannon turned into the driveway of a tiny wooden bungalow.

'This is it ...! home sweet home. It's not bad when you get used to the mosquitoes ... crickets ... frogs ... heat and humidity! It's all yours when I go ... complete with mod cons ... especially the running water ... through the roof ...!'

He laughed heartily.

To Sandy it looked marvellous. The open fronted veranda overlooked the drive which was bordered by tall red and yellow canna lilies. The long spiked flowers appeared in the half light and early morning breeze like small children waving flags of welcome. The dull, rain-laden, skyline was broken by two coconut palms that leaned crazily outwards from one of the gables like two drunken men, their heavily burdened fruit tops just out of range of the roof below.

They pulled up at the bottom of the steps leading to the entrance. Cannon got out, shouting,

'Abdulla ...! where the devil are you ...? Get down here and collect the new *Tuan*'s baggage ...!'

From nowhere the stocky figure of a Malay appeared, dressed in white shirt and trousers. The white cap of a Haji adorned his head, denoting that he had made the pilgrimage to Mecca. His momentarily impassive face burst into a smile on seeing Sandy.

'*Selamat hari Tuan* ...!'

'*Selamat Abdulla*, ...' Sandy replied politely to the greetings of the day.

Elias got out of the back of the vehicle with the baggage and handed it over to the house steward, then climbed into the driver's seat and waited. Cannon called over his shoulder as he went up the steps.

'Come back at nine ... *Baik*!'

'*Ya ... Tuan* ...!' he replied and drove off.

The house had only three rooms. The main room, in the centre of the building, was both lounge and dining-room; it had a bedroom at each end, the bathroom and kitchen abutted each other at the back and were joined to the main structure by a roofed walkway.

Cannon showed Sandy to the room that had been prepared for him. 'You can sort yourself out when I've gone if you don't like this one – there's really no difference in them except mine's nearer the bath house! By the way Alexander, I'm known to my friends as "Bang" ... hate being called Alf or Fred, so don't forget ... I'm the *big noise* around here!'

He laughed.

'What do I call you – Alexander's a bit of a mouthful!'

Sandy grinned and said,

'I'm usually known as Sandy …'

'Well, Sandy, we'll go to the office after breakfast and I'll introduce you to the Police Lieutenant … he does all the ground work with the SCs in the rubber estates. After that we'll go to Circle HQ to meet our boss, Senior Superintendent John Thwaites, then the ASP Special Branch and the Transport and Signals *wallahs* …' he paused. 'You can get some shopping in too if you like, since the place is much bigger and has more shops than we have … I always take advantage of a trip there … breakfast is at eight … see you then …!'

Left to his own devices Sandy began to unpack his bags. He glanced round at the made-up bed with mosquito net, at the finished appearance of the room and it dawned on him that the responsibility of stocking and running the household was now all his!

The aroma of bacon and eggs drifted through, heralding breakfast. Bang was already seated at the table and looked up as Sandy entered.

'Hello there … got yourself organised?'

He swallowed a mouthful of food and continued,

'Elias is your driver – he's a good steady chap and dependable … however if you want to drive yourself you can, he won't mind. You'll also have two chaps as an escort … one armed with a rifle and the other with a Sten gun.'

He took another mouthful of food and Sandy waited for him to finish before asking,

'What do I have in the way of weapons?'

'You'll be armed with a Sten or 300 American carbine if you prefer that … I'm afraid that's all we get! And you do have to be careful not to create a pattern of movements to places out of town! The CTs are very active round here … always stopping buses and burning them in the hope of a quick reaction that might lead us into one of their ambushes!'

He half turned in his seat towards the kitchen and chided,

'Chop-chop Chan!'

And with that the cook, a large Chinese of generous proportions, came ambling in carrying Sandy's breakfast.

'Watch out for this slit-eyed heathen,' he said in a jocular voice. 'He'll eat you out of house and home! I only put up with him because he's a damned good cook and his wife's a first class Amah – I advise you to keep them!'

The fat Chinese grinned at the dubious compliment and disappeared, shuffling into his kitchen where the radio was blaring out the popular Chinese tune '*Rose, Rose I love you!*'

The Land Rover pulled up outside and Bang nodded to Sandy

indicating that it was time to go. The two got up and Cannon went to his room and returned with an American carbine tucked under his arm, then made for the veranda. Elias was already out of the vehicle waiting for him to take the wheel. Sandy got into the passenger seat and Elias, plus carbine, got into the back.

It was a short journey to the Police Station where Sandy would soon take over. He was introduced to the Chief Inspector, a Malay who was the crime officer, and the Lieutenant, a red faced Yorkshireman.

Robert Sutcliffe was Sandy's age and had been in Malaya only three months. He was a quiet, unassuming man, well liked by his colleagues. He saluted Sandy.

'Good morning, Sir ... hope you had a good journey?'

Sandy took a liking to him straight away and, returning the salute, said,

'I'm told you were in the Green Howards ... you didn't by any chance serve in Burma with them?'

'Yes Sir – in the Arakan ... we were attached to the 4th Brigade ... 82nd West African Division ... I finished up in Sandoway!'

'Ye Gods!' exclaimed Sandy, 'that was my outfit! We'll certainly have to get together and talk over old times!'

'Thank you, Sir!' Sutcliffe answered.

After a quick inspection of the premises and transportation Cannon took Sandy to the armoury and asked what he would like as a second weapon. Sandy had already made up his mind and chose the American carbine which was semi-automatic and had a good rate of fire. It was comfortable to carry, accurate and more reliable than the sten. Two Malay SCs were marched in by the Lieutenant, who informed Sandy that they would be his personal escort whenever he left town. Their names were Bujang and Mohammed. Both were family men in their thirties and Sandy was assured they had been chosen for their reliability. They were given orders to make themselves available for duty whenever required. It was suggested that he could use them that morning for his visit to Segamat.

Segamat was about ten miles up the main road and Bang was impatient to get there as soon as possible, having said he would take Sandy to the Rest House for lunch. So, amidst a cloud of dust they drove off, with Elias and the escort in the back and Sandy, plus carbine, riding shotgun up front with Cannon.

The route took them through the sprawling outskirts of the township then past a palm oil plantation, which petered out into virgin jungle that encroached menacingly on either side of the road. The tall, dark trees formed a canopy over them and a dank, unhealthy odour polluted the air from the depth of the jungle's oppressive silence. The road, thickly bordered by tall *lalang*, snaked up through a number of sharp hairpin bends to the top of a steep hill.

'Windy Corner!' Bang growled tersely through his teeth. 'More ambushes here than hot dinners! Lot of bloody good chaps have wet their pants going through this sector ...'

His venom unfettered, he drove on in silence.

Sandy quietly acknowledged it all, his eyes monitoring the green impregnable wall for any sign of movement; the hairs on the back of his neck standing on end! He knew from experience the jungle's mastery at hiding an ambush party, so the CTs would have first 'crack of the whip'.

Eventually they reached the summit and started the downward run, snaking as before, but this time much faster. He saw ahead that the *lalang* had been cut back on each side of the road to the jungle edge which would keep the CTs from getting too close but would, nevertheless, also increase their field of fire. It was a no-win situation – just down to Lady Luck!

They gathered momentum and Bang did his best to get the maximum out of the engine. The road finally levelled out, passing through a mixture of open paddy and scrub.

'Used to be a squatter area this, before the "Briggs Plan". All the Chinks are now in the New Village of Kampong Bedenak which we'll be going past very shortly.'

He gave a huge sigh.

'Bloody glad we got through 'windy corner' without a shoot-out! Must be getting leave happy ... roll on the boat ... it's hard to believe I'll be on the *Chusan* at the end of next week ...!'

Cannon's face was simultaneously one of expectation and disbelief.

'I can't say I blame you ... let's face it, three years is a hell of a long time when you live under these conditions,' Sandy commiserated.

'Well, Sandy boy, always treat this road with respect ... *never* ... let it lull you into a false heaven! ... repentance comes too late.'

They were now passing the large double gates that led into the *Kampong*, which was completely encircled by a high barbed-wire fence. Tall watch-towers could be seen strategically positioned around the perimeter, each manned by the local Home Guard. Five miles on, after passing through some flat scrubland, they crossed the bridge that led into Segamat, and Bang turned to Sandy.

'We'll go to Headquarters first and get the visitation over!'

They went through the gates of Circle HQ, taking the salute *en route* and stopped in front of a single storied building with a veranda running its full length.

Bang led the way smartly down the long, cool corridor to the OSPC's office. He rapped the '*bar doors*'.

'Enter!' a voice called briskly.

Cannon disappeared; the sound of feet clicking sharply on the cement floor was heard followed by muffled voices, then Bang poked his head over the top of the door.

'Come in, Sandy, and meet the Gaffer ...!'

Sandy passed through the door and halted, saluting the seated figure. He saw a long, gaunt man who must have been in his late thirties; his prematurely lined face showed signs of emaciation and the scull-like face had an unhealthy yellowish tinge – a legacy of being a prisoner of war in the infamous Changi jail. The thin, almost shapeless figure uncurled slowly from the chair, and stretched out a bony arm at the end of which a skeletal hand appeared. Sandy, mesmerised, took the proffered hand with some concern.

'*What a difference from the CPO*,' he thought.

A well-spoken, modulated voice brought him back.

'Glad to have you with us, Sandy. I know our friend here is just champing at the bit to get you installed to make way for his departure ...!'

'You can say that again ...!' Bang interrupted.

The OCPC continued unabashed.

'Nevertheless, listen to him when he's giving advice ... he's a prime example of how to survive and still be a good officer ... I won't keep you long, you need to "make your number" with the others. I'll see you another time when you don't have so much to do ... you can always come in and see me if you need to!'

'Thank you Sir ... I'll call in the next time I come ... Bang tells me that's the normal procedure when visiting Segamat.'

'Yes ... that's right. I hope he's also told you to be careful in your neck of the woods! There's a lot going on ... the Gurkhas will be on operations here very shortly which I sincerely hope will ease the situation for us ...'

His voice trailed to almost a whisper. They shook hands again; the officers saluted, then left for the Special Branch office.

'John Thwaites is a great chap and the best OSPC I've ever served under!' Bang said when they had got out of earshot.

'You'll like the SB wallah ...! he's a Scot like you, Sandy, comes from somewhere outside Oban ... his name is Tam Mactavish ... I just call him Mac ...! it's easier and he's the same rank as we are anyway ... but never wears uniform!'

They walked to the other end of the corridor into an almost identical office. A large man in his late thirties was sitting at a desk in the corner of the room, whilst in the other a European lady banged away at a typewriter.

'Hello Mac! I've brought my relief to see you ... Alexander MacIntyre – a fellow Scot, so you'd better look after him!'

A red, boyish face with an impish look glanced up and broke into a grin. The man pushed aside the pile of papers on the desk and heaved his bulk to his feet. The sunburnt face beamed at them as he strode forward to grasp Sandy by the hand.

'It's about time we had some more Scots blood here ...! Is it Alec or Alexander you're known by?' he queried in the soft lilt of the Western Isles.

'Just plain Sandy to my friends ... I'm pleased to meet a kindred man ...!'

He laughed, then jokingly added,

'I know just how you feel amongst all these sassenachs!'

Bang interrupted.

'Mac, we're having lunch at the Rest House, how about joining us?'

'That's a grand idea ... the usual time?'

'Yes, we've only to see Taffy Williams and Bill Harvey and we're finished here.'

'Right ...! I'll be waiting for you with a cool Tiger beer.'

Bang led the way out of the building to the transport workshops and park. Taffy Williams, the Lieutenant in charge of transport, couldn't be found and enquiries indicated that he had gone to pick up a broken-down vehicle, so Bang carried on to an adjacent building surrounded by wireless masts. Here they found a Lieutenant fiddling with a 19 set. Bang introduced him to Sandy.

'Meet Bill Harvey, better known as "Sparks" – the chap's a wizard when it comes to the old chat box ... we couldn't operate without him!'

Harvey was a lanky, well spoken, ex RAF radio technician who'd joined the Police as a specialist. He was well respected for his reliability and knowledge of communications.

'Pleased to meet you, Sir,' he said, welcoming Sandy.

'It's funny you should come today, Mr Cannon, I wanted to see you about a new radio set for your HQ ... I suppose I'd better deal with Mr MacIntyre now that you're going on leave?'

'Yes ...! you do that small thing ... but not today, we don't have time ... I'm only showing him around.'

'Oh, that's all right, I'm not quite ready ... but forewarned is fore-armed! I thought I'd better mention it.'

'Fine – I'll be seeing you,' replied Sandy, as Bang, looking at his watch, chipped in,

'I say, old chap, we'll have to be on our way if we're to get anything to eat ... Mac will be drinking all the beer!'

They took their leave and walked the short distance to the Rest House.

It was a solid building made of wood and brick and was surrounded by a number of chalets which were self-contained. The dining room and bar faced onto a long veranda which overlooked the town. Planters and their families, as well as the local European residents of the district, used its facilities most of the time, making it a popular meeting place.

By the time Sandy and Cannon arrived the place was packed. Mac waved them over as they entered; he was sitting in the corner – just as Bang had predicted – with the two bottles of *'Tiger'* and two glasses, awaiting their arrival.

'Thought you'd never come ...! had to get the drinks in to keep the seats for you, they seem busy today ...'

'Thanks, old chap, don't know what we'd do without you. *Yum Sing*!' and Bang took a long swig at the now lukewarm beer.

They had a couple more rounds followed by an enjoyable lunch and a tour of the local shops, after which Bang became impatient to leave. Elias and the escort looked relieved to see them return and were soon ready to depart. Sandy made a mental note that it was not a good idea to spin out a visit longer than was necessary. Soon they were passing the gates of the new village and travelling through the desolate area before the climb up to 'windy corner'.

After negotiating a sharp bend they saw three armed figures dressed in khaki crossing the road in front of them. Bang slewed the vehicle to a halt, tyres screaming.

'Bandits!! ... after them! ... Elias! ... stay with the Land Rover ... remainder follow me!'

He ran after the figures which had disappeared behind a small deserted building, a one-time schoolhouse, on the other side of the road.

'Sandy, quick ...!' he pointed. 'Take Bujang round that side of the *basha* and I'll go the other side with Mohammed ...!'

Sandy reacted instantly.

'Right ...!' and ran flat out, both getting to the corners of the building at the same time. They heard the crack of bullets overhead followed by the familiar chattering ring of a Bren gun.

'Bloody hell ...!' Bang yelled. 'The bastards have got a Bren on the ridge ...! For heaven's sake get down and under cover ...!'

Sandy dived into the building, Bujang following quickly behind him just before a long burst of fire from the Bren. Bang entered the other end of the building with Mohammed.

'Hell's bloody bells ...!' Bang exclaimed. 'That was a stupid thing to do ...! I should have known better ...! The bastards must have a backup section covering the withdrawal of a foraging party to the *kampong*. You two all right?'

Before Sandy could answer, there were further bursts from the Bren and its bullets ripped through the thin wooden walls of the building, ricocheting like peas in a colander and accompanied by the constant thump of rifle fire.

To his horror, Sandy realised that the floor they were lying on was concrete and no way could they get down lower. Behind them bullets began to ricochet off the wall making it impossible to move backwards. He made a quick appraisal of the situation and noticed that the wall sides were open at the bottom some eighteen inches from the ground, making it possible for them to crawl through to the outside. But, since the Bren was sited on high ground and its trajectory fell behind them into the back of the building and the ground to their rear, they would have to go forward. He crawled towards Bang and indicated his observation.

Cannon nodded that he too had seen the possibility. The light was beginning to go fast and he said tersely,

'We can't hold this place ...! They can just creep up when its dark and pick us off one by one ...!'

His voice was immediately drowned out by the rattling quick fire of automatics coming from the direction of the road. Bang shouted above the din,

'Someone's helping us out ...! We'd better give them supporting fire!'

Aiming in the direction of the ridge they opened fire for the first time through the bottom opening. After a couple of minutes the CTs ceased firing and Bang indicated to Sandy to make a tactical withdrawal with Bujang and that he would follow on with Mohammed.

Sandy and Bujang crawled quickly through to the back, praying that the CTs would not open fire, and carefully made their way to the roadside where they were joined by Bang and Mohammed. There they found another Land Rover and Robert Sutcliffe with a Jungle Squad of SCs spread out in firing positions on the embankment along the road.

'Am I glad to see you, Bob ...!' Sandy gasped. 'You arrived just in the nick of time ...! what are you doing out here ...?'

'I received a message that some CTs were prowling around the new village perimeter so ... I thought that as you'd be coming through here I'd better be in the area in case they intended to ambush you on your way home!'

'Thanks Bob, I owe you one for this little lot and I reckon so does Bang ...!'

'Yes, I endorse that ... thanks Bob ...! It's too late now to mount a follow-up ... it'll be dark in quarter of an hour so we'd better get the hell out of here and report to HQ about our contact for the Sitrep tomorrow. Strikes me a stiff drink's in order ...!'

4

Farewell Luncheon

The next few days passed quickly for Sandy, there was so much to do and learn about his new appointment. Alfred Cannon was a great help and a fount of information; he knew everyone that mattered which made the transitional hand over easy.

He was introduced to a great many people: local government officials, planters, timber men and district members of the Malayan Chinese Association, to name but a few. At the end of each day he found it difficult to place many of them in their relevant position but somehow, as the days passed, he began to cope and sort out the mass of information and intricate details of his command.

To honour Bang, a farewell luncheon party was arranged by members of the Malayan Chinese Association of Labis. It was to take place at noon on his last day and, as the final handover was the same day, both Bang and Sandy agreed that the transition should be completed early in the morning.

Everything ran smoothly and before lunch they returned to the bungalow to change into civilian clothes. The function was to take place in the chambers of the Association, which were situated in the main street not far from the Police Station, so Sandy decided to have Elias standing by with the Land Rover ready to pick them up when required.

The roles were now reversed so Sandy took over and Bang sat in the passenger seat. It was a short drive and they pulled up at the front entrance of the elaborately carved facade of the Association building on the stroke of twelve. The Chairman, Tai Kuang, was waiting in the entrance to meet them; he was dressed in the standard European style of shirt and long trousers. He bowed to Bang and welcomed him in Malay.

'*Selamat datang tuan!*'

'*Selamat hari Tai Kuang!* I hope you and your family are keeping well?' Bang answered politely as they shook hands.

Tai Kuang turned to Sandy and addressed him in the same manner, shaking his hand, each bowing to the other as the greetings were passed.

'*Silakan masok Tuan tuan!*' he said.

He ushered them into the interior of the dark, musty entrance and led them up the steep wooden staircase to the first floor, where they crossed a small landing and entered a large airy room that smelt of incense, spices and coffee.

Lined up and waiting to greet their guests were the other five members of the committee, all prominent businessmen of Labis district.

Bang passed down the line of beaming faces addressing each in turn by name and in Malay, shaking their hands.

'*Selamat hari* Wat Lee ... Tai Thong ... Aw Boon ... Hong Fat ... Bee Chang ...!' each bowing to the other as he passed down the line into the room. Sandy followed, imitating Bang, but got their names mixed up which caused a great deal of laughter.

Tai Kuang was a Straits born Chinese with a good command of English, having attended a mission school when he was a boy. Two other members also spoke well, but the remainder had only a smattering of the language and fell back on their native Chinese or Malay to converse. Sandy found this difficult to follow.

The occasion was his first social meeting with the local Chinese businessmen and they seemed determined to make a good impression.

Tai Thong, a rotund little man, looked like a miniature Buddha and hung on to Sandy, saying,

'*Kamu darimana datang?*'

'Scotland!' he answered, grateful that he understood the question.

His inquisitor looked baffled, grinned wickedly then queried,

'You like Scotch?'

Realising the connection the Chinese had made, Sandy replied with a twinkle,

'*Terima kaseh* ... Tai Thong!'

The little man's face lit up and he trundled off towards a table sitting in the corner of the room which groaned under the weight of bottles.

Briefly on his own, Sandy tried to absorb his surroundings and observed that the area was laid out similar to a boardroom. Standing in the centre of the room, set with an Oriental banquet, was a long, teak conference table, deeply carved from end to end with Chinese dragons and peacocks. Placed all around were equally intricately carved, heavy teak chairs with long-backs.

The walls were adorned with beautifully carved and painted Oriental screens, interspersed with framed photographs of benevolent looking Chinese in national dress.

The little man came puffing back with the whisky – which almost filled the glass! – and out of the corner of his eye Sandy noticed, with relief, that Bang had been similarly well looked after.

Tai Kuang attracted their attention by banging a mallet on a hard wooden platter. Silence descended on the room and Sandy waited in anticipation.

'*Salamat datang kapada para tamu*!' Tai Kuang called out, at the same time lifting his glass. The committee shouted in unison;

'*Yum sing*!' and downed the contents of their glass in one swallow.

It was now Bang's turn to toast his hosts and he rattled something off in Malay which Sandy couldn't fathom, but it made them all laugh and he turned quickly to Sandy and said under his breath,

'Do as I do …!!' and he raised his glass to his hosts and in a loud voice said,

'*Yum sing*…!!!' and finished his whisky in one. Sandy followed, spluttering, as the raw spirit went straight to the pit of his empty stomach, its warmth causing a flush to his cheeks.

'*Good grief, I won't last long,*' he thought.

Casting an eye in the direction of Bang he noticed with surprise that he was chatting to those around him in fluent Malay and appeared to be in his element.

Tai Thong had definitely been assigned to Sandy as his guardian angel! As his glass emptied it was promptly refilled … even his partly filled glass was recharged so many times he lost count of how much he'd drunk!

To Sandy's amazement the room somehow became very crowded, everyone had a twin! Even Bang appeared to have a brother who looked the spitting image of him, and he began to wonder how the hell he'd kept it secret! Sandy heaved a sigh of relief when the two brothers Wat Lee came up to him and said as one.

'*Tuan mau makan seka-rang* …!'

'*Terima kaseh* …' Sandy replied readily as he was led to the chair at the bottom of the table, whereupon sitting down, he espied Bang and his twin at the other end.

Their hosts, all talking at the same time in Chinese, Malay or English or a mixture of all three, took their places at the table. At the same time, an indeterminate number of pretty Chinese girls, beautifully attired in cheongsams, came into the room carrying dish after dish of Chinese food, all deliciously cooked.

Sandy by now was having trouble eliminating the twin that had attached itself to anyone he looked at – even with one eye shut, he found it impossible to get rid of the blighter! As for the food, visually he could recognise nothing but carried on regardless, sampling all that was put in front of him.

Sitting on his left was his benevolent, plump, guardian angel, Tai

Thong, who somehow now appeared to look more like the devil from the pages of Don Camillo. His cherubic, smiling face beamed all the time at him and tempted him with strange morsels of food from the end of his chopsticks, and when he wasn't doing that, he would toast him,

'*Yum sing ...!*'

Sandy began to wonder if the little devil hadn't hollow legs ...

'*Where's he putting all the stuff?*'

However, Tai Thong eventually overplayed his hand and Sandy caught one of the girls topping up his glass with dry ginger ale instead of brandy, which he'd originally been drinking. When Sandy chided him about the deception he just grinned and declared,

'Velly solly ...!' and burst into laughter.

The lunch seemed to be drawing to a close when Sandy thought he spied something he recognised – ice cream! The girls were now placing a small plate and a deliciously creamy looking block in front of everyone. Patiently he waited his turn, but couldn't for the life of him think how he was going to eat it.

'*Surely not with chopsticks?*'

No one appeared to be interested in the contents of the plate in front of them so Sandy, seeing an unused spoon on the table, asked Tai Thong to pass it to him. So armed he pushed the spoon into the ice cream.

'*My God it's hard ... block of ice ... push man, push! ... by Jove it is hard ... oh – got a piece ...!*' and feeling self-righteous he put the spoonful into his mouth.

Meantime, his antics had not gone unnoticed. In fact Sandy, task in hand, was oblivious to the fact that the assembled company was hanging on his every move.

Too late! It was already in his mouth and the foam forming as Sandy's taste buds discovered what it was.

'*Soap!* ... within seconds the girls completed the task they had started; fingerbowls of water and hot face towels to mop up the residue of the meal!

Tai Thong, convulsed with laughter, tears streaming down his face, nearly fell off his chair, and the scene was one of tittering, grinning Chinese, squealing with good-natured delight. Amid the hilarity the party broke up and a message was solemnly delivered to Bang and Sandy,

'*Motokar ada dimuka rumah ...!*'

As Bang and Sandy made their exit – Sandy with the help of Bang! – their hosts shouted after them light-heartedly.

'*Selamat jalan datang ...!*'

'*Selamat tinggal ... terima kaseh ...!*' Bang called – and Sandy did his best!

5

Operations

After lunch the next day Sandy received a coded signal concerning future troop movements and planned operations in his district, and was also informed that the additional officer he so desperately needed was travelling up from JB on the night train and would arrive in the morning. His name was William Beaumont, a Police Lieutenant.

On hearing the voice of Sutcliffe in the outer office he called through the open door,

'Bob ... come in here a minute ... I've got some news for you!'

Sutcliffe entered briskly, grinning.

'Afternoon, Sir ... hope it's good news? I say, that was some send-off Mr Cannon got last night ... I thought we'd never get him on the train!'

'Yes ...! and he's not the only one suffering from the after-effects of yesterday's party! However, life goes on. Bob, I've a job for you, close the door and have a seat ...!'

Sutcliffe took off his beret and pulled up a chair.

'Our new Lieutenant will arrive on the train from JB in the morning. I want you to meet him ... his name is Beaumont ... William Beaumont. Meantime I want you to accommodate him and put him in the picture concerning his duties ... and you might also care to mention the paltry recreational facilities there are here! By the way ... could you put up another two Lieutenants for the odd night or so ... just on a temporary basis, you understand?'

Bob hesitated a moment.

'Yes, I could do that all right ... the bungalow's got two bedrooms but it would still mean doubling up ... they'd have to bring camp beds ... however, we could get by, I reckon ...!'

'Good chap ...! I thought you'd come up with something ... It's all hush-hush at the moment ... we're shortly going to have a series of "operations" ... I'll fill you in later ... bring the new chap in to see me after breakfast ... 09.00 hrs. will do fine.'

'Right, Sir ...! will do!'

'Oh! one other thing Bob ... I'm going to change this business of you going round the estates at the end of the month paying their Special Constables ... far too dangerous! I think we should all take a hand in it ... especially now we have an extra Lieutenant. In actual fact I might just get rid of the task altogether ...! I'm going to speak to each of the estate managers and ask if their own people will pay the SCs ...! I'm sure they'll co-operate if we give them the money – and it would eliminate the danger!'

'Yes, Sir ...! that's the best idea yet ... I don't mind telling you it's a bit hairy paying out large sums of money all over the district at the end of the month ... eventually someone's going to get ambushed!'

'Right, Bob, I'll look into it. Meanwhile, this month we'll confuse the blighters by changing the order of visit ... that's all for now ... see you in the morning.'

The following morning Sutcliffe arrived with Beaumont and entered Sandy's office, giving a salute that would have put a guardsman to shame.

'Morning, Sar ...! Lieutenant Beaumont for interview ... Sar!'

Hiding a smile Sandy said,

'Thank you, Bob, send him in and wait in the Inspector's office ...!'

Of the newcomer he didn't know quite what to expect, never having met him before. Or had he? Through the open door a figure emerged which caused Sandy's mind to flash back to Heathrow.

To his utter astonishment the figure in the doorway turned out to be *"the mystery man in the raincoat"*. Only he wasn't wearing the battered old raincoat now, he was immaculate, resplendent in uniform, buttons glistening, shoes burnished black. He halted in front of the desk and gave a smart salute.

Hiding his surprise, Sandy stood up and offered his hand. 'Morning, Beaumont ... hope you're well again ...? I've been looking forward to your arrival ... pull up a chair.'

'Yes, Sir.'

'We haven't really met ... have we? I think though I've seen you somewhere before?'

'Heathrow, Sir ...! I nearly spoke to you ... but changed my mind at the last moment. I wasn't sure if you were one of the officers they told me would be travelling on the same flight.'

'Ah ... yes ... I remember now ... I see that you're an old soldier, Northwest Frontier! I see too that you're wearing the Pacific Star?'

'Yes, Sir ...! Singapore, Sir ...! I was put in the bag by the Japanese.'

'Sorry to hear that ... I suppose you'll see a change in the place now?' Sandy asked.

'Yes, Sir!'

Judging by the staccato replies Beaument was obviously ill at ease, though his tanned face gave nothing away. Sandy decided to question him no further but simply let him settle down and find his feet.

'I've instructed Sutcliffe ... the Lieutenant at the station ... to brief you on your duties and show you around today. Tomorrow we're all going to carry out firearm qualifications ... no doubt we shall then find out how good we are! Any questions?'

'No, Sir – not at the moment.'

'Well ... if there's anything bothering you just come and see me, I'll help all I can. I'll see you in the morning at 10.00 hrs! Dress ... jungle green. Sutcliffe will fill you in on the shoot. That's all for now. Ask him to come in ... he's in the Inspector's office.'

Beaumont stood up, scraping the chair along the floor, saluted, turned and put it back against the wall before leaving the room. A few moments elapsed then Bob returned and he and Sandy got down to planning the shoot which was to take place in the nearby Chaah Palm Oil Estate. Since under the circumstances it would have been foolhardy not to do so, it was decided that they would take two Land Rovers and the jungle squad to act as guard on the surplus weapons and ammunition.

Next morning the jungle squad plus the two Lieutenants were lined up in front of the vehicles waiting for Sandy's inspection. The various weapons and relevant ammunition were already stowed away leaving only the personal weapons visible. Sandy decided to drive himself so asked Beaumont to accompany him in the front of the vehicle; Elias, as usual, got into the back with the two escorts.

The estate was only a short distance away and the manager had been warned of their coming. On arrival they immediately erected the targets on the makeshift range, setting them at various distances according to the weapons to be used.

Sandy put forward a suggestion. 'Since we're the only ones going to shoot, how about a competition?'

'OK by me, Sir!' Bob replied and turned to Beaumont who gave a thumbs up.

'Say, ten dollars each in the kitty ... highest score takes all?' Sandy concluded.

They shook hands on it and tossed a coin to decide the shooting order. Bob went first and put up some excellent scores with his Browning automatic and carbine, qualifying as a marksman with the Bren and Sten. Next came Sandy who also made a good score. Beaumont was last to shoot and astounded them by scoring *'bulls'* with all the weapons. He even went as far as to demonstrate his skill with a handgun by hitting ten cent pieces at ten paces with his Browning automatic! There wasn't any doubt he was a marksman! He scooped up the kitty saying,

'Drinks on me ...!'

A few days later the Gurkhas arrived in force and began a series of concentrated patrols through the rubber estates. Ambushes were laid along jungle paths leading to known areas of food supplies. The Chinese timber felling groups (known as timber *'kongsis'*) who were working for contractors deep in the jungle under the control of the Forestry Department, were cordoned off and used as *'Judas goats'*. As heavy labour of this kind required plenty of food to keep them going they were always a security problem, being an obvious source of supply to the terrorist.

The weather was now gradually worsening as the rain became heavier and more persistent. The principal features of the Malaysian climate are copious rainfall, high humidity and a uniform temperature. The year is commonly divided into the south-west and north-east monsoon seasons, except on the east coast where the differences of climate normally associated with the monsoon are barely discernible. Rainfall averages about one hundred inches a year, though the highest and lowest averages for certain areas are one hundred and ninety-eight and sixty-five inches a year respectively.

The average maximum temperature in the plains is rather less than 90°F and the minimum about 70°F. At the hill stations, depending on how high they are situated, the temperatures are considerably lower.

Nevertheless, at certain times of the year, it was almost possible to tell the exact time of day as the laden sky emptied itself in bucketfuls, especially in late afternoon. Consequently, operating in such a climate made it extremely difficult for the security forces to stay in the field for long periods.

Despite this, results began to come in, contacts and kills were made and the score began to rise. In the early mornings in and around the Batu Anam and Kg Tenang rubber estates, pitched battles occurred between large groups of terrorists and the Gurkhas. The 7th Company, North Johore Regiment of the MRLA was decimated, losing 47 killed in three actions. Yap Piow and Tan Keng Kiat were at last dead! The morale of the rural populace was not only restored but rose to heights not seen for a long time.

Because of this it was decided that the operations should move further north and a maximum effort be exerted to stamp out straggling groups trying to get away. Sandy was asked to provide two jungle squads with Lieutenants. He was also pre-warned to anticipate the likelihood of a further two squads being attached, and passed the information on to Sutcliffe.

A regiment of Artillery was to be used to systematically shell a tract of jungle the terrorists had been driven into. They were to provide a creeping box barrage to the Sungui Kepong where the jungle squads were spread out in ambush positions over a thousand yards on the high ground, in rubber trees overlooking the river bank. Lincoln bombers of the Royal Australian Air Force were also to be used to pattern bomb the same area. The remaining forces, Fijians and Gurkhas, were to be deployed in mobile patrol groups along the edges of the jungle box.

The initial operation was to last a week and Sandy briefed the Lieutenants prior to moving off. He'd been given the task of co-ordinating the jungle squads, getting them onto the ground, supplying them in the field and providing communications with the other participants. For this latter task he had co-opted Lieutenant Bill (Sparks) Harvey.

To create as little speculation as possible they mustered and moved off in the early hours before dawn and within three hours were strung out along the Sungui Kepong, digging in and laying down enfilading fire positions.

Later in the morning the Artillery moved in, about eight hundred yards behind them, and set up their guns on one of the estate roads. Events and men moved quickly and the guns were soon pounding away, shells screaming over the squad's heads and thumping into the distant jungle. Above the din, aircraft were heard followed by the *chump-thump, chump-thump* of their bombs. Now, it was only a matter of time!

The first, second and third days passed and an irregular pattern of Artillery fire, intermingled with sporadic bombing by the RAAF, carried on late into the night.

Time passed slowly and hot food, which could only be prepared further back in the rubber plantation, was brought up once a day under cover of darkness. The same applied to washing and other facilities and the mosquitoes had a field day! The rubber estates were plagued with them, the larvae being hatched out in the latex collecting cups attached to the trees. The jungle-greens were no protection and only feet and ankles were spared, protected by jungle boots; the constant rain was a nightmare!

On the third night Sandy, who was in the centre of the ambush sector, heard the Bren gun on his right flank open up; the sector being covered by Beaumont. Orders were, 'not to open fire unless a target is clearly presented;' terrorists scouting forward were expected before any large group would cross.

The Artillery were now laying their barrage closer in to the ambush positions. They had been slowly creeping forward daily, as was the aerial bombing – so contact was imminent!

The Bren chattered on accompanied by the intermittent thump of rifle fire. A second Bren opened up and the tracer arched away into the dark jungle wall.

The gunfire put the whole sector on alert and everyone 'stood to', straining to differentiate between the sounds of artillery fire, the screams of shells overhead and the likely movements of CTs crossing the river.

Sandy could only wait for the outcome, which had to be assessed in daylight. He kept in close radio contact with the squad positions during the rest of the night; after the initial firing of Beaumont's squad this was only punctuated by the big guns at their rear.

Eventually morning came and with sufficient light he moved down the sector to investigate the night's action. Beaumont had made a top score again – a terrorist scout had moved forward crossing the river in front of his position. The CT almost reached the ambush position but the men held their fire. He had halted and without moving looked around, then apparently satisfied, crossed back over the river. A few minutes elapsed and he reappeared leading a party of about seven, which he guided over the river and up to where previously he'd stopped in front of the ambush. Beaumont fired the first shot at about ten yards range, killing the scout instantly with one bullet. The ensuing action accounted for another three. The remainder doubled back across the river and returned to the jungle. No other contacts were made during the remainder of the night and no casualties were suffered by the squads in action.

In the middle of the morning of the fifth day orders were received to withdraw the jungle squads and the Artillery. The Fijians, in co-operation with the Gurkhas, were coming up to take over their sector and carry out patrols along the fringes of the jungle tract.

The squads, however, were only pulled back to Segamat for a twenty-four hour rest, as they were required to carry out a cordon and search operation in one of the adjacent rubber plantations to the Sungui Kepong Estate.

Special Branch had received information that an unknown number of terrorists were hiding in the quarters of the Chinese tappers. Three squads were to be used, Sutcliffe and Beaumont together with Crawford, one of the visiting Lieutenants.

The operation was straightforward. They went in after midnight, walking the last two miles into the estate, and laid down a cordon around the living quarters of the workforce and waited for 06.00 hrs when the tappers were called to muster.

The object of the exercise was to hold everyone under guard until the SB came up with their interrogation units when everyone would be checked out and segregated. It was hoped that any terrorists trying to hide amongst the rubber tappers would be either identified or pulled out because they were not on the estate muster roll.

Holding a loudhailer and speaking in Chinese, one of Mactavish's men ordered the tappers out of their lines and told them they were surrounded by the jungle squads. All went according to plan; they came out in orderly fashion, the women and children separated from the men, and were placed under heavily armed guard.

Then the unforeseen happened! It was still half light and Crawford entered one of the lines to see if it was empty. This was against orders since the quarters were not to be entered until full daylight, when a tactical search would be carried out and the cordon would have a better chance to stop an escape.

He led three of his men in single file through the main door of the communal longhouse and proceeded down between the draped mosquito-netted aisle of raised sleeping platforms. In the dim light it was difficult to see. A terrorist lay in wait and shot Crawford at point-blank range in the centre of the body – and the SC behind him. In the ensuing confusion the CT bolted for the door at the far end of the building, passed through it, put his back to the wall and shot the other two SCs as they came charging out after him. He then ran between the cordon and disappeared through the rubber in the direction of the jungle, which was only about five hundred yards away.

Two SCs were dead and one wounded. Crawford was still alive, much to Sandy's amazement and relief. On examining him he found he'd been shot just above the navel and a small blue puncture mark was visible – no blood and no exit wound! Sandy was later told that the bullet had lodged in his spleen and the Lieutenant only survived because the charge behind the bullet was either damp or faulty. Crawford and the wounded SC were evacuated and taken to the Hospital in Segamat, as were the two dead men.

Meanwhile the operation carried on. As soon as there was sufficient light Sandy, plus two SCs, began tracking the terrorist through the rubber trees. Sandy had only gone about a hundred yards when he came upon a .38 Smith and Wesson revolver lying on the ground; it had a long cord attached to its butt, the loop of which was caught on the branch of some low scrub that had obviously snatched the weapon out of the hand of the running CT. A patrol was sent into the jungle after him but lost his tracks and he got away.

On returning to the estate lines Sandy helped Mactavish to check out the tappers who'd occupied the quarters the terrorist had been in. They were a sullen lot and wouldn't give any information regarding the man they'd been harbouring. The questioning drew a blank, failing despite a bit of subterfuge … 'Russian Roulette' with a revolver! The Operation was finally concluded with a number of suspects being arrested.

6

The Wild Boar

Sandy was making one of his periodic visits to the new village Kampong Bedenak when he was approached by a delegation of the male Chinese inhabitants.

With growing concern they told him that a wild boar was rutting through the planted fields, uprooting and eating their crops in the adjacent cultivated land outside the wire perimeter. All their efforts at finding a solution had so far failed and now, exhausted and despairing, they asked his help to solve the problem by killing the beast.

Hunting and shooting were hobbies which Sandy enjoyed, and since he didn't get the opportunity to do so very often he was pleased to help. He decided that the Stevens single barrelled shotgun which he used for dog shooting (a chore he hated but sadly sometimes found necessary) would be the best weapon, if used with an SG ball cartridge.

His escort, always at his side, acted on his instruction immediately.

'Elias …! go to Labis and tell the Inspector I want the Stevens shotgun and a quantity of SG cartridges from the armoury … and explain that I'm going to use it to shoot this marauder! Take Bujang with you, I'll be OK here with the Home Guard.'

'*Tabe tuan* …!' Elias's face took on a puzzled look. 'What is *"Marauder" Tuan* … That is new word, *Tuan* …?'

Stuck for the Malay equivalent Sandy turned on one of his smiles.

'*Tidak menjadi* …! off you go now …! I'll have to speak to my *"Guru"* and ask him what it is in Malay …!'

They both grinned widely at him and departed. Sandy then organised the group of farmers and their families into a number of beating parties.

'I want you to find yourselves big, stout sticks, large tins – anything in fact which you can beat and make a noise with, so the boar can be driven into the open where I can take a shot at it.'

Within the hour Elias was back and Sandy and the beating parties were ready and anxious to go. The village headman was reasonably certain that the animal had made its lair in a bamboo thicket in the jungle's secondary growth at the end of an old paddy field, so they didn't have to look far or long before one of the farmers came running up.

'*Tuan ...! tuan ...! datang sampai ...!*' he shouted excitedly, pointing to where the boar was. Sandy signalled to the beaters to get into position and they started thrashing through the bush hoping to drive it out into the open, dried up, paddy field.

This would be his first boar! He had seen a few in India and Africa but never a Malayan boar. Still, he reckoned he wouldn't have a problem!

He recalled some old hunters saying their skulls were exceptionally thick and that a kill should never be attempted by aiming for the head since a bullet would simply bounce off.

On just such an occasion at the end of the war he'd surprised his Army colleagues by tracking a man-eating tiger for the better part of a day in the Arakan hills in Burma. Afterwards they jokingly referred to him as 'the intrepid hunter'.

... Burma! ... what an awful time that was ... he reflected

'A' Company, under the command of Duba, Major Harold Birchley, left Sandoway two months after the end of hostilities and made their way back to Taungup by landing craft. They were a unit of the West African Frontier Force who, prior to April and together with the Green Howards (the last remaining battalion of 4 Indian Brigade left in the Arakan), had jointly with the East Africans taken on the Japanese holding the town of Taungup.

The enemy had fought a stubborn rearguard action determined not to be hurried in their withdrawal to give up possession of the pass to the Prome area before the monsoon broke.

The Company's task now, however, was a peaceful one. They were to clear the road through the pass to enable the West African Division to travel to Prome, 110 miles away, and eventually to Rangoon for en-shipment to West Africa. The road needed rebuilding, so did the culverts and bridges, many of which had been destroyed by the RAF bombing of the retreating Japanese, so all available units were co-opted for the operation.

Taungup was at the western end of a motorable road from Prome and had been used since 1942 as a base for all Japanese operations in the Arakan. 'A' Company moved up to their sector at milestone 52 and prepared a campsite on the high ground above the road.

Sandy reckoned that for the rest of his life he'd never forget that first night sitting outside his makeshift bamboo hut. It was a magnificent location – on a level with the clouds overlooking a great valley. He could see for miles!

He imagined he was on a peaceful, tropical island, one of many dotted amidst a tranquil sea. Looking into the shimmering distance over the darkening hills he saw the sun go down, a circle of orange fire casting flickering light into the fleecy clouds. He watched, spellbound, as the sky appeared in all its majesty, life's caldron glowing, until the dying embers fell away over the rugged hills, changing their green into shadows of blue.

The day's last light raced ever onwards across the sky and Sandy, in his solitude, felt the creative hand of God and realised it was not the end but the dawning of another day.

He relished the evenings watching the spectacle unfold – not unlike a theatre's first night, albeit orchestrated from the jungle by the whoop ... whoop ... whoop of monkeys and the constant cooing of collared doves and pigeons mingling with the sounds of baboons, cicadas, crickets, frogs and the unseen animals deep in the forest. Sounds halted abruptly by the sun's disappearance over the horizon.

As time elapsed the peaceful interlude was broken and the unit experienced a rude awakening which marred the two month sojourn on the pass.

A man-eating tiger had carried off a soldier from a Company further down the road. It was thought that the tiger was old and had survived in the past on a Japanese menu, thereby developing its liking for the easily obtained morsels of war!

One such evening became their turn for a visit. Screams could be heard coming from the direction of the perimeter where the latrines were located.

'What the hell's going on ...?' Sandy shouted, leaping into action. Investigation revealed that one of his platoon, Tyjani Mahomadu, had been attacked, fortunately making such a hullabaloo it saved him from being dragged off into the jungle and eaten. His wounds were superficial lacerations and scratches, indicating that the animal was almost toothless. Mahomadu shook with fear.

'That was a near thing but we'll soon have you patched up ...' Sandy said as he tried to comfort the terrified man. He made a mental note that in the morning something would have to be done – permanently; the constant threat they were living under could not go on. Meantime, the perimeter guard must be strengthened and everyone warned to be 100 per cent alert!

Early next morning he made a recce around the area where the tiger had been and found pug marks which clearly indicated that it had retraced its tracks into the jungle using an old game path into the valley in the direction of what would almost certainly be a watering hole. He reported his findings immediately to Major Birchley.

'Harold ... do you mind if I go after the tiger?'

The Major was a couple of years older than Sandy and from their first meeting they'd become staunch friends. He was a quiet, thorough man and had been aptly nicknamed by the Africans 'Duba' since he was always on the lookout. Nothing much missed his eye!

'Good idea, Sandy ... but be careful ... heaven knows what else is out there!'

Sandy was confident. 'Oh ... I reckon I'll be all right. I'll take my platoon Sergeant with me, he's a reliable chap and a good tracker ... he could take a Sten to give me a bit of extra fire power should it be needed!'

With Duba's permission ringing in his ears he went off to get his batman's rifle. It was kept in mint condition and he knew it was accurate.

Sandy, with Sergeant Audu Bannana covering him about five yards behind, followed the pug marks of the tiger. They wound their way down the old game track which was flanked by thick bamboo and tall trees. The process was painfully slow due to the steepness of the hillside and the fact that he had to feel his way forward in case the tiger was lying in the bamboo thickets or the equally deep, dark undergrowth.

Down and down they went, at times sliding on their backsides, the ground was so damp under the tangle of lush foliage. Surrounding them bedraggled creepers dropped from the tall tree canopy, whilst high above them gaps let in fierce slashes of light. Ghostly shadows appeared between the trees and both the hillside and game track were covered with rotting vegetation which gave off a dank, putrid smell.

Slowly they descended into the valley leaving behind the sound and bustle of the camp and road. At one point in the middle of the morning they came across the toed boot footprints of a single Japanese crossing their track on another old game path along the contour of the valley. It was so fresh that Sandy thought at first it had been made that morning, but Audu, an old experienced tracker and hunter, convinced him otherwise. He explained that the track had only stayed fresh because of the trees and undergrowth that had protected it from being dried up by the sun, or washed out by the rain.

Further on another larger path cut into the one they were following, this time with elephant signs. They too had been travelling along the contour but now went down, preceding the tiger, to what was becoming evident as a watering hole.

Sandy and Audo continued to slither down the slope following now a combination of elephant and tiger tracks. They could see where the great beasts had slithered on their rear ends in a waltzing 'free for all'.

Eventually, around midday, they arrived in the valley and saw the large water hole which was fed by a fast stream. Audu searched amongst the multitude of tracks around the salt-lick and drew Sandy's attention to the mutation of the Mimosa pudica which abounded along the side of the well worn game track leading away into the valley.

'Baturi ...! Audu exclaimed. 'This path be fit for plenty animal ... not know which ... plenty go follow giwa ...! no good, Sir ...! big cat he go off into bush ...!'

... and so the running dog

'Right, Audu! This is the point of no return, I'm afraid — it's going to take us all our time to get ...'

He lifted his right hand ... paused and listened. A faint sound like the snapping of a twig came from the nearby thicket. His eyes darted in that direction and picked out the fawn coloured haunch of a small deer moving away from him across a small glade. It must have come out of the back of the thicket directly to his front!

They were downwind so the deer was unaware of their presence — so far! Audu was still as a rock. Sandy felt the fawn must have seen them! Suddenly, there was a flash of colour and the tiger sprang from a tongue of tall grass, hitting the deer on the shoulder and bowling it over, at the same time biting into its neck bringing its head to the ground. In a simultaneous motion it lashed out with its hind legs, claws ripping down the stomach of the deer, disembowelling it. A ravaging, piercing cry of terror rang out across the glade — then silence!

Sandy indicated to Audu to standstill and, moving to his right, put the thicket between himself and the tiger. Cautiously he moved forward, one step at a time, in the direction of the kill. On reaching the bamboo clump he meticulously began to skirt it, alert for a sight of the tiger which he reckoned should be about fifty yards ahead.

His hands were sweating and his ears thumping.

'Ye Gods ...! mustn't make any mistakes now ...!' he thought.

He made one last check on his rifle to ensure that the safety catch was off, then painstakingly placed each foot on the ground, making sure there was nothing to give his presence away.

At last, clear of the thicket, he could see the tiger down on its haunches in front of him, its head buried deep into the stomach of its prey. The whole length of its body was visible. Sandy slowly — very slowly — raised the rifle to his shoulder, sighted it, taking a deep breath. His curled, damp, finger squeezed the trigger, the weapon bucked, the thump of its fire vibrating across the glade and echoing over the valley ...

Quickly he reloaded and fired again, his shots thudding home between the shoulders of the tiger, which momentarily rose, then slumped, motionless.

Nothing moved and he carefully reloaded, stalking forward, picking up on the way a stone the size of a cricket ball. Getting a little closer he threw it at the silent, huddled figures on the ground. Nothing stirred and he found himself sucking the air back into his lungs, little realising he'd been holding his breath! Audu came up at the double, grinning.

'Al hamadu lillahi ...! madala Baturi ...! you good shot, Sir ...!'

'Heavens, Sergeant ...! I wouldn't like to do that many times ... certainly not on foot ... look at the size of him ...! I didn't realise it was so big ... we'll never get it out of here ...! I'll just have to cut off the tail to prove it's dead ...!'

The tiger was a magnificent, fully grown male which had been wounded in the lower jaw; the vital teeth necessary to bring down and kill its prey, were missing. Sandy was sure it was the same one that had paid them a visit, only the beast wasn't old as he'd first surmised. The wound, having forced it to look for easier pickings, made it necessary to use its weight and speed of attack to bring down animals such as the deer. No doubt in a normal kill, the tiger would grab the victim by the throat, hold the head down on the ground with its cavernous jaws – keeping clear of its prey's kicking feet – and the deer's movement would either dislocate or break its own neck. This tiger, however, because of its lack of killing teeth, had developed a kicking-killing action with its powerful hind legs and vicious claws.

Audu cut two prime portions from the haunch of the deer and they each put a bloody piece of meat into their haversack. It was all they could carry back up the valley side. The tail of the tiger he cut off and stuffed also into his haversack.

It had taken them about four hours to get down into the valley, it would take them longer to reach the road again. First things first, however: a welcome brew of tea!

Slowly they made their way back up the difficult, steep slope. They had been going steadily for over an hour, having just cleared that part of the track Sandy had christened the 'elephant slide', when the crashing sound of whipping bamboo got louder and louder. He turned to Audu.

'Sounds as though the elephants are coming back …!'

The Sergeant's eyes rolled to the heavens.

'Quick, off the track … get into some cover …!' Sandy yelled. They crouched in the undergrowth behind a large tree and listened. The noise increased and the bamboo cracked like rifle fire. Below him he could see it swaying as though in a high wind, just like a vast green and gold sea.

'Hell …!' he muttered under his breath, 'it must be the elephants … we're right in their path!'

They waited, enveloped in bamboo which whipped and cracked alarmingly about them. Then, above, they saw a large family of baboons swinging and chattering overhead – mercifully veering away out of sight.

'Hells bloody bells – that was a near one, Sergeant …! if they'd spotted us they'd have attacked and we wouldn't have got out alive …!'

Audu remained silent and Sandy thought he detected a pale tinge in his black complexion!

They moved on and eventually, just as the sun went down, reached the road – to the relief of Duba who was waiting to greet them as they emerged from the jungle …!

The whoops, shouting and rat-a-tat-tat beating of old cooking utensils and compo ration tins echoed across the empty expanse of ground and, shaken, Sandy came back to reality.

'*Too late now to evaluate the Stevens shotgun ...!*' he reflected. '*Still, I have my automatic to fall back on if I need extra firepower.*' Carefully, he positioned himself in front of the thicket about thirty yards out on an old paddy bund which elevated him about eighteen inches above the normal level of the field.

The noise from the beaters continued to reverberate around him when his eye was suddenly attracted by a movement in the tall *lalang* which was a continuation of the thicket in front of him.

He waited, tensely holding the Stevens at the ready ... moments passed by ... then, in an explosion, the boar broke out of cover and stood, quivering, in front him. The biggest, ugliest and most ferocious brute he had ever clapped eyes on. It must have weighed at least three hundred pounds and was over two feet tall ... and its tusks! ... they were like the battering rams on some medieval galley, with the capability of ripping a man to pieces in seconds!

Sandy's instinctive reaction was to run ... but where? To his rear there were no trees to climb or get behind ... besides, he couldn't run ... he was rooted to the spot, as though his feet were encased in boots of lead!

The boar pawed the ground and with its tusks ripped out a large furrow, flicking the pieces over its shoulder in rage. It then shook its head from side to side and appeared to squint at him through its beady, red rimmed eyes. There was no doubt it had found something to vent its rage on in revenge for being so rudely disturbed from its afternoon nap. The beast quickly decided Sandy was the one to attack and, with a blood-curdling squeal, followed by a thunderous grunt, it charged.

Sandy stood fast, the Stevens held firmly, the barrel pointing to the ground at an angle of forty five degrees. He only had one round, he must make it count; there would be no time to reload – and therefore no second chance!

A cloud of red dust rose about the charging animal, its snarling grunts becoming louder the closer it came. Sandy was oblivious to the perspiration dripping off the end of his nose, only conscious of the boar charging in front of him.

The pounding of its hoofs sounded deafening – on and on it came. He waited, motionless, until it was within six feet, then he fired and stepped swiftly to one side. The beast's haunches dropped, but its body continued on with the momentum of its ferocious charge and hit the bund with a crunch, where seconds before he had been standing!

The boar was dead, the single ball of the SG cartridge had hit it squarely between the shoulder blades, severing the spine. With sheer relief he heaved a great sigh as the cheering Chinese descended on him, shouting ...

'*Tuan ...! tuan besar ...! Terima kasi tuan ...!*'

The villagers erupted in a frenzy of excitement, yelling or laughing and trying to get to him to clap him on the back. His 'audience' had watched it all, having broken out into the paddy after the boar.

Quickly they cut a length of bamboo from which they hung the beast by its legs, then cut its throat. It took four men to lift and carry it back in triumph to the village, where it was shared out between all those who had suffered through its marauding.

Sandy never again shot another boar but he did go on a number of tiger shoots on his journeys throughout the country, and many a time encountering the odd Malay tiger crossing the road; however, he never repeated the thrill, nor knew the fear, of the Taungup tiger or the Kampong Bedenak boar.

7

Under Fire

Curry tiffan was the usual Sunday fare and Sandy received many invitations from planters to join them on their estates. Whilst his duties necessitated him getting around his district he was never keen to take up these offers at weekends, unless it was a planter with a family in which case he made a special effort. Accepted regularly the lunches could create a movement pattern that would be noticed by CT informers. However, since he had not visited the Ayer Panas estate for some time, and so far never on a Sunday, he accepted gladly and set off attired in civvies and accompanied by his uniformed, armed escort.

The monsoon season was just about over but there was still a lot of water in low lying areas on the way to the estate, which was situated in the midst of thick jungle. The Land Rover, with Sandy driving and Elias beside him, bumped and splashed through the puddles in the still water-logged laterite-surfaced estate road. Later in the season everything would dry out and to traverse over it would, in contrast, cause a cloud of fine red dust to billow out behind, then be sucked forward, covering the occupants. It was a no-win situation, you were either too wet or too dirty, depending on the conditions prevailing at the time!

Whatever the state of the road it was an unpleasant drive and Sandy began to hate the jungle as it lay dark and menacing on either side. The narrow stretch ahead was particularly nasty and he felt as though he was driving through a long, ill-lit tunnel. The still dark, cloudy, sky provided little light under the foreboding thick jungle canopy and he began to feel its threat, wishing whole-heartedly that he'd refused the planter's invitation.

'God, it's all right for them', he thought ruefully, *'sitting in their big, heavily armoured American cars that can take the first onslaught of a CT ambush, and are hardly ever preceded by land-mines or whatever!'*

The powerful engined American-built limousines were the only vehicles available that could carry the thick, heavy armour plate that encased them. Many of the vehicles were so armoured that the occupants could often withstand a siege until help arrived.

'Hell ...! what's the matter with me ... must be getting bloody selfish in my old age ...! who'd envy those blighters ...? they've got the worst end of the stick, stuck in one place and mustering every morning at six ... and they travel in and out of the same place six days a week more or less at the same time. No alteration of movements! – my God I'd hate to be trapped like that ...!'

Ridding himself of the remainder of his thoughts, he said out loud,

'Still ...! it's time the Police had some protection ... we've only a few armoured cars and those are used to escort VIPs on the move through dangerous areas – plus they're allocated only to certain districts!' he grumbled.

Elias, eyes darting everywhere, said nothing.

At last the road broke out of the dank, steaming, jungle and wound its way through avenues of rubber trees, presenting a more open vista. Line upon line of them stretched away until they too became a distant solid green wall. Only in the foreground could he see the slanting rays of the fleetingly visible sun, giving the illusion that figures were dodging between the uniform upright tree trunks which, fortunately, were unlikely to provide adequate cover to an ambush party!

On and on the road twisted, gradually winding around the contours of a small hill. On negotiating a sharp bend Sandy and Elias were rewarded with a spectacular view of the plantation manager's house which was situated on the forward slopes of a miniature plateau, the highest knoll in the estate. They were now on the last leg of the journey and the house and blaze of colour in the surrounding garden was a welcome sight.

The plantation was long established and the garden had matured over the years, the Japanese occupation having passed it by leaving it almost untouched. There were Jacaranda, Tulip, Flame trees, magnificent Magnolias and Frangipani – Sandy could remember the names of only a few but allowed nature's beauty which stretched out before him to momentarily wash away the stress of the journey.

Because of the state of emergency, the house and garden were now completely surrounded by a high, double, perimeter wire fence, which had four medium sized, sandbagged *sangars* (sentry posts) at each corner, two on the sky line covering the high ground and two on the lower slopes. The whole area was roughly eight hundred yards square.

Slowly he approached a junction in the road which, to its left, continued on down to the tappers' lines in the centre of the estate about half a mile away. Sandy travelled straight ahead, making for the entrance gate that could be seen clearly in the wire fence where the guardroom was situated. The estate had a complement of Special Constables at infantry platoon strength who were similarly armed.

He could see some activity just beyond the gate, so the lookout in one of the *sangars* must have spotted his approach and alerted the platoon Sergeant; the Sergeant could be heard calling out the guard. To return the compliment he would be expected to stop and inspect them, which would also forewarn his host of his arrival. They were a smart lot and didn't often have a chance to show off, so Sandy was glad of the few minutes spent with them. It didn't take him long to get through the formalities and soon he was on his way up to the house where he was greeted by the manager, a man in his late forties.

Will Penrose, a tall, grizzled, thick-set Welshman, was a pre-war planter with over twenty years service in the country. He'd gone into the jungle at the beginning of the Japanese occupation and at one time had been a wireless operator with Spencer Chapman in Force 136. There was nothing he didn't know concerning the duplicity of his, then, Chinese communist comrades. However, being a humble man, he was reticent to speak about his experiences.

The main house had been built on two levels and was encircled on both by wide verandas, giving the impression that it was bigger than, in reality, it really was. On the ground floor were a number of stores and offices and a reception room, and the whole building felt cool and airy.

The living quarters were situated on the first floor and a magnificent, wide, teak staircase, adorned with trophies, rose from the centre of the entrance hall, the floor of which was so highly polished that Sandy could see his figure reflected in it as he crossed gingerly over.

'How are you, Sandy?' The soft undulating tones of the Welsh valleys fell on his ears.

'Fine, Will, thank you ... you're looking fit, how's the family keeping? Hope they're all well!'

'Oh ...! they are Sandy ... so I gather ...!' he answered, with a tinge of loneliness in his voice.

'Enjoying themselves too, they are ... always do when they go to Hong Kong on a shopping spree ...! I'd a letter from Dione yesterday telling me that she and the two girls are staying on for another week ... they don't really like it here and it's no place for two teenagers ...! The emergency has spoilt everything ... no tennis parties or anything and they can't move about freely and visit the other plantations ... I can't blame them for wanting to stay on and they might as well make the best of it when they have the chance ... you understand Sandy ...?'

'Yes, Will ...! and I absolutely agree with you ... I wouldn't want to live up here all the time ...!'

The two men began to climb the wide, teak staircase, and halfway up Sandy turned to his host.

'I say, Will ...! I do admire that tiger rug you have at the bottom of the stairs ... haven't seen it before ... is it a new acquisition ...?'

'No-o-o! I've had that for years but it's been away having a repair job done to it.'

'How'd you come by it ... a Malayan tiger, isn't it!' Sandy queried.

'Quite right ...! and you may not believe it, I shot it just where it's lying ...! the bloody thing wandered into the house one night ... mind you', he concluded with venom, 'it was before the emergency!'

They walked on in silence, crossing the landing and going into the comfortable lounge/dinning room, where two young assistant planters were chatting over a glass of Tiger beer. On seeing the manager enter with Sandy they stood up.

Both were in their early twenties and had been in the country a matter of weeks, their predecessors having gone home on leave. Introductions were made and Sandy was pleased to learn they'd completed their National Service in the UK and were taking a special interest in the estate platoon. They occupied a small bungalow adjacent to the house.

'By the way, Sandy ... I've taken the advice you gave me the last time you were here – what do you think of that ...?'

Walking into the centre of the room Penrose kicked aside a small Persian rug and pulled up a trapdoor in the floor.

Sandy rose smartly to his feet and peering down through the opening saw what appeared to be a child's slide, complete with sides, made of polished teak. A thick mat was placed strategically at the bottom to ensure a safe landing!

'By Jove, Will, that's an excellent job! I hope you haven't had to use it in an emergency yet?'

'No! and we don't want to either ...! however we feel that much safer being able to get down quickly. As you pointed out ... we're rather like sitting ducks up here!' He gave a bellowing laugh which was rather half-heartedly taken up by the two young assistants!

After a couple of pink gins it was time for lunch and the conversation dwelt on the recent successful operations by the Gurkhas and the number of contacts that had been made.

'We're fortunate in having an Indian work force on this estate, they're less likely to be communist inspired. Nevertheless, I'm informed that some of my younger workers have been approached to help the communist cause and there's been some canvassing going on for recruits!'

The two young assistants nodded their heads in agreement, letting their senior lead the conversation.

'I think you'll have to ensure that the SCs constantly patrol when the work force is out in the rubber. It's the only way', Sandy concluded, 'that you can stop this kind of infiltration and, as you know it doesn't stop there – the CTs are getting short of supplies!'

... crack! thump ...! crack! thump ...!

The sound of rifle fire abruptly interrupted the conversation. Startled, they instantly exchanged eye contact.

'Bloody hell ...! bandits – just my luck ...!' Sandy blurted through gritted teeth.

'Quick, Sandy ...! down the shute and answer the phone that'll report in from the nearest *sangar* ...! I'll get into the house armoury for extra arms and ammunition ...! you two as well ...!' Will roared the order at his young assistants.

Sandy obeyed at once, followed by Hugh and Ivan, who stood at the ready as Sandy picked up the ringing instrument.

'Number one *sangar*, Corporal Omar reporting, *Tuan* ...! We're under attack by unknown number – from rubber on our left flank – range about two hundred yards – rifle fire only – no casualties ...!'

'Roger one ...! return fire only when you see target – stand by for further orders ...!' Sandy instructed, and immediately rang up *sangar* number two.

'Hello, two – anything to report?'

'No, *tuan* ...!'

'Roger two! – stand by ...!'

These were the two posts commanding the high ground overlooking the house compound and the rubber trees to the jungle edge. Sandy then rang the guardroom where the main body would be stood-to awaiting orders. All this was general procedure when the manager was in the house. When he was not, the reports would go on the underground telephone line to the Sergeant in the guardroom, who would take the necessary action.

'Hello Sergeant ...! OCPD here ...! This is the situation ...!' He then repeated the message received from number one *sangar*.

'Orders ...! Despatch immediately a section with Bren to the house and alert number two *sangar* that I'll take the section out of their gate. I'll make a flanking attack from the right – got that ...! Roger ...! Inform number one of intention and tell them to return fire on the CT positions in exactly five minutes to provide covering fire – they're to keep it up until they see a red Very light fired at them ...! then must stop ...! Got that ...!'

'Roger *tuan* ...!' the Sergeant replied and Sandy put the phone down.

'Ivan ...! you'll come with me ...! Hugh! stay by the phone until Mr Penrose tells you otherwise ... Oh! he's here!'

Sandy then put Will in the picture, explaining the action taken so far.

'OK, Sandy …! we'll leave it as it is …! except that I'll go up to number one and direct their fire – so not to worry …! Hugh can stay here with another section to reinforce any sector that needs it …! the Sergeant will stay with the remainder in the guardroom …! Any questions …?' he concluded.

The sound of running feet and the sharp crunch as they halted, heralded the arrival of Sandy's section as Will handed over a Very pistol and some cartridges.

'Good luck, old chap …! take care and don't take any chances …!'

'OK …! I'll try not to …!' Sandy gave a dry laugh, picked up his carbine and, turning to the pale-faced young assistant, jokingly said,

'Come on, Ivan – let's see how terrible you are …!' and off they went to the waiting section.

'Corporal …! *Siape nama anda …?*' Sandy asked the saluting Malay.

'*Nama saya Ahmad tuan …!* came the swift reply.

He asked him if he understood English. The Corporal did and Sandy explained his intentions and asked him to pass them on to the men so they would know what was expected of them. It only took a minute or so, during which time, Sandy turned to Ivan.

'Keep close to me and if I should be knocked out – you take over … Right?'

The young man swallowed hard and nodded his head in agreement.

'Follow me …!' Sandy ordered and set off at the double to the number two *sangar*. Moving in the dead ground out of sight of the terrorists it took only a few minutes and, once out of the gate, Sandy ensured that the men kept the regulation distance between each other. He went straight out, away from the post in the opposite direction along the ridge for approximately two hundred yards, counting the number of paces as he went, then made a ninety degree left turn from the line of the perimeter, moving over the ridge in the direction of the jungle edge at the base of the rear slope away from the perimeter.

He kept going in the rubber for about four hundred yards, again judging the distance, before halting.

He directed them to turn left again, facing in extended order, the direction of the now faint rifle fire. Sandy positioned himself and Ivan in the centre of the section, by moving the Bren group to his right flank.

'Now Ivan! one foot on the ground … understand? … as per battle drill! I'll move ahead in bounds of fifty yards – you'll follow on when you see me in a covering fire position. We'll move like that until we either make contact with the CTs or I indicate otherwise! Any questions?'

'No Sir …! I understand …' Ivan answered quickly.

Sandy then in point position about five yards ahead, led the Bren group out in arrow-head formation through the rubber, where possible keeping behind a line of trees for cover.

They continued to move like this for four hundred yards or so, making eight bounds in all. As they tactically advanced over the undulating ground the sound of firing grew louder. Sandy calculated they were now approximately halfway down the line of the perimeter fence and that the CTs must be about two hundred yards ahead, slightly to their left in the direction of the fence. He estimated that his own position was most likely midway between the terrorists and the jungle edge.

They had been gradually climbing a spur off the main ridge and had made no contact, and as yet there was no evidence that the CTs' attack was a diversionary one to hold their attention whilst a party did some rubber tree slashing. Sandy anticipated therefore that the force was a small one and that they would concentrate their attack on the one *sangar*. So far, his hunch was paying off!

His plan was to outflank the terrorists and attack. The sound of rifle fire was increasing, so to establish the situation he took Ahmad and decided to scout forward himself.

Leaving the rifle and Bren gun sections behind under the control of Ivan, they crept forward until they were overlooking a small defile, across which they spotted a number of terrorists strung out over another spur off the main plateau.

Sandy made a quick appreciation and decided he'd bring up the whole section in one bound, still keeping the Bren on the right flank where it would be best served to give an assault party covering fire – and also act as a cut-off fire position on any CTs retreating to the jungle edge! As there was little likelihood of the section coming into the line of fire from the *sangar*, he decided to use the Very light as a signal for his small command to open fire on the terrorist positions. He sent the NCO back to Ivan, to inform him of the plan, and waited for them to come up to the assembly point in the dead ground from which he would place them out into firing positions.

It didn't take long for Ivan and the section to get forward and Sandy quietly outlined the plan, stressing the need for stealth in getting into position without being seen. The Bren group was first into place and then the riflemen, two at a time, spread out five yards between each, with Sandy and the Corporal in the centre. Ivan, now with the Bren group, was to open fire immediately Sandy signalled.

'Fire ...!!!' Sandy yelled at the top of his voice as the Very light hurled in the direction of the number one *sangar*. The Bren opened up, chattering away in bursts, together with the rapid fire thump ...! thump ...! thump ...! of the riflemen.

The CTs were taken completely by surprise and Sandy saw two fall, hit in the opening burst. At first they didn't know where the fire was coming from and when they did, it was too late. The attack had put them in complete disarray and they were unable to regroup and return fire. Sandy had the initiative and the terrorists only managed to get a few rounds off as they retreated down the spur and, as he'd anticipated, in doing so they ran into the cut-off position covered by the Bren and he witnessed another go down as the chattering bursts of fire continued.

The red Very light signal had got through to the *sangar*, fire from that quarter having ceased. Sandy and the riflemen moved around and down along the spur the terrorists had been on, his intention being to clear it and press on with the attack.

They followed him at the double in arrow-head formation through the rubber, then down the spur they charged in extended order. Sandy saw two crumpled figures lying behind a fallen tree and wasted no time as he ran past, firing twice into the huddled bodies. Out of the corner of his eye he saw Ahmad, who was running alongside him, do the same. They raced on down the now sloping ground – another shot rang out – they never faltered, slipping and sliding until they broke out into the open flat ground below which stretched out to the jungle edge.

He stopped, chest heaving, holding his carbine at the ready, looking right then left, and was glad to see the rifle section were all present, though also a little out of breath!

'OK …! we'll follow them up to the jungle edge, so be careful …! We'll move in bounds, myself and right flank first! Move!'

They doubled forward about twenty-five yards and stopped, taking up a firing position. The left flank then repeated the operation and Sandy got up and bounded forward again coming up to a large expanse of swampy ground which barred his way.

'*Tuan* …!' cried Ahmad.

'Over here! … this way *Tuan* …!' He pointed to a series of old fallen trees that appeared just above the oozing mass of short swampy undergrowth.

'Follow me, *Tuan* …! he shouted again. Sandy turned and ran along to the point where he was standing.

'Hell, this isn't so good …!' he exclaimed.

'We'll have to cross in single file …! one at a time in case the CTs are in the jungle edge waiting …! I'll go over with two men first and make a recce. Take up covering positions, if I want you I'll wave you on when we get across!'

With that he began to pick his way across moving from tree to tree, frequently having to jump the gaps between them. He'd got about halfway across when he misjudged one of the jumps, lost his footing and slipped, falling into the swamp up to his knees. He was stuck, unable to move either forward or backwards, and felt himself slowly being sucked down.

'Don't move, *Tuan* ...!' Ahmad called and edged forward with the two SCs that had been behind Sandy. They grabbed him by the shoulders and gave an almighty heave, struggled and tried again, then with a squelch and plop he was free. They hauled him back onto the log, this time minus a shoe which had been sucked under when they'd extricated him.

'Damn it ...! I've lost my shoe ...!' Laughing he bent down and shoved his arm into the water-logged puddle which was now forming where his right leg had been. Fortunately, the shoe had come off just as he was being pulled out and was within eight inches or so of the surface. What a mess!

Sandy decided that the initiative was now lost, precious minutes having been taken up removing him from the swamp, and the remaining CTs had disappeared into the jungle. It would be extremely unwise to follow since any pursuing party could easily be ambushed!

He put on the mud filled shoe and limped back across the logs to firmer ground.

'*Terima kaseh*, Ahmad ...!' he said thanking the Corporal.

'That was bloody nasty ...! we'll go back now and see if any of the CTs are alive ...! I made sure those I saw wouldn't be shooting us in the back as we pressed on ...!'

'Yes, *Tuan* ... me too!' Ahmad nodded his head vigorously.

Sandy then led them back tactically to the position from which the terrorists had been firing, regrouping his small force. A search of the area revealed three young Chinese dead, armed with SMLE .303 rifles in fairly good order, and from the various firing positions nearly two hundred rounds of ammunition were collected. Sandy then called in the Bren group and Ivan was jubilant on seeing him and the remainder all intact. He shouted as he came running up,

'By Jove, Sir ...! we were lucky to get away without any casualties ...!'

'Yes, Ivan, we were ...! come with me to number one *sangar* and we'll make our report together ...!' Turning to Corporal Ahmad he said,

'Corporal, I'll send a stretcher party for the bodies ... be careful on your way back and put out a rearguard, understand ...?

Ahmad came smartly to attention and saluted as Sandy and Ivan made their way back to the perimeter fence.

'My God ...! Ivan ... these chaps have done well today – you too ... I'm proud of you all. We really gave 'em a shock and that's the way to do it ... remember there's a lesson to be learned!

'Speed is the aim in attack and – *anticipation*! Keep your plan simple and cut down verbal orders to the absolute essentials ...! If you're in command keep forward so that you can deal at once with the situation ...!'

'Yes, Sir ...! I've certainly learnt something today ...!' Ivan declared.

They were now within hailing distance of the *sangar*, Will Penrose had already spotted them walking through the rubber trees and was waiting for them. He clapped them both on the back as they came through the gate.

'Jolly good show, chaps ...! three CTs killed you say and no casualties ...! Bloody good show ...! bloody good show ...! We'll have to open a bottle of champagne to celebrate ...!'

A stretcher party was quickly organised and Sandy was whisked off to bath and given a change of clothes. Hugh was about the same build as Sandy and offered him shirt, shorts and stockings and made sure his muddy shoes were cleaned.

Sandy left word that he'd visit the guardroom later and speak to the men, in particular those who'd been out with him.

'By the way, Will ...! a patrol will have to go out first light tomorrow and comb the swamp area for CT casualties, but I don't advise they go into the jungle ...'

'OK, Sandy ...! I'll get young Ivan here to take it out as he knows the situation.'

It was 3.30 p.m. when they returned to the lunch so abruptly interrupted earlier. The action only lasted about an hour but to Sandy it felt much longer.

They finished off a couple of bottles of champagne and were delightfully mellow – one and all! Will tried to get Sandy to stay the night but since he had a meeting to attend the next day it was out of the question and he thought he'd better be going before it got dark. He made his farewells then went down to the guardroom to thank the SCs for their magnificent participation in the action.

The journey back this time with Elias driving, did as always appear quicker. He was certainly in a better frame of mind and felt pleased with himself and the Special Constables.

8

A Taste of Honey

The Government of the United Kingdom continued to monitor affairs in the Colonies and Protectorates and made no exception with the Federation of Malaya. When Sir Thomas Lloyd, the Permanent Under Secretary for the Colonies, made a tour of the Federation he decided to begin in Johore and Sandy was called to Circle Headquarters to be briefed in the role he would undertake when Sir Thomas arrived.

The tour was to be extensive, beginning in Johore Baharu, where Sir Thomas and Lady Lloyd would stay with the British Adviser. An armour-plated Rolls Royce with bullet-proof windows was to be put at their disposal by the Federal Government and the British Adviser was to accompany them in his own Rolls whilst they were in his area of jurisdiction.

The Police Field Force Company operating in the region were to provide the escort, which would be at platoon strength. Their duties were to protect the two VIP vehicles, fore and aft, by travelling in a number of Land Rovers. The CPO directed that Sandy was to command and lead the motorcade in a Ferret armoured car provided for the occasion by the Federal Police HQ in Kuala Lumpur. Communications would be by radio between all Police vehicles and Operational Control at Contingent Police Headquarters JB.

The route Sir Thomas wished to take to Malacca was via Bandar Penggaram and Batu Pahat and it was arranged that the party would stop for lunch at the Bandar Penggaram Club, where Sandy would hand over his charge to a Captain of the Fijian Regiment who was to provide the guard from there onwards to the Malacca state boundary. After the transfer Sandy would be free to escort the British Adviser back to the Residency in JB.

The whole operation was top secret and Sandy had to return to his district and go about his duties until he was called.

Meantime he was completing his part in the 'Briggs Plan', resettling the so-called Chinese squatters; the plan being in its last phase in his district. In the course of his duties he'd negotiated with the District

Resettlement Officer for the supply of timber from the local sawmill. Large quantities were required for the building of houses in the new village, which had been designated to accommodate the last of the families brought in from the outlying areas.

The sawmill manager was an Anglo-Indian whose father, a Scot, had been a Judge in India before the war and had married an Indian lady of high cast. Ian Buchanan, their only son, was an intelligent man and well educated, having been sent to study in Scotland. Ian and Sandy, who were of similar age, had a lot in common and became good friends. During the school holidays Ian had stayed with his Scottish relatives and travelled widely to many of the favourite haunts that Sandy visited as a boy.

Ian was tall, good looking, of slim build and with an excellent, resonant, speaking voice. Life had been hard for him on leaving school and on returning to India he'd been packed off to Malaya to make his own way in the world. At the outbreak of hostilities he joined up in the Straits Volunteer Force and served as a medical orderly until he was eventually interned by the Japanese in Singapore. The fact that his skin was almost black saved him and the Japanese, not knowing his true history, allowed him to return to Johore where he'd made his home.

He was a rather solitary man, had few friends and wasn't accepted by either the pre- or post-war Europeans, nor by the coloured and indigenous populace; he was too well educated for them and this, regrettably, left him a loner and social outcast. But Sandy instantly liked Ian, enjoying his company. He was also an untapped mine of information. Often in the evening they would listen to records or, whilst having a drink, talk about places they'd known in Scotland; Sandy, as a matter of course, learned all the local gossip!

The days passed quickly and in time a coded signal was received informing him that he was to report for duty to Contingent Police HQ in JB. Bob Sutcliffe was alerted to arrange for the train to be stopped in the evening enabling him to board it on its overnight run to Singapore. His cheerful number-two entered the office and gave Sandy a questioning look.

'Bob ...!'

'Yes, Sir!'

'Make yourself available to drive me to the station tonight ... I don't want Elias or anyone to know where I've gone – and that goes for Beaumont too! ... this is just between the two of us ... I'm off on special duty to Contingent HQ ...!' he paused a moment looking straight at Sutcliffe.

'Understand?'

'Yes, Sir ... mum's the word!'

'If anyone does start asking questions – just say that I've gone on a few days local leave – that should keep them quiet. Actually it won't be untrue because I intend to have a few days in Singapore if I can arrange it ... don't worry about the OSPC, he knows where I'll be ... Right, now you know what to do ... you're in charge whilst I'm away – and don't swan off on any patrols – delegate others!'

Just after midnight Sandy slipped away and boarded the train, which was on time for once. There weren't many travelling so he had no difficulty in finding a quiet position in the first class saloon and settled down in one of the vacant comfortable armchairs. He observed, everything appeared the same as on his first journey a long time ago. He could hardly believe it was over twelve months since that memorable night when he'd started out from JB venturing into the unknown and Bang had met him. Bang hadn't returned to Johore after leave but had been posted to Kota Bharu, Kelantan to take command of the Jungle Company stationed there.

'I could do with a spot of leave,' he thought. *It'll be good to have a change of scene and Singapore has so much to offer. I'll contact Dinger!'*

Dinger had written to him often and now with the family there he had a standing invitation to stay with them.

'Once this job's over I'm in just the right place to take some days local leave, which is well overdue.'

He dosed fitfully throughout the night, always waking when the train stopped at the numerous stations on the way or for the necessary security checks.

The train eventually arrived half an hour late and Sandy found the HQ Orderly Officer patiently waiting with transport to take him to the officers' mess where he was to be billeted.

'Morning, Sir!' Mallet greeted him in his usual friendly manor.

'Morning, Mallet, nice to see you again, hope all's well with you?'

'Oh, I'm all right, Sir, glad to see you again and in one piece. You're a bit of a celebrity here, what with one thing and another – your parish certainly keeps hitting the Sitrep headlines!'

'What's the drill this morning, Mallet?' Sandy asked briskly, wanting to change the subject.

'The CPO wishes to see you at 09.00 hrs, Sir! – which should give you time to change and have breakfast, the Land Rover will be at the mess at 08.45 hrs!'

'Right! then let's get moving!' Sandy replied curtly, being in no mood at such an early hour to waste time discussing with Mallet his district's notoriety.

'I need as much time as possible!'

Mallet took the hint and picking up one of the bags replied briskly over his shoulder, 'Follow me, Sir …!'

They made their way in silence down the station platform through the throng of alighting passengers and out to the waiting Land Rover. The short drive to the Police Mess, located along the Straits road, was also undertaken without conversation and Sandy was eventually installed in the guest room.

The building was a small rambling bungalow with only one resident, since most of the Contingent officers were married and had their own quarters. The officer living there, a member of the Marine Branch, was out on patrol in one of the converted naval motor torpedo boats so Sandy had the place to himself. He changed, had something to eat and at 08.45 hrs was once more being escorted by Mallet to HQ.

The CPO gave him one of his crushing handshakes as he greeted him.

'We meet again, MacIntyre! Sit down, make yourself comfortable. I must tell you I'm very pleased with the way you've carried out your duties, very commendable! This next job is damned important, we must ensure that our visitor is given the utmost protection … you do understand, don't you?'

'Yes, Sir!'

'I've chosen you specially, you're the man to see it through to a safe conclusion.'

As he spoke his unblinking, piercing eyes took in Sandy and a smile hovered around the corners of his mouth.

'Thank you, Sir! I'll do my very best, Sir …!'

To his horror, the words echoed like the recording he'd once heard of a Peter Sellers' party piece entitled 'Fool Britannia': brilliantly funny but not something he wanted the CPO to twig precisely at this moment! He just managed to stop himself smiling.

'Right-oh …! here are the details,' the CPO continued, handing Sandy the tour itinerary – a bulging file of papers.

'Guard this with your life – it's for your eyes only! At 11.00 hrs this morning you're to see the British Adviser, he'll fill you in as to his own requirements. The platoon and transport are standing by and will only need an hour's notice to get them to start point.' He paused, looking intently at Sandy, then resumed,

'Carry the instructions out to the letter … but … do use your discretion should anything unforeseen occur … you know what I mean! The OC Company, Field Force and the Lieutenant Platoon Commander are in the picture, as are the Transport and Signals officers you'll meet when you see the SO Operations this afternoon.' He hesitated momentarily, letting his instructions sink in.

'It's all there in your orders ... read them now!' he finished briskly.
'Yes, Sir!'

Sandy opened the file which outlined the complete plan of operation.
A silence fell and the CPO patiently waited whilst he read through the
contents.

Raising his eyes Sandy directed his gaze at the waiting figure to indicate
that he'd finished.

'Any questions?' The CPO shot him a quizzical look.

'No, Sir ...! it's all very clear.'

'Right-oh ...! off you go and the best of luck ... I'll see you when
you get back ... take a few days in Singapore when its all over.'

'Thank you, Sir ...!'

Sandy felt elated, everything was going well – but he wouldn't contact
Dinger until he was free! The briefing over he returned to the mess and
studied the orders again in greater detail.

Before long he was on his way to the British Adviser, a pipe-smoking,
genial old Colonial Civil Service Officer, with rather a look of Noel
Coward about him, who immediately put him at ease.

'You'll meet Sir Thomas and Lady Lloyd in the morning; they're at
the Istana at the moment seeing the Sultan ...' He walked to the window,
then turned to face Sandy before continuing,

'There's a minor change of plan for you to note, MacIntyre. I'll travel
in the Rolls with our visitors. My car will go up empty as reserve and I
hope will only be used on my return.'

Sandy acknowledged the instruction.

'That's OK by me, Sir, as long as I'm kept informed where everyone
is!'

'Right! See you in the morning ... I won't keep you, no doubt you
have a lot to do,' and with that the meeting ended.

Early next morning the Scout car took Sandy to the Residency where
the escort was waiting in the drive. The previous day Sandy had met the
platoon commander in the Operations room and, as he dismounted from
the Scout car, the Police Lieutenant saluted and briskly made his report.

'Morning, Sir!'

'Good morning, Hardy ... everything in order?'

'All present and correct ... all radios have been checked and are
operational – including yours, Sir!'

'OK! We'll move off as soon as our charges are in their cars, I'm
assured they'll not keep us waiting. It's going to be a long day!'

The time was now a little before seven o'clock, and with that, the VIPs
made their appearance on the steps of the great house. Sandy approached
the waiting party, halted and saluted Sir Thomas, whom he addressed.

'We're ready, Sir!'

'Right, MacIntyre ...! we are too ... we'll not keep you!'

Everything went according to plan and they began their journey making their way first to Kulai where a new village was inspected and a palm oil estate visited. By the middle of the morning they had passed through Ayer Hitam and were well on their way to Batu Pahat, travelling through the picturesque coastal plane bounded by paddy fields and swaying coconut palms. At midday they reached their rendezvous with the Fijians. The luncheon in the Bandar Penggaram Club House, a rambling wooden structure with a colourful covered porch, was presided over by the Colonel, a New Zealander, and the 2i/c, a burly Fijian international rugger player – and a Paramount Chief to boot! Sandy and the Lieutenant were invited to join the party and he sat across the table from the Chief who carried on a lively conversation with him.

Hors-d'oeuvre over, a suckling pig was placed on the table and the Fijian Major remarked that it was a favourite dish of the Islands ...

'Apart from the traditional one of "*long pig*" which is no longer available!'

One of the lady guests showing great interest, asked in all innocence.

'What is "*long pig*", Major?'

He roared with laughter.

'Don't you know ...?!! We were once cannibals ...!' and without stopping to draw breath he looked straight at Sandy, eyes twinkling.

'So you're a Scot, are you!'

'Yes, I am ... on both sides of my family.'

'Ah yes ... so be it ...! However, I've very likely got as much Scottish blood in my veins as you have ...!' and gave another deep-throated chuckle as though he was relishing some private joke.

The luncheon guests were agog waiting for the outcome of this unusual conversation and turned towards Sandy, waiting for him to ask the inevitable.

'Well, Major ... may I ask how you come to that conclusion?'

'Oh ...! that's very simple – my grandfather was a great man for the traditional dish – and very partial to Presbyterian Ministers!'

The assembled company laughed in sheer delight at the improbable story and the lunch was pronounced a great success. When it was over Sandy rejoined the escort and waited for the British Adviser to bid farewell to Sir Thomas, his Lady and the Colonel. The Fijians were efficient and eager to be on their way and on waving their visitors goodbye the BA turned to Sandy.

'Right, MacIntyre, we'll make our way back to JB. You can, if you'd like, ride in the Rolls with me – you must have had a pretty uncomfortable journey up here ... the Lieutenant can take over your duties in the Scout car and look after us for a change!'

So it was that Sandy returned in style to make his report to the CPO who was eager to learn the outcome of the operation. It was late when he finally called it a day, but he'd enjoyed his meal at the Residency with the BA and his wife, and before turning in decided that, tired or not, he was going to telephone Dinger to arrange a spot of well earned leave in Singapore.

'Hello, Dinger? Sandy here ...!' he shouted down the crackling line.

'What ...? ah ...! oh ...! yes ...! Sandy!!! the voice at the end of the line queried.

'I'm in JB on a job ... hope to be finished tomorrow!' Sandy heard Dinger's voice in the distance asking if he'd like to stay.

'... love to, thanks, can do ... four or five days at least! Right, that'll do. OK, I'll give you a ring and let you know what time to pick me up at the Mess – you know where it is.'

'Bloody awful line this ... fine ...! family all right? Great! looking forward to meeting them too.' Dinger faded away into the distance.

'Oh! you're on call tonight ...! ah ...! I'd better get off the line ...! OK, I'll give you a ring at the office tomorrow. Cheerio ...!'

With that he put down the receiver, feeling tired but at ease and looking forward to Singapore.

Early next morning Sandy saw the CPO and was granted local leave. He sent off signals to his OCPC and to Bob so they would know where he was should he be needed. He then rang Dinger who turned up at 3 o'clock. The first thing Sandy noticed was that his face seemed to have filled out, looking much better with the full set of teeth he was now sporting!

'No doubt his wife's doing!' he mused.

This was their first reunion since arriving in Singapore and there was lots of back-slapping and the urge to tell all at once their individual experiences.

'By Jove, Sandy, I *am* glad to see you, we've been getting all sorts of stories about you! Anita's dying to meet you and so are the girls! You'll like the house; we live just off Cannon Rise, nice and quiet, but easy for the centre of town and, of course, the *"Cockpit"* in Oxley Rise. That's my local for your info.'

As they drove life took on a slightly nightmarish air, with Dinger behind the wheel of his new Citroen completely oblivious to other road users! Sandy, feet hard on the boards, gripped the seat with both hands as they had several near collisions with bicycle-rickshaws, pedestrians and other vehicles, which he didn't appear to see! The Citroen's gear lever was in the dashboard and he simply couldn't remember where it was; his hand fumbled between the seats and he kept looking down in despair in the area where he thought it ought to be!!

'Hell …! Sandy, I'll never get used to this bloody car – trust the French to put the gear change where you least expect it!'

Sandy stared straight ahead, replying through clenched teeth,

'Well, if it's OK with you I'll drive you any time – in fact …' he added with a flash of inspiration. 'I'd like to try out this car since I've never driven one with front wheel drive before.'

'Right, old bean, you can have it next time out. I don't like it at all, especially in Singapore!'

Sandy breathing a sigh of relief, crossed his fingers.

'Be nice if I could meet Anita whilst I'm still breathing!'

After a further couple of near misses they drew up outside a pleasant half brick and timber colonial house set on the hillside overlooking a distant view of the city and harbour.

Dinger's wife and daughters were waiting in anticipation of their arrival and on hearing the car coming down the short drive were out of the house like a shot. Anita, a small, pretty, plump woman in her thirties greeted them; her dark brown hair was tied back in a yellow ribbon matching her blouse and dirndl skirt; sandals encased her feet setting off her tanned legs.

She offered Sandy her hand and her steady gaze came from lovely deep brown eyes; her voice was soft and modulated.

'I'm glad you could come, Sandy, Ted's been so looking forward to a visit from you and I've been quite intrigued with the stories we've heard about you. The girls think you are some sort of knight in shining armour, slaying dragons up and down the country.' She laughed and Sandy immediately felt at ease with her.

'How's my little poppets?' Dinger roared, as his girls rushed out screaming,

'Daddy … daddy …!' The girls flew into his outstretched arms from where they looked up shyly at Sandy.

'Well, Sandy, what d'you think of this lot?' he asked looking down with a father's pride at the wriggling figures.

'Come on now, Sandy … let's get in and have a drink – I'm sure you're ready for one – and I'll tell you what we'll do this evening. I've a little trip set up for you, we've been invited to a party on board a cargo passenger ship …!'

Sandy followed Dinger up the wooden steps of the veranda which ran the full length of the house. The double doored entrance opened into a spacious combined living and dinning room; a comfortable place which had the air of a woman's touch – the choice of curtains, the artistically arranged flowers!

Dinger, carrying the younger girl in his arms, made straight for the sideboard where there were a number of bottles. Putting her down he poured two large measures of whisky and from a syphon squirted a short blast of soda into his glass, then handed the other to Sandy, saying,

'Help yourself to the soda, old sport ... by Jove, I've been needing this all day ...! Cheers ...!' and he downed half the contents.

'Ah ...! that's better,' he exclaimed and let out a long sigh. Sandy noticed the quick glance Anita gave her husband and felt a slight tension in the air.

'Hitting the bottle perhaps?' he wondered.

'Sandy! ...' Anita exclaimed, breaking the silence. 'I'd better show you the guest rooms ... we have two ... you have your own shower and toilet so you'll be self contained ... it's much more comfortable for you ... and you won't have the children underfoot getting in the way ...!'

'Right, off you go,' Dinger said, helping himself to another large scotch. 'Anita'll look after you ... she's the boss! I'll tell you later about tonight.'

Sandy left his tumbler of whisky on one of the side tables and followed Anita down a short passage to the staircase at the rear of the house. Eventually they entered a bright airy room which looked out over the veranda and drive.

'There you are, Sandy ... I hope you'll be comfortable – you're our first guest. By the way ... I'm not going with Ted and you tonight!' She gave him a long, searching look then continued,

'Try and not be too late ... I get a little worried when he goes off on one of his jaunts ...'

'Anita, please don't worry – I'll keep an eye on him,' Sandy quickly assured her. 'For one thing I'll be driving, so I shan't drink too much – especially with a car I've not driven before and in a city I don't know!'

'Oh Sandy, I'm so relieved – I'm glad you're driving – because that's part of the trouble ... Ted isn't a good driver at the best of times and Singapore gets him down.' She gave his arm a squeeze and the troubled look disappeared, her face brightening.

'I'm so glad you've come ... he needs a friend ... someone like you.' With that she turned to leave, hesitating in the doorway before saying over her shoulder,

'Dinner is at seven but come down as soon as you're ready – I suspect Ted wants to tell you about where he's taking you ...' She closed the door quietly behind her.

Now on his own, Sandy had a quick look about the room and the adjoining bathroom, both of which were more than he expected; he was going to be very comfortable. He was already feeling quite at home and the break from the stress of life upcountry would do him the world of good. He'd liked Anita as soon as he'd met her, but Dinger was definitely a bit edgy. A bad sign drinking his whiskies so fast ... there must be a reason why!

It was six thirty before he realised it and, refreshed after a quick shower and a change of clothes, he made his way downstairs to the lounge. Dinger was sitting waiting for him with a large whisky in his fist.

'Thought you were never coming ... been studying for the staff course!' he said peevishly. Sandy pretended not to notice, assuming it was the drink talking, and wondered how many Dinger had had already.

'It's time you had your sun-downer, help yourself and freshen up that glass you left.' Taking a long draught and putting down his glass he said in a more jovial tone,

'Well, Sandy, what d'you think of the house, not bad, eh?'

'Dinger, you're a very lucky man – the place is marvellous and so are you all ...! I've been looking forward to making a visit for a long time and I know I'm going to enjoy myself.'

'Well I reckon you will tonight ... we don't have to go far – just down to Clifford Pier ... I'll direct you there. We pick up the harbour Police launch which'll take us out into Keppel harbour where the ship is now riding at anchor, ready for docking in the morning ...' He peered down into his glass apparently uncertain whether he should finish it off. He decided to carry on talking.

'I get an invitation every time the ship comes in from UK ... the first officer generally gives me a ring when they get alongside – but at the moment the berths are full and they passed a message by way of immigration control ... which I'm attached to!'

'Velly interesting ... as our slit-eyed brothers would say,' Sandy mimicked. 'I like ships ... I suppose you get a lot of this kind of thing?'

'Well ...! once or twice a week at least, but most of my duties are in the docks ... where I work closely with immigration and customs.'

At that moment Anita came in with the children who, having eaten earlier, were now ready for bed. The girls rushed into their father's arms and each gave him a quick kiss. Anita, ever watchful, said,

'Say goodnight to our guest ...' and in chorus they cried,

'Goodnight Uncle Sandy ...' and dashed out of the room in childlike glee before he could answer them.

They all burst out laughing.

'Would you believe it.' Anita said. 'I've been trying to get them to say that for the last five minutes ... they're really not used to visitors and are naturally shy. You'll see a difference tomorrow, Sandy – when they get used to you ... must get off to the kitchen and see how cookie is getting on ... dinner should be ready.'

Immediately on Anita's exit Dinger turned to Sandy and said, in a tone which suggested collusion,

'By the way Sandy ... we'd better get off as soon as we've had dinner ... the launch will be standing-by at eight o'clock and I don't want to keep it waiting.'

Dinner was enjoyable, if rather hurried, and soon they were on their way. Brief instructions from Dinger on the Citroen's controls and Sandy was soon enjoying the feel of being behind the wheel of a car for a change ... a world away from driving the Land Rover!

The journey was short and they pulled up at the pier, parking opposite where the launch was moored. Dinger greeted the boatswain, a Chinese Police Inspector, who was waiting for them at the end of the gangway.

Sandy couldn't clearly make out what was being said but it sounded like instructions as to their return. He overheard the word '*midnight*' and saw Dinger nod his head in agreement. Once on board Dinger explained,

'We'll be picked up at midnight at the end of their patrol so ... *whatever* ... don't forget to get me moving or we'll be stuck on board all night and will only get ashore when our friends dock in the morning – and that's quite a way from where we've left the car ...!'

Sandy made a mental note of the instructions, his mind flashing back to Anita's troubled face.

Slowly they edged out into the harbour, weaving amongst a number of ships riding at anchor, then set course in the direction of Sentosa Island. Standing on the small bridge of the launch with the steady, assuring thump of the powerful engines beneath his feet, mingled with the swish of water alongside, Sandy looked back towards the stern. The rolling wake in the moonlight appeared like jet black silk studded with diamonds. A feeling of elation swept over him; the arduous months up-country seemed to belong to another world of which he was no longer a part.

It didn't take them long to reach the cargo ship with its stark, foreboding shape looming out of the darkness. The vessel was some ten thousand tons, with a capacity for twelve passengers all berthed in cabins on the boat deck.

A swaying, clanking accommodation ladder, slung over the port side, came into view and the launch, with the Inspector at the helm, slowly and expertly came about to approach the small landing stage. One of the crew standing-by with a boat-hook made fast the launch to allow each of them in turn to jump onto the pitching platform. Dinger was first, then Sandy – the heaving swell requiring quick co-ordination and agility. They climbed with care, for the swaying movement of the steps clanking against the ship's side threatened to send them hurtling into the water. At the top they were met by the officer of the watch.

Dinger was first to speak.

'Hello, Tim, had a good voyage? By the way I've brought along an old pal of mine – Sandy MacIntyre. He's in the Police upcountry and on a spot of leave.'

'Fine …! how goes it, Dinger?' Tim shook his hand.

'Oh, I shouldn't grumble …'

'Howdy, Sandy …! glad to have you aboard.'

'Thank you …' Sandy replied, shaking hands.

'Follow me, everyone's in the wardroom where we're having a dance – of sorts!'

The sound of music and laughter drifted towards them as they proceeded down a companionway. The air was heavy with cigarette smoke and through the approaching doorway a number of couples could be seen dancing in the overcrowded room.

As Dinger entered people waved to him from different directions. It looked as though the party was made up of more than just the ship's officers and passengers and later Sandy discovered that the guests were a mixture of Police and Customs officials and their wives.

After introductions the ship's first officer asked what they'd like to drink, and charged with a large whisky and soda each they were at last free to mingle. It was explained that the passengers were couples returning from leave.

'All except one rather attractive nursing Sister who's travelling alone,' said the officer, eyes twinkling, indicating a tall redhead attired in floral silk.

Sandy looked across to where she was standing. He watched her steadily and found he couldn't keep his eyes off her; he was sure he'd seen her somewhere before – but where …?

Harry, the Number One, was a friendly chap who'd served in the Royal Navy during the war and, since leaving the service, had been with the shipping line about four years. There were few places he hadn't been, since the line traded back and forth between the UK and the Orient. Sandy found the older man very interesting, all the more so when Harry mentioned this was to be his last trip for a while because on return to the UK he was to commission a new cargo vessel on the Clyde.

Deep in conversation and unconscious of the hubbub of voices and people around them, Sandy was startled when a soft voice whispered in his ear,

'Hello, Sandy …!'

He felt the hair on the back of his neck rise; the past flashed before him as recognition dawned. Spinning round, he faced the caller.

'Kay ... Kay Sutherland!' he gasped in surprise.

'What on earth are you doing here? Heavens ... you're a sight for sore eyes.' Instinctively they embraced and Sandy kissed her on the cheek.

'You two know each other?' queried Harry.

Sandy and Kay, oblivious to the interest they had kindled in the ship's Number One and those near by, looked up a little embarrassed as they disentangled themselves. Turning, they answered as one,

'Yes ... we do!' and burst out laughing.

'I can't believe it ...!' Sandy exclaimed, gazing at her in amazement.

'Harry ...! Kay and I met after the war when I went back to Kaduna, Nigeria – she was a Queen Alexandra Nursing Sister at the Military Hospital – but we haven't seen each other since then – and that was nearly four years ago.'

'How extraordinary that we should meet again, Kay – and in the middle of Singapore harbour of all places!'

'It is good to see you, Sandy ... I've often wondered what had become of you ... I'm now a Sister Tutor and have a teaching post with the General Hospital in Singapore ...! But tell me what on earth you're doing here?'

'Well I'll be darned ...!' Sandy said under his breath, unable to believe the turn of events.

'I'm almost next door as it were – in Johore – serving in the Police now – have been for over a year ...! I'm on a few days leave and staying with a buddy of mine – he's about somewhere ... in fact he brought me here!' The words tumbled out.

Harry laughed.

'Don't mind me butting in, but I can see I'll have to leave you two on your own. You'll have a lot of catching up to do, so I'll see you later!' With that he moved away.

Sandy studied Kay with interest and realised she had changed very little, though she looked sadder than he remembered. They were about the same age and although she was tall, he towered above her. She had a lovely figure and a sensuality which pervaded the print dress she wore. Sandy remembered well the natural elegance of her lithe and graceful walk; the distinctive face and creamy textured skin set off by her long, auburn hair.

He realised that she was a part of his life he missed and a yearning deep within him awakened. He must see her again!

'I'm so glad to see you, Kay ... this time we'll have to make sure we keep in touch!'

'I'd like that, Sandy,' she replied.

Never lovers – they could (should) have been had he stayed on in Kaduna!
There were all sorts of questions he wanted to ask her ... but dared not give
voice to.

'*Are you married, Kay?*

His mind raced on.

'*Are you engaged, Kay? Oh Sandy! ... this'll never do ... get a grip ...*
you've only just met her again ... give her time to tell you!

Over her shoulder across the crowded room he caught sight of Dinger who
was on his way over, glass held high, face flushed and already hailing them.

'Trust you, Sandy, to get the belle of the ball ...! I've been watching
you ...! Don't fret, Madame, I'm coming to your rescue ...!' he cried
out in mock gallantry.

'You've got it all wrong, Dinger ... come and meet an old friend of
mine from Nigeria.'

'Good heavens, you actually know her ...! wait till I tell Anita ...! she
won't believe me,' he babbled cheerfully.

Sandy introduced Kay, telling Dinger about her post with the General
Hospital.

'That's great news ... the hospital isn't far from where I live and quite
often some of the senior staff are guests at functions in our Police Mess ...
you'll have to come over and visit us – my wife'll be only too pleased
to see you ...'

Turning to Sandy he said,

'Say ...! you could bring Kay over for a sun-downer and dinner
tomorrow evening then we could all go to the Swimming Club ...
Saturday night's always a good night ... they've a live dance band ... I
was going to suggest it anyway ...'

Sandy looked eagerly at Kay and, taking her hand, cajoled,

'Yes? You'll have plenty of time to settle in tomorrow, you'll be ashore
early ... please ... I won't be here next Saturday ...!'

She smiled at him.

'You're as persuasive as ever, Sandy ... thank you ... Yes, I'd love to
come.'

'Well, that's settled ...!' he answered, suddenly feeling rather boyish,
happy ... and a little embarrassed!

'Now, let's have a dance before someone takes you from me.'

They joined the throng milling around the middle of the floor and
danced to music played on an old gramophone. At the end of the dance
Kay whispered,

'Let's go up on deck and get some fresh air ... I want to know what
you are doing in Johore? No doubt it's dangerous!'

He followed her through the door, down the companionway and up to the boat deck out into the warm humid air. They had a magnificent view of the harbour with its ships riding at anchor and the twinkling lights of Singapore as a backdrop.

They stood silently, leaning against the rail, looking out over the moonlit water. Quietly she put her hand lightly on his arm and he turned to face her.

'Forgive me for asking this, Sandy – but are you seeing anyone at the moment?'

Taken aback by the speed of her direct approach, he hesitated.

'Well ... no! No, to be honest, there's little chance of meeting anyone where I am ... this is the first break I've had since coming out!'

'Oh ...! I'm sorry, forgive me but I had to ask you. I feel so ... so unprotected ... I don't want to get involved again ... you mustn't expect too much of me.' Her voice trailed off as she looked away.

Sandy turned her face gently towards him and wiped the glistening tears away. He drew her into his arms and cradled her head against his shoulder, discerning the stifled anguish within.

'I've been very unhappy, Sandy ... and such a silly fool – I met someone, a man I thought I could trust, but really should have known better to keep away from. It's all over now ... but it still hurts ... that's the reason I don't want to get involved ... with anyone!'

'That's all right, Kay,' he assured her. 'I understand. Remember ... we were always good friends and we always will be ... come on, dry those lovely eyes of yours and let's try to make you happy ...!'

'Oh Sandy, you haven't changed ... you know just the right thing to say! Yes you're right, and of course I shouldn't inflict my troubles on you ... it's just that meeting you again suddenly brought it all home to me ... I was sad to see you leave Nigeria and return to your Regiment ... after you left ... I missed you!'

This little confession pleased him and he gave her a light kiss on the forehead.

'Cheer up, Kay ... life's too short and there will be better days ahead ...!'

'You're right ...! and I will, but only when you tell me who this Anita is!?'

'Oh, you must be feeling better, I detect a hint of jealousy in there already ...!' Sandy jibed. 'Well ... all will be revealed when you meet her tomorrow evening – I'm sure you'll like her?'

'Sandy ...! you're teasing me ... you'll break my heart ...!' she replied with half-hearted banter.

Without another thought he relented.

'Anita, my sweet Kay is ...' he paused for effect ... 'Dinger's wife and has two charming little daughters.'

'Ah ...! I was beginning to think you had a girlfriend tucked away after all ... and I wouldn't relish getting caught in the crossfire!' she laughed. 'After all you're quite a catch!'

'Compliments ... naughty, naughty ... this will never do,' Sandy scolded her and they both laughed.

'Marvellous ... I feel better already. Tell me, what are you doing here? ... let's sit down over there.'

She led the way, appearing to relax as Sandy painted a generally rosy picture, intentionally eliminating the danger and anything that would be considered a security risk. Conversation was easy and she too covered her last tour of duty, likewise managing to make it sound less gruelling than it undoubtedly was.

Eight bells denoted the end of a watch.

'Heavens, it must be midnight ... and the launch will be coming any time now to pick us up ...!'

'I say, would it help if I came down to the docks tomorrow morning and transported you up to the hospital ... I can borrow Dinger's car!'

'Oh, you are sweet to think of that Sandy ... thanks! ... but as it happens I'm being met with transport to take my baggage. Can I have your telephone number and as soon as I'm settled I'll give you a ring and let you know what time in the evening to pick me up!'

As the launch approached Sandy gave her one of Dinger's cards with his home number on. He checked over the side, saw the Police pennant flying and the Inspector standing on the bridge. Quickly he grasped Kay by the shoulders, gently kissed her on each cheek then let her go.

'Thank you, Sandy ... it's been marvellous seeing you again – watch how you go with that awful ladder ... I don't want to lose you!'

'You won't ...! but I must get hold of Dinger!'

'Right ... I'll say goodnight here ...!' Suddenly she clasped her arms around his neck and kissed him on the mouth, then before he could hold her she was out of his grasp.

'Night Sandy, see you tomorrow!' The words floated across the deck as she disappeared out of sight.

Sandy's stomach churned! Reluctantly he retraced his steps to the deck below to find a well-oiled Dinger.

'Hello old cock!'

His voice was thick and rasping.

'We've got extra bodies to take back ...! where's that girlfriend of yours ... got everything fixed for tomorrow night?'

'Yes ...!' Sandy answered as they made their way to the head of the accommodation ladder.

Harry was on duty to see everyone off the ship. Beside him was stationed a seaman equipped with a lifebelt and on the platform below another was positioned to assist the guests returning ashore. Everyone was bubbling over with laughter but there were no incidents and soon they were safely set ashore to pursue their own way home.

They arrived back at the house, which Sandy was relieved to find in darkness. He declined Dinger's offer of a night-cap, instead making his way to his room feeling distinctly happy and looking forward to seeing Kay again. He hoped he'd have the chance to see more of her in future.

The scene he faced at breakfast next morning amounted to an inquisition. Dinger had put Anita 'in the picture' (as he saw it!) and she was dying to know more about Kay.

'How long have you known her? ... where did you meet? ... how old is she ...', the questions went on and on.

He was certainly put in the 'hot seat' and had great difficulty in convincing them that Kay was just an old friend. In fact he didn't succeed, so in the end he gave up and agreed to go along with their assumption that she was his girlfriend. It seemed to please them both!

Poor Sandy – respite only came much later, in the form of a suggestion from Dinger that they should pay the Mess a visit for a Saturday lunch-time drink.

The remainder of the day dragged and he found with alarm that he was much more anxious to hear from Kay than he'd realised.

Around tea-time the telephone rang!

It was Kay!

Sandy became a changed man!

At 6 o'clock on the dot he was outside the Sisters' quarters; Kay was already waiting for him.

He felt good – warm, more complete as it were, with a pretty girl beside him, and so with a quick about-turn he drove her back to introduce her to everyone.

They arrived at the bungalow to find Anita waiting for them. There was almost an air of triumph in her welcoming of Kay. They hit it off instantly and the dinner which followed was a delight, with tasty food, beautifully served, and lots of goodnatured banter around the table; it was obvious they liked Kay.

Coffee over, they made their way to the Swimming Club. Sandy drove and Dinger sat back, content to give directions. They danced into the early hours, giving them time to renew their acquaintance and ease back into the intimacy they had enjoyed in the past; the evening was a great success!

Sandy grasped the golden opportunity offered by the ambience of the evening and asked them to join him for a meal the following day.

'How about the Cockpit for dinner?' he suggested.

Graciously Anita and Dinger bowed out, saying they should enjoy an evening on their own. Anita, almost imperceptibly, winked at Sandy!

Borrowing Dinger's Citroen for the evening Sandy collected Kay about 6.30 p.m. The "*Cockpit*" was unusual, in that the hotel contained a number of bungalows and a house which previously had been used as an interrogation centre during the occupation by the Japanese. The restaurant and bar were popular with expatriates.

Soon they too were enjoying the cosy atmosphere of the restaurant, so well known for its delicious rijstafel always served on a Sunday.

As they ate, there was little need for idle chatter; each delved deftly into what made the other 'tick', reassessing their relationship without committing themselves. The evening passed all too quickly and both were inwardly dreading the time to part.

Across the table Kay looked intently at Sandy.

'Do be careful, Sandy, I know your job is more dangerous than you make out ... hospital talk is that it's rough!'

'Don't worry, Kay, I'll be all right ... I've got some jolly good chaps around me and we keep our heads down when the flak's about ... we've been lucky up to now ... I'll keep my fingers crossed for you, too!'

'You'd better ... I'm ... fond of you!'

She blushed. 'There, I didn't mean to say that ... but I am ...!'

Sandy reached out and took her hand. Looking into her eyes he said quietly,

'I wasn't going to say this either, but I'll miss you ... I didn't realise before ... until it was too late ... that you're my kind of girl! I won't leave you willingly this time!'

Her eyes misted and her fingers gripped his hand.

'Oh Sandy I'm so glad ...! I'll look forward to you coming to Singapore ... and you never know, I might be able to wangle a visit to your local hospital on some pretext or other and see you if I get a chance!'

'Great, and there's always local leave ... I've only had a few days so far. Now I know what to do with it!'

She had a busy day ahead so Sandy took her back to her quarters early. As she stood in the doorway he put his arms around her unresisting body, gently kissing her lips. They were soft and yielding. Gently she pushed him away, saying,

'No more, Sandy ... I'll be thinking of you ... I'll ring!' and with that she was gone.

The following day Sandy drove Dinger to the office and later took Anita and the girls to the Swimming Club. On their return home in the late afternoon they picked up Dinger. He'd had a gruelling day and was pleased to spend a quiet evening at home replete with countless whiskies discussing the events of the last few days.

Towards the end of the evening Kay rang as promised. They talked small talk, neatly skirting round their newly found relationship, so fresh and fragile. Despite the urgency that war brings to every relationship they sensed that, at this moment, speaking without seeing, touching, could spirit away a little of the magic.

Next morning – early – and after a fitful night, Sandy caught the train. His last sighting was of Dinger and Anita disappearing into the distance, waving as the Kuala Lumpur train pulled slowly out of Singapore station and onward to Labis via JB.

Sandy's thoughts traversed a lighter path on that journey. He remembered it as feeling sweet.

... at last he'd had a *'taste of honey'*!

9

SO Operations

Sandy returned to running the district. There had been no major incidents whilst he was away and Bob Sutcliffe dealt efficiently with most of the immediate actions. However a few CT sightings were reported and some minor cases of 'rubber slashing' had occurred. This, of course, was not always attributable to terrorist activity! A disgruntled labour force often got their own back on a planter or his assistant by slashing some trees which would then bleed uncontrollably, knowing full well that any skulduggery would first be laid at the door of the terrorists! The Inspector had a number of suspect cases in hand and with very little crime generally for him to get his teeth into, he was in his element with this type of investigation.

Sandy found it increasingly difficult to keep his mind on the job and the first few days dragged. He thought of Kay constantly; life just wasn't the same any more. He kept silent about meeting her. Once or twice in the evening he was tempted to telephone her but thought better of it and decided to wait for the letter she had promised to write.

He pondered on how long that would be; the mail was notoriously slow. Outwardly he was unchanged – at least he thought so – hoped so! Inwardly he felt impatient, sick at heart, wanting to see and be with her.

'Hell ...! pull yourself together, Sandy ... a slip could be bloody fatal! Damn, damn, damn ... keep thinking about her ... stupid ... she's so lovely ... makes me feel ... happy ... I could fall for ...'

His thoughts were abruptly interrupted. The frown on Bob's face – which meant trouble – brought him back to reality.

'Bad news, Sir ...! Lieutenant in the Segamat district just shot an assistant planter ...! I've decoded the message ... Circle Headquarters want you there right away.'

He handed Sandy the signal which outlined briefly the situation, giving no indication on how, where or when it had happened. It instructed Sandy to report immediately and attend a meeting at midday.

'Alert my escort and driver, Bob ... I want them ready in ten minutes.'

'Do you want me to come as well?' Bob asked expectantly.

'No ...! hold the fort here ... heaven knows what this is all about – we'll just have to wait and see ... it's going to cause trouble whatever!'

He made a fast, but mercifully uneventful, journey to Segamat and arrived at headquarters just in time to meet Clive Thurgood and Mactavish heading in the direction of the OSPC's office.

'Hello chaps ... what a bloody mess!'

Clive rolled his eyes to the heavens, exclaiming,

'Just my luck, Sandy ... the Lieutenant is one of mine ... a new man, just out, and this happens!'

'Aye, Sandy ... it's a great pity so it is!' Mac commiserated.

The OSPC, sitting grim-faced at his desk, acknowledged their entry.

'Be seated, gentlemen, and we'll get down to the business in hand. This is a very serious matter and I want you to ensure that the instructions I've initiated are carried out to the letter! Apart from Sandy here, you are already in the picture as to what happened yesterday afternoon ... and Clive, I'm grateful for the swift action taken by you and the thorough investigation you carried out at such short notice!'

At this point his secretary handed each of them a memo. Sandy read it quickly; in short, it outlined a number of guidelines that had to be taken by Police Lieutenants when dealing with visits to plantations.

The incident apparently occurred after a Sunday curry lunch where, as a matter of course, a considerable quantity of beer and pink gin was consumed by the assistant planters – mostly young and single! They were reported to be a bit of a wild bunch. The Lieutenant in question was off-duty that morning and on his own in the rest house bar, so he'd been invited back to the estate for lunch. He was new and, since he had no previous experience to fall back on, didn't realise what he might be letting himself in for. Sunday was the only day the planters could relax and let their hair down!

Generally on such occasions the younger element indulged in some good humoured leg pulling and horseplay and the Lieutenant fell into the almost inevitable trap of accepting a senseless challenge which, without the stimulus of copious amounts of alcohol, would probably never have happened.

They were all wearing handguns of one kind or another and he was asked how fast he could draw the Browning automatic he was wearing at his hip. Someone bet him that he couldn't beat the reputed fastest draw in the district – a certain young assistant planter.

Consequently he accepted the gamble and a western style stand-off was arranged. The two contestants each prepared themselves by unloading their weapons, the planter his revolver and the Lieutenant the magazine from his automatic. The duel was set up and the referee started the contest with the drop of a hat. What happened next stunned the onlookers and so the winner was never declared. The befuddled officer, having consumed innumerable beers and gins, drew his gun, instinctively pulling the trigger ... *and fired the round he'd loaded into the breech before travelling out to the estate!*

The planter was shot in the upper right shoulder and luckily only received a flesh wound. The OSPC took a serious view of the incident – the shot could have been fatal! It was highly undisciplined of the officer to forget the rule imperative to anyone using handguns – *clear the breech* – and furthermore, he should have known better than to use firearms in any kind of 'game'. It certainly didn't do the Police image any good.

'Right, gentlemen,' the OSPC sternly concluded. 'That is all ... you know what to do ... we must *never* have a incident of this nature again!

'Sandy! stay please, I want a word with you ... I won't keep you long. No doubt you'll be having lunch at the rest house with these two rapscallions!'

Laughter broke the solemnity of the meeting.

'We'll keep you a place, laddie!' Mac called over his shoulder.

As Clive closed the door the OSPC looked hard at Sandy.

'Now ... tell me, what kind of officer is Sutcliffe?

The question caught Sandy off guard.

What the devil had Bob been up to whilst he'd been away?

Before answering he drew a deep breath.

'We ... ll as far as I'm concerned he's first class!'

Then putting aside all caution he carried on,

'He's an excellent officer who performs his duties with a high sense of responsibility and considerable initiative!'

'I'm glad to hear it, because he's going to take over from you! ... and will have to do the job until I get another ASP!'

He ignored the shocked look on Sandy's face and resumed,

'At the end of the week you will be posted to Contingent HQ Johore to take up duties as Staff Officer Operations ... it's a Deputy Superintendent's (DSPs) post ... so ... you're also promoted!'

Sandy was stunned, the news was tremendous; he didn't know what to say. His heart missed a beat as Kay flashed through his mind ...

'By Jove, Sir ...! I'm delighted ... and surprised, I didn't expect this.'

'Well, I'm not in the least surprised ...! the CPO is very impressed with you and you deserve the promotion and a decent position. I shall certainly miss you, and I'm sure your compatriots will too ... but I can't stand in your way ...! I wish you all the best. You can inform Sutcliffe – so begin to hand over. I'll be in touch!'

The OSPC smiled, stood up and offered Sandy his hand.

'Congratulations, you're just the chap for the job, you can tell the others over lunch!'

Sandy took his leave and walked over to the rest house as though he was walking on air!

He found his two friends already installed, their chilled Tiger beers in front of them, the glasses sweating, droplets trickling down the sides. Clive, on seeing him enter, alerted the steward to bring another beer.

'Well, laddie, you look as though you've pinched the cat's cream!' Mac gibed, looking at Sandy's flushed face.

'Come on, Sandy boy, something's a foot!' he badgered. 'You've no' got some poor wee lassie in the family way?'

Sandy chuckled.

'Sorry, Mac, to disappoint you! Actually it's a great piece of news ... you're now looking at the future SO Operations ...! I've been posted to JB! So ... lunch and drinks are on me!'

'Jolly good show ...!' Clive grinned.

Mac pumped Sandy's hand up and down, slapped him on the back, causing him to splutter, and in mock sarcasm said,

'We've got rid of you at last ...! No, frankly, I'm glad ... the opposition will find it harder to get you ...! you've earned it, Sandy boy, and the best of luck to you!'

Peels of laughter and goodnatured bantering accompanied the lunch. Sandy found it difficult to suppress his feeling of elation, but not once did he let slip that Kay was the reason, and he was longing for the evening when he could telephone her. Before taking his leave of them they made him agree that on his last evening there would be a farewell party in the rest house.

On his return to Labis, Bob was waiting in the office. He was unsettled to learn that Sandy was leaving and apprehensive on being told he was to take over. They were a good team and a genuine respect and friendship had grown between them.

'I'm glad the OSPC has given you the chance to show what you're made of, Bob, but you'll have to ensure that there's no nonsense from Beaumont ...! I'll see him in the morning, inform him of events ... and give him the gypsy's warning!' he assured him.

'Thank you, Sir! I'm glad you're going on promotion, but really sorry you're leaving ... still JB isn't far and we'll no doubt be in touch!'

'Yes, Bob, we will ...! But as from now I want you to start thinking about taking over! In the morning hand over your duties to Beaumont, but don't say anything tonight ... I want to speak to him first. Now, let's get out of here and have a drink at my place to celebrate.'

With that they left the office and took the waiting Land Rover to the bungalow. It was too early to contact Kay and Sandy felt in need of some congenial company to while away the time. So, over a couple whiskies he and Bob discussed the hand-over which had to be completed by the end of the week.

Once Bob had left Sandy tried to get in touch with Kay. He had difficulty in getting through, but after a number of tries eventually tracked her down in the Sisters' Mess. The sound of her voice made his pulse quicken.

He tried to sound relaxed.

'Hello Kay ...!'

'Sandy! are you all right?' she queried. 'There's a letter in the post to you ... I would have 'phoned but it isn't easy from here!'

The line crackled and his answer was drowned.

'What's that, Sandy ... the line's awful ...!' she shouted.

'Kay ... I've got some great news ... I've been promoted ... and posted to JB!'

'Oh Sandy! That's wonderful, I'm so glad ... when?'

'Sooner than you might think ... at the end of the week in fact ... I'll be arriving on Saturday morning and will take up my duties the following Monday ... so keep the weekend free!'

'Yes ... yes I will! ... but first,' she teased, 'I'll have to get rid of all my newly acquired boyfriends!'

'You'd better ... if they want to stay in one piece!' he countered.

Remembering his manners he asked, 'Anyway, how are you ... how's the new post going?'

'Fine! especially now ... on hearing your news ...!' she replied excitedly.

'I'll get in touch with you when I arrive ... give Dinger and Anita a ring for me and pass on the good tidings.'

'Yes ... I'll do that ... take care ... I'll be waiting for you to call!'

'Right ... it won't be long now ... 'bye Kay ... must go!'

With her voice ringing in his ears he replaced the receiver.

Her letter to him duly arrived, full of news of trips into Singapore and the kindness shown to her by Anita and Dinger. They sounded as though they'd adopted her! She even hinted that she might be able to make a semi-official visit to the Segamat Hospital. He grinned to himself, acknowledging that this would not now be necessary!

The next few days flew as he put Bob in the picture concerning the intricacies of command. The OSPC also called to see him and whilst there gave the personnel a pep talk.

On the Friday afternoon Bob went with him to the Segamat rest house, dismissing the escort so that he could accompany Sandy on the midnight train as far as Labis.

When Bob got off the train Elias, Bujang and Mohammed were on the platform to see him off. It had been officially decided not to broadcast his leaving, so the send-off was kept to the minimum.

Looking back, his recall of the party was hazy, however he did remember Bob's last words when they parted at Labis:

'Don't forget, Sir ... if there's any shooting on the way, keep your head down!'

The remark itself jolted into focus the crystal clear memory of his first journey up-country. Voices echoed and shimmering figures floated before him ... it seemed so long ago!

The train picked up speed and Sandy settled down into a comfortable club chair. With the steady, rumbling rhythm of the wheels lulling him to sleep he dreamt of Kay.

The train was delayed a couple of hours at Kluang which allowed him to sleep undisturbed and as Kulai approached he awoke refreshed. The journey had been peaceful.

He arrived in JB in the murky dawn of Saturday to see Harry Mallet, cheerful as ever, waiting for him on the platform. He greeted Sandy with a nonchalant salute.

'Hope you've had a comfortable journey, Sir ... I've a Land Rover outside ... it's at your disposal until you have your own transport!'

He picked up Sandy's gear and whisked him off to the Mess, blathering non stop about bandits, weather, good luck and God-knows-what. Sandy, thoughts of ringing Kay uppermost, was oblivious to it all. He came to when he heard Mallet say,

'.. and the CPO wants to see you at 10.00 hrs., Sir!'

'Fine, Mallet ... fine! No problem there.'

He reviewed his idea of ringing Kay straight away.

The meeting with the CPO was brief and to the point, simply putting him in the picture. He learned that he was to take over a Joint Operations staff which comprised personnel from the Army and Air Force as well as the Police. All would be revealed on Monday; until then he was free to settle in.

'Glad to have you here, MacIntyre!' roared the genial CPO, giving one of his crushing handshakes.

'Go off and have a jolly good weekend ... come Monday you're going to be busy!'

With George Picthall's voice still ringing in his ears and the numbness of the handshake only beginning to wear off as he got back to the Land Rover, he returned to the Mess and chose from a number of vacant rooms one which overlooked the Straits. It was a pleasant room from which he could see the shimmering water above the swaying palms that cloaked the hillside along the road below.

At last he managed to contact Kay and caught up with her latest news. She'd bought a Morris Minor saloon and in great excitement informed him that she'd pick him up in the afternoon and take him to Singapore where they'd stay overnight with Anita and Dinger. The intention was to dine out and a table for four had been booked at the Swimming Club.

Sandy felt a surge of elation! He realised that at last life was beginning to have real purpose; his new appointment was a first-class career opportunity and incredibly, in such a war-torn world, his reunion with Kay gave him a chance at happiness beyond his wildest dreams.

10

Bombing Mission

Sandy returned from the superb weekend in Singapore with Kay and his friends and reported for duty on the Monday morning filled with hope for the future.

The Operations room and its supporting offices were situated in a group of long interconnected wooden huts set in the middle of a compound adjacent to the guardroom which covered the HQ gates. The complex was surrounded by its own high wire perimeter fence and Sandy presented himself to the guard at the entrance gate. As arranged, Mallet was waiting to escort him to the SO Operations whose office was down the main corridor beyond the Duty Officer's room. Mallet ushered him in and Mike Seamour looked up expectantly from behind a pile of papers on his desk.

Sandy had met Mike previously on a number of occasions and instantly liked the quiet man. In his late thirties, he was fair and gangly, looking much older than his years; a legacy from his days in captivity in Changi jail. His lined, parchment coloured, aquiline face, was prematurely creased.

'Hello Sandy ... glad to see you again!' he said in a gravelly voice.

'I say, old chap, I'll be bloody glad to hand this lot over to you!' He grimaced, nodding at the papers strewn across his desk. 'I'm really looking forward to my leave ... feeling boat happy already ...!'

He unravelled his emaciated frame from the swivel chair, his skeletal hand outstretched in greeting. Hardly waiting to draw breath he continued,

'By the way you'll find Monday mornings bloody hectic ... catching up with the weekend's incidents ... fortunately it's been quiet for a change ... too damn quiet for my liking ...' He took a deep breath and in a staccato voice continued,

'I reckon something's afoot ... all hell's going to break loose ... one of these days! Anyway ... morning prayers won't take long ... and immediately they're over ... I'll introduce you to all those who matter ...!'

He paused momentarily and Sandy took advantage to reply,

'Good to see you, Mike ... I reckon after three years you must be ready for leave ... and no doubt I'll be the same when my turn comes. Anyway, I'm looking forward to having a go here! The CPO informs me that everything's run on military lines with a GSO 2 and GSO 3 attached – as well as an RAF Liaison Officer to deal with the air strikes!'

'That's right ... you'll meet them this morning as well as the Singapore Special Branch representatives ... by the way ... the CPO and Brigadier won't be attending today – they're at a conference in Kuala Lumpur.'

Mike glanced swiftly at his watch.

'Good heavens! it's time now ... we'd better get off to the Ops. room!' He picked up a sheaf of papers from his desk and turned to Sandy.

'Follow me, old chap ...' He ambled through the door and down the long corridor which appeared to join the two huts together, halting towards the end where he pointed at the notice-board on the wall indicating that they had arrived at their destination.

'Sorry! – I'd forgotten, you've already been here when you did that escort lark!'

Turning, he passed on through the door and into the large room, the walls of which were covered with maps and notice boards. Pinned up on the latter were operational photographs of wanted terrorists, contact kills and on display were captured weapons and other paraphernalia.

The room was crowded with Police and Army officers from the various regiments which comprised the Gurkha Brigade. Facing the far wall, the multi-uniformed assembly sat in splinter groups chatting. Sandy could just see over their heads the huge operational map of Johore and the bordering northern states. Mike marched purposefully down the centre aisle to the front where the coloured map, stuck with pins, was in full view. The pins represented the daily major and minor incidents of terrorist contacts and movements, also the position of the current security force operations.

Slowly, Mike climbed onto the dais which ran the full width of the map. The hubbub of voices lessened and the audience turned their faces expectantly towards him. He raised his hand and in a modulated voice addressed them.

'Your attention, please!' A hush fell on the assembled company. 'Good morning, gentlemen ...

'Before we begin the briefing I would like to introduce to you my successor ... Sandy MacIntyre! He is, I know, known to some of you ... so I won't embarrass him by giving a summary of his considerable experience ... without doubt you'll find out for yourselves! Nevertheless ... I'll say this ... he's no stranger to the type of warfare we're embroiled in and I'm sure he'll leave his mark ...!'

Mike paused for a split second, gazing about the room as though expecting an interruption, then took a deep breath and continued,

'Gentlemen ...! please don't leave the room at the end of morning prayers, I want each of you personally to meet Sandy. Thank you!'

From the back of the room without warning came a stagy, high-pitched voice.

'Please, Sir ...! can I leave the room now, Sir ...!'

'No you bloody well can't ...!' Mike flashed back, causing roars of laughter. Once the clamour had subsided he resumed to the business at hand.

'We shall now get on with today's briefing ...!' and turning to Sandy he indicated an empty seat in the front row.

'Take a pew, Sandy and be enlightened ... the service is about to begin ...!'

Morning prayers over, Mike took Sandy around the various groups of officers ensuring that he met everyone, including the Joint Operations Staff. This included Major Tim Fletcher, the GSO 2, 1/2nd Gurkhas, a tall man in his mid thirties and built like a long-distance runner. His deeply tanned, open face complete with moustache and sideburns, showed evidence of his long service in the Far East. Sandy had met him before, upcountry, and knew him to be an excellent tactician and concise on orders.

'Hello, Sandy! ... we meet again ... glad to see you ... I'm looking forward to working with you once more.'

He then turned to the red faced Captain standing behind him, another Gurkha officer.

'And this is Rory O'Malley from the Emerald Isle ... he's your GSO 3.'

The brawny, raw-boned, Irishman, well over six feet tall and with an air of the grisly bear about him, stepped forward and shook Sandy by the hand.

Reminiscent of some previous occasions Sandy felt himself pumped up and down as Rory's tightly clenched fists wrapped round his gun hand, almost lifting him off the ground.

'*Not again!*' he thought.

'I'm pleased to meet you, Sandy, to be sure. I hope you're not averse to a drop of "*uisce breatha*" ... that, to the uninitiated, is "Tullamore Dew", a smooth dram if ever there was!'

'Indeed not, Rory ... as a matter of fact I'm rather partial to a drop of Irish!'

'Great, we've some in the Mess ... and you're welcome any time!'

Sandy felt at home with these two likeable professional soldiers, who'd spent their entire commissioned life with the Gurkhas. Tim was responsible for Army intelligence and operations, whilst Rory liaised between units, disseminated information and ensured that the movements of the security forces in the field were co-ordinated.

Ken Schofield was the next to be introduced. A Flight Lieutenant in the Royal Australian Air Force, he was seconded from Sembawang, Singapore, where a squadron of Lincolns were based. He was a typical Australian, with khaki drill uniform hanging haphazardly on his gaunt figure as though it had always been there.

'G' dai Sandy! Y' may not believe it, Cobber ... but we three ...', he swept his arm in a grandiose gesture to include the two Gurkhas, 'are known by the rest of these Pommies as the unholy alliance ...! Beggin' y' pa'don Mike ...!' he blurted, glancing quickly in his direction.

Mike, taking the outburst with good grace, grinned.

'And how do we address you, Digger?' Sandy joked.

'G'd for you Sandy ... y'r sma't! Friends call me Ken ... I reckon that'll do for you!'

As they shook hands Sandy had the feeling that, all round, he was accepted!

Introductions continued and the notable ones were the SB officers from Singapore, a Superintendent and a Cadet ASP who was a newcomer apparently, having only recently completed his national service in Kenya with the King's African Rifles.

'Amazing how they kept on turning up from Africa ...!'

Tony Blackett was of medium build, in his early twenties and, true to his name, sported a crop of jet black hair. He was an associate of Dinger's but Sandy didn't get much chance to talk to him.

The Superintendent was a pre-war Colonial Police Officer born and brought up in the East and following in his father's footsteps; his father had been at one time the Commandant of the Shanghai Police. Jack Bellamy was in his early forties and had been in India when Singapore fell. He immediately joined up and was commissioned into the Indian Army, finishing the war as a Major in Burma.

He stood out in a crowd, a stocky figure with grizzled hair and a strong but kindly face. His voice was such that one wanted to listen to him, though mostly he was a great observer and nothing missed his steady gaze.

At long last it came to an end and Sandy lost count of the numbers he met.

The rest of the day he spent familiarising himself with the various functions of the Police and Army staff. Later in the afternoon Ken Schofield came into his temporary office, his Aussie drawl filling the room.

'Listen, Sandy ... we have an operation coming off in a few days time, a bombing mission on a terrorist camp in the Tasek Bera area ... that's the large lake and swamp area on the Pahang-Negri Sembilan-Johore boundary. Some Semelai brought the information in and it's just been confirmed!'

'That's right, Sandy ...!' Rory chimed in from behind. 'I'm going as an observer ... how about coming along?'

There are few things more infectious than enthusiasm and as Sandy listened he found himself eager to add another first to his long list of experiences. As they gave him information on the intended strike, their vibrant attitude rubbed off. He addressed the Flight Lieutenant.

'Is it possible for me to go, Ken ...?'

'Sure ... no trouble at all – I'll fix it with Ops ... but y'd better let Mike know ... he'd hate to lose y' ...!' he joked.

Rory banged the desk.

'You bet he would ... he'd go bonkers!'

'Right, I'll go and see him! You two better wait and hear the outcome!'

Sandy went off, post haste, to Mike's office.

The rattle of an old typewriter greeted his entrance and from behind it Mike looked up.

'Hello, Sandy ... you've just caught me composing my memoirs ... hand-over notes to you! What can I do for you?'

'Well, Mike, I've just been told that a bombing mission is being launched against a terrorist camp in the Tasek Bera ... I wondered if it would be OK for me to go as an observer?'

'That will be Thursday ...?'

'Yes! ... early strike! ... daybreak!'

'All right! I guess it's a good idea and it'll give you some experience as to what the others are doing? ...'

He paused reflectively.

'Good Lord, Sandy ... I'd hate to lose you ... you must swear to come back ... nothing must stop me getting that boat on Saturday!'

He gave a low chuckle.

'Once you're in my seat you can please yourself what you do ... with the CPO's blessing, of course!'

'Thanks, Mike!'

'Don't thank me, old chap ... you'll likely wish I'd said no by the time you get back! Give me the details later!'

'Right-oh ...!' and Sandy doubled back to the waiting pair ... feeling like an excited teenager allowed to take part in an adventure he thought his parents would never give their consent to. He was exhilarated!

He leapt into the room.

'It's on ...! I can go ...! what's the gen ...?'

'Well, you'll have to stay in the Mess the night befo'e, 'cause the take-off in the morning'll be early,' Ken informed him. 'Come to dinna Wednesday evening 20.00 hou's … come ea'ly … Mess dress! For the op … jungle green, wata bottle and sidearms … the usual kit!' he instructed. 'We'll do the rest and give you a room for the night.'

'Great – I'll look forward to it!' Sandy responded as Schofield and O'Malley left to return to their duties.

He spoke to Kay in the evening but made no mention of his forthcoming venture.

'Unnecessary weight on her pretty shoulders,' he reassured himself!

To allow himself greater freedom of movement Sandy ordered a black, soft-topped, Morris Minor from Borneo Motors in Singapore and, the following day, collected it.

Wednesday evening arrived and he presented himself at the RAAF Mess, Sembawang. He received a tremendous welcome from Ken's buddies and in the course of the evening his consumption of alcohol was … excessive! He simply lost count of the whiskies he'd downed and at two in the morning he staggered in a fog back to his room.

His head seemed to have just touched the pillow when at 03.30 hrs. his breakfast call came through!

He dressed, feeling like death warmed up; the banging in his head was unbearable as he bent down to pull on his jungle boots. The room tilted and swayed and his tongue felt stuck to the roof of his mouth. He likened it to the inside of a mynah bird's cage!

They ate at 04.00 hrs. and he drank copious cups of black coffee. Eggs were on the menu, cooked in various ways, and Sandy made the fatal error of having them scrambled! Throughout breakfast the others at the table remained silent, apparently suffering from the same malady! At 04.30 hrs. whilst weaving his way to the briefing room, he bumped into Rory.

'Morning Sandy!' he boomed. 'Sleep well?'

'Don't be stupid …! Bloody awful in fact … somebody woke me as soon as I'd gone to bed!'

Rory laughed.

'Sure, Sandy, your eyes look a bit like piss holes in the snow …!'

Sandy groaned.

'Thanks Rory … bloody hell, you must have the constitution of an ox!'

The briefing was short.

The squadron was to make a low level attack in three waves, each flight pattern bombing the target. The Squadron Leader was to lead the first attack and Sandy would fly with him. Afterwards, the whole area was to be ground strafed by aircraft going in line astern, thus enabling all guns to fire. As an observer Sandy was stationed up front with the bomb aimer in the belly of the aircraft and was provided with a chest harness to clip his parachute to. The chute was carried in a bag.

At last they were ordered to proceed to the lined-up bombers which were shrouded in the dank, swirling air. The attending ground crew of scurrying figures presented an eerie scene in the early dawn.

Sandy followed the young flying officer he'd been introduced to as the bomb aimer/forward gunner and climbed the steep ladder after him into the belly of the aircraft.

'Stow y' chute here ...!' He pointed to the open bin adjacent to Sandy's flying position.

'Y' won't need it unless y' have to bale out ...' his companion explained laconically.

'At take off, y' better stay he'e ...!' again he pointed; this time to a small, pull-down seat in the gangway.

'Remembe' to fasten y' belt ...!' I'll let y' know when it's OK to come fo'ward ...!'

Sandy nodded his head ... and wished he hadn't!

One by one the engines roared into life and he listened as the crew reported to the captain on the intercom. All went well as the aircraft gave a shudder and taxied down the runway to the take-off point. Looking through a small porthole he saw the others flanking, making up the flight, and had a vision of the remainder of the squadron taking similar positions in a queue behind.

Dead on 05.00 hrs. came the flash of a green Very light from the control tower, and with a mighty roar the aircraft hurled itself down the flare path and into the air. Squinting below Sandy caught a glimpse of the mud flats on the island shoreline shimmering in the dawn light and the clusters of stilted, tin roofed, houses of the fishermen. Skimming over the straits the navigator droned over the intercom.

'Navigator to Skipper ...!'

'Roger, Navigator ...!'

'Navigator to Skipper ...! Course zero ... zero ... five ... heading north ... north ... east ... Tenggarho lighthouse ... ETA ... twenty minutes!'

'Skipper to Navigator ... Roger ... Wilco ... Out!'

As they ascended to five thousand feet over Kota Tinggi Sandy settled down in his position and watched the unfolding landscape through the tiny observation window. His concentration was abruptly interrupted by the intercom.

'Navigator to Skipper ...! Position Tenggarho lighthouse ... change course ...! zero ... zero ... eight ... heading ... Pulau Teoman ... ETA ... six minutes ...!'

The island was the largest of a volcanic group off the coast of Mersing in the South China Sea, and the last bastion in the peninsula of the once numerous mouse deer. Here the squadron was to reform for the quick, low-level attack on the target. On crossing the coast and leaving the mainland behind, Tioman's twin 3,373 ft. peaks were seen ahead and the island spread before them like a gigantic emerald set in a molten gold and turquoise sea.

Dead on time they circled the mighty jungle clad peaks, with 'B' and 'C' Flights reporting that all was correct. *En route* the navigator had been continually working out the change in course in regard to the target.

'Navigator to Skipper ...!'

'Roger, Navigator ...!'

'Navigator to Skipper ...! change course ... two ... six ... zero ... north ... north ... west ... ETA ... twenty-eight minutes!'

The captain once again acknowledged.

The aircraft banked steeply, swinging round into its new course and heading towards the distant coast, beyond which lay thousands of square miles of impregnable jungle and mangrove swamp.

In a short while they crossed the eastern mainland coastline, over the darkened, muddy mouth of the Sungui Rompin, which initially wound its way inland in tight curves from the sea. They passed over dark green mangrove interrupted by occasional feeder streams, which made it look, Sandy thought, like the exposed roots of a gigantic tree!

Eventually, the multifarious undulating carpet of the towering rain forest could be identified by the elaborate pattern of crowns, the leafy canopies rising and falling with the rolling ground beneath. In the distance could be seen a blaze of a hundred different shades of green, through which flashed the reflection of the new sunlight bouncing off the tin roofs of the houses in a *kampong*.

Sandy looked at the row of selector switches in the bomb compartment and watched the prone figure in the nose, methodically testing the switches and the bombsight settings.

A thrill passed through him at the anticipated action! Suddenly his ears popped and he realised they were descending to three thousand feet for the bomb-run. He looked at his watch and noted they were due over the target.

'Navigator to Skipper ...! target coming up!'

'Roger ...! Skipper to Bomb aimer ... Bomb doors open.' A few seconds elapsed and the engines were throttled back; he caught the faint sound of the air-stream over the wings. Looking out he noticed the flaps had been partially let down.

Abruptly the intercom crackled into life.

'Bomb aimer to Skipper! Right a bit ... steady ... steady ...!! steady ...!!! Bombs away!'

Sandy felt the aircraft lift a little as it disgorged its heavy load into the trees far below.

'Bomb aimer! look for bomb bursts ...!'

Sandy looked back through the escape hatch window and saw the mushrooms of the blasts reaching up into the sky, and witnessed 'B' flight coming in on its run. At the same moment he was thrown sideways as the aircraft went into a tight, banked, turn, the engines roared and momentarily his seat seemed to be glued to his bottom.

The first indication of the origin of his breakfast manifested itself as his stomach flattened, then wanted to turn itself inside out! He denied it the privilege! But it crossed his mind that he would not be able to withstand very much punishment of a similar nature!

To attempt to keep his mind off the subject he stared at 'B' flight and identified the aircraft Rory was flying in, 'N' for Nuts! He spotted it executing an almost identical manoeuvre ... and swallowed hard!

For the moment they maintained the same altitude and flew in a circle round the erupting jungle. The terrorist camp was located in a small valley surrounded by hills and caused little difficulty to the bombing mission. However, the ground strafing was another matter!

The bombers would have to dive low and accelerate out, banking sharply to get all their guns firing!

'Ye Gods! ...' he thought. '*Another turn like that and I'm lost! ...*'

The terrible urge to throw up those awful scrambled eggs brought him out in a cold sweat, water surged into his mouth and he was prompted to address the bomb aimer, who was still in the prone position observing the strike.

'I say, old chap ...!' he stammered ... 'You don't by any chance have some sick bags on board? I'm afraid I may be in need of one shortly ...!'

'Sick bags ...!!! f ... hell ...! this ain't no bloody airliner ...! Y'll have to use y' chute bag ...! but don't let the Skip see y' ...!'

Temporally this ominous threat steadied him; he took a deep breath and the spasm receded!

They stooged around until the bombing was completed and he heard the captain instructing the rear, mid upper and forward gunners to stand by and begin firing when the ground target presented itself. The bomb aimer now got behind the guns in the forward turret which left Sandy to take his place and observe.

Again his ears popped, indicating a change of altitude; they were in fact in a shallow dive duplicating the earlier run, except much lower. Down and down they went, the bomb aimer rattling away on the forward guns first. Then in a tight turn they zoomed up, banking to the port side and the mid and rear guns took their turn to hammer away.

Sandy was oblivious to the turmoil around him and with the lightning speed of a cheetah took his chute out of its bag and replaced it with the erupting eggs!

In those last moments, like a drowning man, he simply didn't care!

Finally the operation was completed and they re-formed at five thousand feet.

'Skipper to Navigator …! Course for home!'

'OK, Skipper …! Course … one … four three … heading south … south … east … ETA … thirty-seven minutes …!'

They were bang on time at the base, landing at 07.00 hrs. having spent five minutes over Tioman and twenty-four over the target area.

Nonchalantly he disembarked, managing to carry his 'cargo' to the shower room undetected, where he scrubbed the chute bag before handing it in.

To the best of Sandy's knowledge the Skipper didn't find out … and the stores personnel were very sympathetic!

11

Jungle Fort

The Director of Operations ruled that a fort should be built to protect the aborigines in the Tasek Bera and, though not in the state of Johore, the operational area did come under the CPO; consequently Sandy was directed to ensure that the location for the fort was convenient for all concerned. Accordingly, he ordered a platoon of the Police Field Force to survey the area for a suitable site in the region of Kampong Aur where reports indicated there was a large group of aborigines.

On discussing the best overall plan for him to carry out a personal inspection of the area, Sandy was informed by the GSO 2, Major Tim Fletcher, that the logistics of his visit would be finalised by the GSO 3, Captain Rory O'Malley, who was familiar with the 'Modus Operandi' for such a visit. He suggested that Sandy might go part of the way out of Segamat to the jungle fringe using the rubber plantation roads and then proceed on foot through the jungle to the Sungai Terbang, where it was possible to travel by longboat up river beyond Kampong Kempas, and thereafter continue again on foot to his destination.

It was agreed that tactically his visit should coincide with the relief of the platoon already on operations there, as this would enable him to experience at first hand the problems that had to be faced to maintain a presence in the area. The feasibility of using helicopters as backup for supplies and emergency evacuation would involve the building of a landing pad but this could only be considered after inspecting the site.

The remainder of the staff were alerted, including the RAF liaison officer, Ken Schofield, who was co-opted to help with the air logistics and, together with Rory, was called into the office to discuss the task.

'Morning, Sandy ...!' Rory boomed on entering, Ken trailing behind. 'Sure we have some news for you ...!'

Ken nodded in silent agreement.

'Morning, chaps ... good, I hope!'

Rory shrugged his shoulders.

'We ... ll ... it depends on you old son ...! You'd better tell him, Ken ...'

'Gee, Sandy, I'm sorry ... I couldn't get a helicopta to take you in ... as far as we know there isn't a suitable landing site where the platoon is ... afraid you'll have to go on foot and use the river for pa't of the way.'

'Doesn't surprise me ... I expected as much ...!' Sandy answered with a frown and a shrug of his shoulders in resignation and regret.

'What about my return?'

'That may be the same, Cobber ...! unless you fix up a landing zone when you're there ... we could fly over and check it out!'

'OK ...! we'll leave it at that for the moment ... rest assured I'll make the landing pad my first priority on arrival ... I can't spend too much time on this now but I'll be depending on you two chaps to see that an air recce is carried out when I give the signal!'

'Wilco ...!' Ken affirmed.

His colleagues were unanimously agreed that, for the time being, it would be an overland journey and Sandy was equally determined that, if humanly possible, a temporary helicopter landing site would be constructed.

'Thanks, chaps ... I'll let you know when I'm likely to go.'

The staff officers left and Sandy mulled over the project before sending off a coded signal to the Field Force Company Commander informing him of the plan and requesting that the platoon in the area make a recce for a suitable fort and helicopter landing site. At the same time he arranged to go in with the next relief platoon in about ten days time.

Arriving at the Mess that night he began to put together his operational gear, the basic attire, rations and equipment, and he also gave his 300 carbine a double check. Past experience dictated that he would have to carry everything and it was vital he took only the mere essentials. It was no good leaving it to the last minute.

Next morning he went to see the CPO to put him in the picture concerning his proposed trip, he also began making plans for the handing over of all outstanding operational matters to the GSO 2; his Duty Officers would take care of the routine Police responsibilities. Sandy pondered on how to get to Segamat where he was to join the relief platoon and eventually decided to drive up in the Morris on his own. The days passed quickly and he was soon on the first part of his journey which was thankfully without incident. On arrival he made his number with the OSPC John Thwaites who, pleased to see him, offered to put him up for the night. Sandy, however, declined the kind invitation since he had made a prior arrangement to stay with Mactavish. Thanking John, he made his way to Mac's office. It was just like old times; the SB officer was his usual jolly self.

'Hello, Mac, how are you, you old rascal ...!'

Mac looked up, his face bursting into a huge grin on seeing Sandy standing in the doorway. He got up from his desk, strode across the room, grasped Sandy by the hand and vigorously shook it.

'Hello to you, laddie ...!' he exclaimed.

'By Jove, I'm glad to see you ... things haven't been the same since you left ... even the Tiger doesn't taste as good!' Laughing, he drew a deep breath and rattled on.

'How's that wee lassie you tell me you've met ...?'

'Very well the last time I saw her ... she's looking forward to meeting you!'

'Aye, you'll have to bring her up here ... I could put you up in the spare room – a double ... no questions asked!'

Sandy feigned shock.

'I'm not sure she'd like that, Mac ... the double room I mean ... we're not that close ... yet!' he laughed.

'Well, it's about time you were, Sandy lad ... life's too short, you should find yourself a lass and settle down!'

'Profound words from someone who's still a bachelor!'

'Trouble is, Sandy, who'd want to take us on with the lifestyle we have! Take a pew, laddie, or would you like to freshen up at the bungalow? I won't be long here, then we can have a sun-downer before dinner.'

'Yes ... I'd like to get settled in and get my kit sorted out for the morning ... it's going to be an early start.'

'Right! Off you go. I'll fill you in with any info. over drinks.'

He took his leave and made his way to Mac's bungalow and was welcomed by a smiling Abdulla, Sandy's old house servant.

'*Selamat datang tuan!*' the familiar stocky figure greeted him.

'*Selamat pagi* Abdulla! I didn't know you were here.'

'*Ya tuan* ... after you left ... much better work for *tuan* Mac!' Abdulla said bluntly.

More surprises were in store for Sandy when later he met Chan Lee the old cook, and his wife the Amah.

Mac followed shortly afterwards and Sandy mentioned how delighted, but surprised, he had been to see them.

'Well, laddie, they weren't happy after you'd gone to JB ... so I took the initiative before the new chap arrived and asked if they'd like to work for me ... Bob said he didn't mind ... so here they are!'

'Good show, Mac, I'm glad you did ... for much as I'd have liked to, I couldn't take them with me!'

They enjoyed a couple of sun-downers and sampled Chan Lee's fine cooking, after which they were joined by the platoon commander

Lieutenant Pat Kennedy, and Mac discussed with them the latest intelligence on the Tasek Bera.

Like O'Malley, Pat was an Irishman from the south, in his early thirties and on his second tour of duty. He spoke Malay fluently and his jungle experience was impressive. The evening was to prove invaluable.

The following morning at 06.00 hrs. Sandy joined the platoon waiting in their vehicles in the Police HQ yard. In the cool, half-light of dawn a soft southern accent broke into his thoughts; it belonged to the six-footer standing in regulation jungle green beside one of the Land Rovers.

'Mornin', Sir ...!' the shadowy figure greeted him. 'I've made a seat available for you in the second Land Rover ... you can put your gear in the back ... I've detailed one of the lads to be your Orderly while you're with us ... his name's Mahmet!'

'Thanks, Pat, that'll do me fine ... now we can get on our way!'

The first section of the journey through the rubber plantations to the jungle edge took only an hour and the long trek to the river began, the shafts of sunlight coming up over the jungle canopy to light their way.

The platoon, spread out over two hundred and fifty yards, proceeded in single file, and as the column trudged on and on down the hot, dank jungle path Sandy's thoughts turned to his time in Burma. It felt, as it always did ... endless!

Their route passed through virtually untouched primary jungle with row upon row of huge tree trunks, many with enormous buttress roots, which caused the indistinguishable track to wind and undulate. Hampered by the bad light filtering through the canopy of the green foliage far above, visibility began to vary from five to twenty yards. The undergrowth consisted of bushy shrubs alternating with gangling young saplings, all struggling for light; small streams were constantly forded and swampy areas negotiated, huge fallen trees crossed and blood sucking leeches lay in wait for a meal from animals and unwary travellers.

They trudged on late into the afternoon, wading and slipping along the ever winding track which eventually came out into a broad clearing overlooking the Sungai Terbang. Here, changing direction, they continued up river for about fifteen minutes when they saw, drawn up on the bank, four longboats.

A Malay boatmen was engaged in tinkering with a large outboard motor and three others were hunched-up over some cooking pots on a low fire. At first they didn't take much notice of the emerging platoon who automatically spread out up and down the bank in strategic positions.

Kennedy indicated that Sandy should stay with the platoon HQ section whilst he went forward to converse with the boatmen. Sandy, on one knee, his carbine at the ready, watched and after some minutes observed Kennedy nodding his head in apparent agreement; he turned and beckoned to Sandy.

His face was grim.

'We've a problem with one of the outboard motors ... we'll have to stay here tonight and go up-river in the morning ... they hope to get the motor fixed ... however we'll move out even if they can't ... we'll just have to tow the bloody thing! I'm not splitting my force ...!' he spat the words.

Red-faced and irritable, Pat instructed the platoon Sergeant to move the men in and cover the boats for the night. Each section took up a suitable position, with the HQ section in the middle; guards were set up and meals prepared and a radio signal (Sitrep) was sent off to give their progress and position. Sandy, with the end of a cigarette, set about burning leeches off his feet and legs. He shuddered involuntarily.

'Bloody awful things!'

The task done, he ate the cold meal old cookie had prepared for him and drank the mug of tea so gratefully received from Mahmet, before getting ready to bed down in the bivouac he had constructed at the side of one of the boats. Meanwhile, Pat and the Sergeant moved between the sections making sure the men were fed and giving orders for the night guards before returning to Sandy.

Pat expressed his opinion quietly.

'These boatmen ... I'm not certain about them ... they're an idle lot and don't give a fig ... we've got to be careful just in case they're in cahoots with the CTs.

'The problem is ... they'd to be recruited some five days ago by a section specially sent in ... which could have given the game away ... I don't want to have the boats too close together on the river tomorrow ... we'd stick out like a sore thumb and be an easy target!'

'Yes ...! I agree with you, Pat ... however, let me point out that if we're forced to tow a boat ... half the force will be in danger of an ambush anyway!' Sandy advised.

Kennedy gave him a quizzical look.

'Well ... we'll just have to wait and see, won't we?'

Changing the subject he continued.

'You're in the picture and you know what to do should we have a visitation in the night ... keep your head down ... I'll see you in the morning!' He crept into the night to take up his own position.

As dawn approached Sandy was awakened by Mahmet bearing a mug of tea in which a shot of rum had been splashed (an old Burma concoction called gunfire!). The platoon were standing too and Pat turned up a few minutes later with good news, the defective engine was working and they would be on their way.

In the half light of the cool dawn the boats were slipped into the water and the four sections were allocated. One section up front to lead, followed by Pat in the second, then the third with Sandy and the fourth in the rear as backup. Bren gunners got into each boat first and took up a position in the prow, with Pat and Sandy behind them in their respective boats, followed by the remainder of the section. Once seated, everyone was ordered to remove their jungle boots, unfasten their belt and place packs and haversacks at their feet. Carbines were to be carried across the body at the ready. The boatmen sat in the low stern with the engine and tiller and had been instructed on what was expected of them in an emergency.

The occupants were alerted to watch the adjacent banks and, to ensure they didn't bunch up, they put off at intervals into the centre of the river. Travelling against the current the journey was anticipated to be slow.

Progress throughout the morning was irksome, the brown muddy water concealing hidden snags such as fallen and rotting tree trunks, broken branches and the debris of monsoon rains. The winding banks of the river constantly changed and evidence of old clearings indicated some form of cultivation had been undertaken in the past, but the menacing dark green jungle fringe was ever enfolding to the water's edge.

By midday it was hot and sticky and the current became faster; the sullen brown, rolling surface of the water showed flecks of dirty white in the swirling troughs, forcing the engines to rev and roar a note of defiance. Sandy was beginning to suffer in the cramped position and on rounding a bend in the river observed the number two boat with Pat, tack to the left bank where the occupants of the number one had already landed and taken up defensive positions. Sandy followed suit and on landing was approached by Pat.

'Rapids ahead ...!' he explained.

'We'll have to carry everything up and over them ... there's a small *kampong* fifteen minutes away ... I'm going to leave you here and get help – I'll take a section with me ...!'

He gave a whimsical smile.

'So you're in charge, Sir ... until I get back ...!'

'OK by me, Pat ... but don't be too long!' Sandy laughed.

Kennedy then departed with the section and one of the boatmen, passing out of sight over a rocky bluff up a track parallel to the river bank. The platoon Sergeant left behind with Sandy gave instructions to one of the HQ section to get a fire going and brew up for the remainder.

Forty-five minutes later Kennedy emerged with eight Malays, a motley bunch of varying ages and unlikely candidates to porter the boats. Dour-faced he approached Sandy.

'Don't say anything, Sir! ... it's all I could muster! We'll just have to do it ourselves and get them to carry the kit-bags. It's going to take the rest of the afternoon to get them up and the engines are going to be the worst!'

'Good heavens ...!' Sandy exclaimed. 'How in the devil did the boats get into the river in the first place?'

'In a nutshell, Sir ... they shot the rapids!' he explained. 'They managed that all right ... but it appears they don't often come this side because it takes them two days to get back!'

Pat got everyone busy and instructed the platoon Sergeant to detail a couple of men to cut lengths of stout bamboo for use as poles to sling the engines on. One section was detailed to get the first boat out and the Malay instructed to unbolt the engine, which was then slung on a bamboo pole between two men. The remainder lifted the boat onto their shoulders and staggered off up the track, with a section doubly armed as escort; the villagers carried the haversacks.

The operation was repeated again with the two remaining sections, leaving two boatmen behind with their boats. Kennedy led the column with Sandy tagging along in the rear. It took over an hour to get the boats up the bluff and back again to the river's edge and it was obvious that it was going to take the rest of the afternoon to complete the operation.

A gruelling task and everyone was exhausted!

A section was detailed to protect the boats and equipment and Sandy volunteered to stay with them. Then the lighter force went back with the villagers for the remainder.

By late afternoon everything was finalised and they were tactically making camp around the boats, a foraging party having been sent along the river to the *kampong* for fresh vegetables.

Later that same day Sandy was astounded when Mahmet presented him with a chicken and vegetable stew with boiled rice ... compliments of the platoon commander! Never had a meal tasted so good!

Next morning, in the half light they left the *kampong* behind and were once again on the river. Progress was similar to the preceding day; the river however became narrower as they advanced and eventually, in the middle of the morning, the boats ran onto some pebbly shallows which marked the end of their journey on the water.

Leaving the boatmen to return to the *kampong* Pat lost no time in getting his small force on the overland route and they were soon in deep jungle again. Moving on a compass bearing they advanced through more primary growth and in the late afternoon made camp in a large clearing straddling a small, fast flowing stream.

Sandy was thankful to see clear water again and took advantage by stripping off, washing, and freshening his jungle green.

That evening, his spare uniform on his back, Sandy sat over a small campfire watching the curling smoke keep the mosquitoes at bay. Pat informed him he'd been in radio contact with the recce platoon and they were to meet at the confluence of two small, fast flowing rivers. He reckoned they were only half a day's march from their destination and should move off again at dawn to enable them to get to the rendezvous early in the day.

Having been plagued by mosquitoes the previous two nights Sandy was relieved to waken refreshed and feeling better for a peaceful night's sleep; the buzzing of the wretched insects hovering round the protective net made quite a din!

Once again he packed his spare uniform into his pack, donned the jungle green – still wet – had a mug of *gun fire* and a few dry biscuits and was off again trudging through virgin jungle.

The route climbed and snaked over a divide, and by mid morning they started the descent into a long valley. Midday saw them break out of the jungle into *belukar* (secondary growth) through which flowed a small river.

Kennedy, his face wreathed in a glowing smile, came dashing back up the column to Sandy.

'I reckon, Sir, we've come to one of the rivers I was told about – the recce platoon can't be far away 'cause they've been on the air and confirmed our position.'

'Jolly good show, Pat ... congratulations on a nice piece of navigation.'

Kennedy flushed and stammered.

'Thanks, Sir ... I appreciate that ... the powers-that-be don't know what we've to put up with ... it's not often we get a compliment. By the way, they're keeping their radio open until we've been sighted.'

'Yes! that's a good idea ... saves us being mistaken for the enemy and fired on!'

Gradually the going became easier and the *belukar* showed signs of being cut as they entered a defined track leading into a narrow clearing along the river bank, which contained evidence that it had once been a *ladang* in which wild tapioca was growing.

They plodded on in the clammy heat following the flow of the river and came to a point where a second river coursed in; they felt sure this was the confluence they were looking for. As they approached, wisps of smoke coiled lazily into the air and an outpost hailed them to come into the protected area further along on the river bank.

The platoon advanced and on entering the fortified camp were met by the commander, Lieutenant Jim Sanders, who eagerly awaited them and turning, addressed the junior officer first.

'Hello, Pat ... am I glad to see you! Bloody awful place to get to, isn't it? I'll be glad to get out.'

Turning to Sandy he saluted.

'Glad to meet you, Sir ... hope the journey wasn't too difficult for you.'

'No! not at all Sanders ... I've had worse,' Sandy replied testily, the tone of voice and manner of the tall officer riling him.

Sanders, without batting an eyelid, turned away and spoke to Kennedy.

'I've prepared a position for your blokes to go into and I reckon you and Mr MacIntyre can come into my HQ area ... when we leave in the morning you can sort things out for yourselves!'

'That's OK by me, Jim ...!'

Kennedy turned to Sandy.

'How about you, Sir?'

'Fine!' Sandy replied curtly and, giving Sanders a steely look, continued in the same tone. 'But ... Sanders ... you're not going tomorrow! I have authority to keep you here for as long as I see fit ...!'

And noting the surprise on his face ...

'I need to know firstly how far out you've patrolled ... secondly, the aborigines you've contacted ... thirdly, all the intelligence you've gleaned, and lastly to discuss the site of the fort ...!'

Sandy took a deep breath.

'I'm afraid there's a lot to do and we shall discuss the matter later when we're settled in ...!'

The two officers looked stunned at Sandy's abruptness. Kennedy was the first to recover.

'Yes, Sir ... there's a hell of a lot to do ... I for one need to see to my men after this long march ...!'

Sanders, his face now sullen, remained silent. Sandy broke the impasse.

'Right, Sanders, where's this HQ of yours? Kennedy and I need to get organised ...!'

Sanders nodded a surly head over his shoulder indicating the direction, and took them into the centre of the camp to a small bamboo, attap roofed shack with a lean-to attached to one side.

'The lean-to's my pitch ...!' he uttered irritably. 'The shack is used as a store and to operate the radio in ... you can put your gear on the other side until you've sorted yourselves out ...!'

Kennedy dropped his kit and, slinging his carbine over his shoulder, replied,

'OK! Jim … let's see where my platoon is to go …?'

He followed the brooding countenance of the officer and went to inspect the position his men had been allocated. He later returned on his own and said to Sandy,

'I've opened my radio and sent off a Sitrep asking for an air drop of a week's rations for my men and a European ration for each of us … I've also taken the liberty to advise Sanders to do the same for himself and his lads …!'

'Bully for you, Pat …! thank goodness someone's on the ball … we've all got to pull hard to get this project off the ground … we'll get together this evening and see what Sanders comes up with regarding information … I shall then be able to brief you both on what we have to do.'

That evening, after they had finished their meal, Sandy questioned Sanders about the suitability of the present site, bearing in mind that the fort needed to cover an area in which the aborigines could settle and cultivate.

It transpired that the aborigines had already visited the camp and asked for protection from the CTs and assistance in felling trees, indicating they would be interested in creating *ladangs* along the bank of the river to plant crops. The clearing they were now in was suitable for airdrops (which had already taken place) and it could be widened by cutting down trees and *belukar.*

Daily patrols hadn't made contact with any CTs, but from intelligence gleaned from the aborigines who'd been robbed of food, there were signs they were in the region.

On hearing this Sandy decided to wait until morning to have a good look round and make an appreciation before committing himself further. He felt that the extra platoon would provide invaluable manpower to begin the project and clear a suitable area for a helicopter pad. Accordingly, he gave the two officers a plan of immediate action.

Briefly, Sanders would continue to be responsible for the daily patrols and protection of the camp. The patrols would be reinforced each day by one of Kennedy's section commanders, plus two of their men so that experience of the terrain could be gained. Their prime object would be to contact aborigines and request them to come in to see what could be done to help them. Grudgingly Sanders agreed and made no further mention of when he was likely to return to base; Sandy didn't pursue the matter!

Next morning he and Kennedy were given the grand tour, providing evidence that the site was a good one. A short distance away from the river a small wooded knoll overlooked the clearing where the fort could be strategically sited.

The problem would be water! This might be overcome, however, if a well could be sunk within the perimeter below the knoll and a pump installed.

As for air drops, there were no great hills near, only a few trees in which the parachutes could become entangled, so a small number needed to be felled to enable a helicopter to fly safely in; thereafter the best approach could be chosen for the helicopter pad. Any trees taken down would have to be disposed of, the felling done with guncotton and cleared by burning, with help coming from the aborigines.

A Sitrep was sent confirming the suitability of the site and an order made for the necessary stores: guncotton, saws, axes, also picks, *chungkels* and shovels. Many other items, such as a water pump, fuel and piping, a lighting generator and relevant equipment, would have to be considered later and brought in by air when the pad was completed. Sandy instructed that the first order, including sandbags, should be on the next airdrop.

Later confirmation was received by radio that the airdrop would take place the next day at noon. Sandy and Kennedy made a recce around the clearing, the essence of which was to find the largest unobstructed touchdown zone which required the minimum number of trees felled.

They didn't have far to look and an ideal site was found between the knoll and the river. They each cut a six-foot section of bamboo to act as a measuring pole and detailed men to cut shorter lengths to peg out the area.

That evening a patrol returned and reported that they had successfully contacted a number of aborigines who'd agreed to visit the camp the next day. Sandy was elated, everything was fitting into the general plan and it was agreed they should get down to the tree clearing immediately the guncotton arrived.

He discovered, however, that neither of the platoon commanders had any experience with its use, so he decided to start the task in hand himself and instruct them in the process.

He explained that the guncotton would arrive separately boxed as would the primers, detonators and cord-fuse. He stressed that, for safety reasons, it was vital at all times to keep everything separate and in their relevant containers. In use, the detonator and fuse should be assembled last and placed into the primer which should then be put into the corresponding hole in the guncotton block. Furthermore, the cord-fuse should always be tested before use by cutting a measured length, lighting it and recording its burning time. This would enable the handler to work out sufficient time to retire to a safe position after lighting.

Sandy assured them that the guncotton on its own was safe to handle and should be placed, in this instance, as a cutting charge against each tree trunk and tamped to make a close contact before inserting the primer and fuse.

Next morning, whilst waiting for the airdrop, Kennedy and Sandy started the job of marking the trees to be felled and, as they were doing so, a number of aborigines were seen entering the camp.

This was a good sign and, anxious to meet the jungle people, Sandy called a halt to the task. It was his first contact with the *Sakai.*

'I'm surprised at how small they are, Pat.'

'Yes, these people are *Semelai* aboriginal Malays and a common group around here. They have a hereditary headman on a *ladang* basis, all the members being related ... more or less ... and the headman is the leader of an extended family group.'

'People mistakenly call them *Sakai,* which isn't right ... and they don't much like being called that; they have their own language and they don't all speak Malay ... so don't be surprised if they can't understand you.'

'Good heavens, Pat, we're going to have our work cut out trying to get through to them ...!'

'Oh ... it's not that bad, Sir ... there's not a great deal we need to explain, over and above a demonstration of what we expect them to do!'

'Well, Pat, I'll leave it to you to negotiate with them!' As the faint sound of an aircraft was heard Sandy stopped speaking. Sanders, also alerted by the drone of the engines, gave the order for the fire in the middle of the dropping zone to be damped down to create smoke; the ground signal panels were already positioned and the radio operator waiting to give their recognition call.

The twin-engined Dakota came into view and made a low run, down wind over the clearing and Sanders fired a green Very light. The aircraft flew on making a steep turn to come back, upwind, and begin its drop.

Roaring down the centre of the clearing it disgorged its first stick of chutes, the weighty bundles falling relentlessly before being drawn heavenwards by the opening of the white, billowing canopies. As the first stores hit the ground the aircraft circled around again to make another run, and on the third and last it spewed out coloured parachutes indicating the arrival of explosives. Finally, the aircraft waggled its wings in farewell and on gaining height was soon lost into the distance.

From the four corners of the clearing, sections moved in to pick up the containers with white chutes, leaving the explosives to be collected by a special group under the command of Kennedy, with Sandy in attendance.

Everything was gathered and the explosives placed in a dugout which had been prepared that morning. Sanders sent a section to the river's edge to fill sandbags to complete a wall around the dugout and to reinforce the Bren gun positions around the perimeter of the camp.

Later, Kennedy spoke Malay to the *Semelai* headman. To Sandy's ear it sounded fluent, but appeared to make little impression on the stout, dark skinned little man. Standing no more than five feet tall, with slightly wavy black hair and a porcupine quill through his nose he looked ludicrous as his immobile face turned upwards to look at the giant European.

'He says he is a *Batin* which is the highest rank in order of precedence in his group!' Kennedy explained. 'His name is *Mat* and he understands some of what I say but not all ... it's hellish frustrating and I think we'll have to show him how clever we are ... what d'you say?'

'Right, Pat ...! let's go and fell a tree with some guncotton and that'll give him some idea what we want him and his people to do.'

Sandy went off to get a block of guncotton which he gave to Kennedy, put a primer in his own pocket and carried the tin of detonators and fuse cord to a tree on the edge of the clearing. Batin Mat brought up the rear; he was escorted by two of his henchmen carrying blowpipes!

The tree was about forty-six inches in circumference and approximately thirty feet tall – an ideal specimen for the demonstration. Sandy went through the ritual of testing the fuse and decided to cut a thirty second length to give sufficient time to get away safely.

He sliced a wedge out of the base of the trunk with a *parang* (machete) and tied the guncotton into the slot making sure that it was well tamped in. Indicating that he was ready to fire the charge, Kennedy took the little group of aborigines back out of danger. Sandy finished off the arming of the primer which he placed into the guncotton and lit the fuse.

Walking briskly away he counted to thirty then turned to check; there was a flash, a puff of smoke and dust, followed by a bang as the explosion vibrated across the clearing. The tree fell with a loud thump, exactly where he had meant it to fall! As it hit the ground a crackling cloud of dust rose into the air.

Later, a grinning Kennedy told Sandy that a goggle-eyed Batin Mat was flabbergasted and convinced that Sandy must be a *bomoh* (magician).

Taking the group up to the fallen tree Kennedy demonstrated with a *parang* what was required of the *Semelai*, who, thereafter, vigorously cut off the remainder of the branches with their small tanged iron axe (a blade about three inches wide) the Malay *beliong* – mounted in a long whippy handle with a rotan bound head. They made light work of the tree and the cut off branches were soon burning on a fire, sparks thrusting into the air as the intense heat sought out the rising sap.

Sandy was delighted. Firstly the trees would be cut down as demonstrated, and so he briefed Kennedy to get all the *Semelai* to come and work in the clearing and the proposed helicopter landing site. They could make their camp on the other side of the river where some trees would be felled to make a clearing for their *ladang*.

It was agreed that payment for work would be in the form of cooking pots, tin plates and mugs, jungle knives, fish hooks and nets, penknives with tin opener, small mirrors, plastic hair combs, sarongs and a medical pack with bandages etc., but containing no drugs. Some rations would also be given: tobacco, rice, tinned fish, coffee, tinned milk, sugar, matches, salt, chillies ... and a dollar a day in coin to the headman! All was to be requested on the next airdrop in seven days time.

Sandy, Kennedy and his platoon Sergeant, with two men to carry the explosive boxes, formed the demolition squad and got to work on the trees that had been marked for the helicopter landing site. By the end of the day they had moved on to those in the dropping zone. Sanders followed with men from the combined platoons, whose task it was to saw or hack off the branches and to reduce tree trunks where possible, the latter being a long, all-consuming job.

There was concern that the explosives had been used up so quickly but, once the debris had been cleared away, a decision was taken that sufficient trees had been felled to enable a helicopter to land safely. As more and more *Semelai* arrived Batin Mat set them to work cutting and pulling out branches and burning the debris.

One evening when Sanders was doing his stint as duty officer, Sandy having suggested they each take a turn, he confided in Kennedy.

'I think, Pat, I may stay on here with you for another week and see in the new batch of explosives. If the *Semelai* do their bit it's possible that Sanders could go at the end of this week. Tomorrow we should concentrate on the helicopter site and get the RAF to make a recce over the area as soon as possible ... the outcome of which must be positive ... then, if they return the week afterwards bringing in the stores to build the fort, they could take me out on their return journey.'

'Yes, Sir, good idea ... we could get on faster without aggravation from Sanders, that's for sure ... between you and me he's a sarcastic bugger and his men are muttering ... the main problem, as I see it, is they don't like to be away from their families too long and no doubt he's spread the word of your involvement in keeping them here ... it would surely make a lot of sense to let them go back before they begin to influence my men ... I don't want that!'

'Yes, Pat ... I understand and agree ... I'll send them back the moment I see a positive improvement in the situation ... I'll decide in a couple of days.'

'Right, Sir, mum's the word ... we've certainly given them plenty to do for the next few days ... and it might just be possible to get more out of Sanders' men if they know when they're going ... the helicopter pad is the most important project and I'll get my men on it in the morning ... with as many of Batin Mat's people as we can muster!'

The days passed quickly and the momentum increased as the project unfolded. Sandy came to the point where Sanders' platoon could return to base so that Kennedy's men could feel they were achieving the target.

The *Semelai* were in their element and set about the tree clearing with a zest that became infectious; everyone doing their utmost to show how much they could accomplish. The helicopter pad and approach was completed within five days enabling a trial landing to be set up. At the same time as Sandy sent a message to HQ informing them he was staying a further week, a signal was despatched for the flight to be undertaken.

The following day brought the news that the helicopter would make its recce at noon and bring in some supplies.

A buzz went around the camp at the prospect and the *Semelai* were told that a great motor bird, but without wings, would come out of the sky, bringing them presents. The air was charged with expectation and excitement as Batin Mat's little people gathered, together with members of the remaining platoon (Sanders having departed that morning to return to base) to watch the bird land in the area they had helped to prepare.

The familiar swishing sound of the helicopter rotor blades could be heard in the distance and as it came closer echoed off the lush foliage of the trees below. The signal fire was already alight and spewing out smoke which hung in the still air. Earlier, in preparation, the recognition panels had been laid out and the wireless operator, on the edge of the clearing, standing-by ready to transmit.

Kennedy raised his Very-light pistol above his head and an expectant hush came over the little group as the helicopter came into sight. He fired, the report of the pistol vibrating across the clearing as the green light rose and arched.

The *Semelai* gasped as the thundering aircraft hovered over the newly defined landing pad. It pivoted, turning in the air as though performing an elaborate dance ... albeit the pilot was actually inspecting the ground below before making his final touchdown! It made a perfect landing, softly coming to rest as the whirling props slowed. Then, to Sandy's surprise, out of the cockpit climbed the familiar figure of Ken Schofield, breezily booming across the landing pad,

'G'dai, Sandy, this su'e is the outback ... nice little pad y' got ...! knew y'd make it ...!'

He ducked under one of the gently revolving rotor blades and made his way across to the small reception.

'What d'you know, Cobber ...? got y' another visitor ...!'

Sandy cast his eye over the familiar broad, burly back climbing out of the cabin of the aircraft. As the figure turned he recognised the red grinning face of Rory.

'Hello, Sandy! Sure you've certainly been busy ... got a little present for you from the Emerald Isle, so you can celebrate ...!' Clutched in his left fist was a bottle of ... The Dew!

Sandy walked out to the pad, surprised and delighted, hand out-stretched ready to greet his unexpected visitors.

'Well, chaps, you're a sight for sore eyes ... never in a month of Sundays would I have anticipated seeing you here ...!'

Some goodnatured joshing followed as they inspected the pad and were introduced to Pat who was left to direct the working party to unload the aircraft of the stores it had brought. In the meanwhile Sandy gave Ken and Rory a tour of the designated fort site.

Later, before take-off Batin Mat and two of his henchmen were given the grand tour of the helicopter. They entered cautiously, but not before they had been separated, with difficulty, from their blowpipes!

The expression on their faces was one of total bewilderment and it was decided that on no account should they be taken on a demonstration flight ... since, in fright, they might just jump out!

Sandy explained to Rory his intention to stay on for a few more days, making certain the explosives and equipment were used to the best advantage. So, amidst a wave of hands, his friends departed.

The next few days proved busy. Sandy and Pat worked well together and there was an air of excitement throughout the camp as the fort began to take shape and the designated water point at the foot of the knoll turned out to be a bonanza.

The well digging had been taken on by one of Pat's men who, as luck would have it, had been apprenticed to his village well-digger. The well, when coupled with a liner, would eventually supply all the needs of the fort.

As arranged, when the next supplies were flown in Sandy took his leave on the return flight.

Before going he thanked the platoon for the tremendous effort they'd made, then taking Kennedy on one side he quietly congratulated him.

'Well, Pat! it's been an experience I wouldn't have missed for the world ...! I'll send a commendation for you and the platoon through to your Company Commander telling him of the excellent work you've all done!'

Pat's face lit up and he stammered his thanks.

'Oh ...! thank you, Sir ...! it's good to know ... it's been a pleasure working with you ... the men'll be pleased ... we've all learned a lot ...! you being with us ...!'

'Well, that's rewarding for me to hear ...! I've really enjoyed myself being with you and hope to be able to see the fruits of your labour when it's all over. Keep your head down!'

With that, Sandy climbed on board and was whisked off, the helicopter skimming the tops of the dense undergrowth before climbing high into the skies.

12

Exit the Mystery Man

It rained all night and the incessant shrieking of flying foxes heralded the wet, sullen dawn. The large fruit bats detached themselves from the laden trees around the town and in gathering hordes, flapped away on their huge four-foot-span wings. Their eerie cries faded into the distance as they made the journey back to the mangrove swamps to join hundreds of restless colonies, hanging upside down throughout the day until sunset, when they would make another marauding flight.

Sandy tossed fitfully on his narrow bed. The high-pitched screams had wakened him over and over again, each time making his heart pound and sending shivers down his spine. On wakening he instinctively reached for the Browning automatic on his bedside table and squinting into the half light filtering through the wooden shutters he withdrew his hand, yet again, from the butt of the gun. He sighed wearily.

'*. . . bloody things never stop!*'

He wished the bats would give him some peace and stop squabbling over the sweet fruit and succulent shoots discovered in the garden. Now awake once more he felt an ominous presence; something dreadful was about to happen! He'd experienced the phenomenon before and some disaster always followed; especially when the menacing spectre of '*The Reaper*' hovered, ready to gather his harvest of souls!

'*Imagination! ... those bloody bats screaming like banshees ... enough to drive you mad!*'

He tried to dismiss the dark thoughts from his mind and after a while slipped into a fractious sleep which ended with Ahmad coming into his room.

'*Selamat pagi tuan!*'

'*Tabek* Ahmad ...!' Sandy replied sleepily.

'Bloody awful night, Ahmad ... those squealing bats again ... they never stop chattering.'

Cocking his head to one side he listened intently.

'Phew! they've gone ... thank goodness!'

The silence outside gave credence to his outburst and he pulled himself up in the bed to accept from the outstretched hand the proffered large, brown mug of tea.

'*Tebeb*, Ahmad! I'll have my KD uniform today.'

'*Ya Tuan!*'

Ahmad didn't ever have much to say ... except when he wanted a day off! ... and he couldn't understand his master's dislike of the flying foxes! So, with a bemused expression he handed over the mug and went about getting Sandy's uniform out of the wardrobe.

The day's routine began like many others with Sandy arriving at the office to a hubbub of activity. Information just received stated that a Police Lieutenant in the Labis area had been killed! The message on the teleprinter was still being decoded and Sandy waited impatiently, thoughts of who it might be racing through his mind.

At last he was handed the completed message and breathed a sigh of relief on seeing that Bob Sutcliffe was the originator.

The Lieutenant killed was Beaumont; he'd died by his own hand in an accident and his body was on its way by road to the morgue at JB General Hospital.

Immediately Sandy informed the CPO, who instructed that the officer be given a ceremonial burial and interred in the Krangi Military cemetery on the outskirts of Singapore. All HQ officers were alerted to attend the funeral, if possible, and a firing party and bugler were ordered from the Training School.

Sandy spent most of the morning communicating with Krangi, re-questing that one of the prepared graves be made ready for the next morning. It was an operational necessity to have graves dug and coffins ready; the latter were held at the BMH Singapore and the General Hospital JB since casualties occurred frequently and without warning.

By mid afternoon Sandy received a call from Bob Sutcliffe, saying he had arrived at the hospital with Beaumont's body and that a post-mortem was being carried out immediately.

Sandy took off in his Morris 1000 and met up with Bob outside the mortuary. He looked dishevelled in his jungle green and his face appeared drawn.

'Awful business, Sir!' he said in a low voice, giving his usual smart salute.

'Yes, Bob ... glad to see you're in one piece ... thought at first it might have been you ... gave me quite a turn!'

Sandy shook Bob by the hand.

'What the devil's this all about? I just can't imagine Beaumont having an accident with a firearm ... how'd it happen?'

'Well, Sir, it's a long story!'

He took a deep breath.

'I've made out a report for the OCPC to send to HQ! However, in short … he quite literally shot himself in the head! We received information that some CTs were in the area of the New Village – they were after food supplies from one of our informers. Beaumont went out with a Jungle Squad the night before last, to lay an ambush which unfortunately didn't come off … so he aborted the operation and returned about six this morning …

'After dismissing the squad he went into town and started drinking with the resettlement officer – they got into a card game with some Chinese – one thing led on to another – and he apparently downed some quick drinks and was lucky with the cards. The resettlement officer was armed with a Smith and Wesson revolver … Beaumont observed this and asked if he could look at it.'

The words rattled out and Bob drew another deep breath before continuing.

'You won't believe this, Sir – it's mind boggling – according to what the chap told me – Beaumont took the revolver and remarked, "*Nice little pistol this …*"

'The resettlement officer had unloaded the gun and put the rounds on the table. Beaumont twirled the cylinder with the palm of his hand making it spin, and at the same time picked up one of the rounds and loaded it into a chamber.

"*Bet you've not seen this little trick …!*" he'd said grinning, and put the gun up to his temple and pressed the trigger … the hammer fell on an empty chamber.

"*Russian roulette it's called – who'll bet me I can't do it again?*"

'The resettlement officer told him not to be bloody silly, but one of the Chinese shouted, "*I'll bet you ten dolla!*"

"No! – that's not much – how about fifty?" – Beaumont had said.

"*Fifty – good!*" said the Chinese.

'According to the account, Beaumont gave the cylinder another twirl and repeated the action, pressing the trigger. Once again the hammer fell on an empty chamber and the money he'd won was duly passed over …

'Beaumont bought a round of drinks … they were by then on brandy and beer chasers and apparently everyone was in jocular mood. Beaumont didn't seem satisfied with his good fortune and pressed on to do it again – the befuddled company all put money on the table and the ritual was once more staged. Beaumont put the pistol to his right forehead and pressed the trigger! Only this time … it fired! … and blood and pieces of flesh spattered the occupants of the table … he fell back, sideways at first ... then toppled across the table with the pistol still in his right hand. There was nothing anyone could do for him ... he was dead!'

Bob's drawn face was now ashen.

Sandy stood aghast and silent. It seemed an eternity before he spoke.

'Dear God! – what on earth made him do such a bloody stupid thing? – what a way to end up!'

He shuddered involuntarily.

'I suppose I'll have to take a look at him ...?'

'You can, Sir – the post-mortem's over – better do it quickly – they'll want to put the lid on the coffin!'

'Right! Let's get it over with – you'd better come with me.'

In low spirits Sandy and Bob passed through the door of the building and walked down the corridor leading to the post mortem room, entering in silence. The body lay in a coffin on one of the slabs and was the only one there. Beaumont's lower jaw was held up by a bandage wrapped round his head and cotton wool was stuffed into his left eye socket where the bullet had come out. Stretched out, still in his rumpled uniform of jungle green, he was not a pretty sight. Sadly Sandy turned to Bob.

'Well, that's that ... give me a hand with the lid – we'll put it on for the attendants to screw down.'

Bob took the head of the lid and Sandy the foot – they carefully placed it over the body.

'Bob!' Sandy suddenly exclaimed. 'Hold on a minute ... I've just noticed something!'

In a flash, he was taken back to London Airport, waiting on his flight out.

He'd been checking the Telegraph *for an en-route weather report to Egypt when he became aware that someone had stopped in front of him. He'd lowered his gaze below the spread-eagled pages and his eyes had focused on the scruffiest pair of shoes he'd ever seen. They were brown, dirty, scuffed and scratched beyond redemption and hadn't seen polish for a long time. Intrigued, his eyes had wandered up the grey flannel trousers which, too, had seen better days and he'd continued his gaze upwards as the rest of the man came into view.*

He remembered the crumpled mackintosh; it enveloped a swarthy, tanned, thickset man of average height with piercing dark brown eyes, who'd looked older than his years. He recalled the 'lost look' that had made the man look ill. At the time he'd subconsciously dubbed him 'The Mystery Man'!

Sandy took a second look, letting out a long, deep sigh; there again were the shoes and in just the same condition, looking incongruous now at the end of the jungle green trousers.

They didn't appear right somehow on the feet of the man – and without another thought he bent over, unlaced them and, taking them off, threw them into the corner of the room, whispering,

'There, that's better old chap ... you can't present yourself in those ... much better in bare feet ...!

'All right now, Bob, we can put the lid on ...! It's just something I noticed and felt an urge to do for him ...!'

The funeral next morning was well attended. The day kept dry and the drive across the causeway to Kranji was short. Beaumont was laid to rest high up on the right slope overlooking the Straits into Johore, joining the company of over forty thousand other comrades of WWII.

The crackle of rifle fire filled the air with an acknowledgement of respect ... which Beaumont would have been justifiably proud of!

As Sandy stood at the graveside with the last post ringing in his ears he paid his respects to his comrade and, once again, found himself remembering the first glimpse he'd had of Bill Beaumont ...

'*Exit the Mystery man.*'

13

One ... Two ... and Three?

In the days that followed, Sandy found it difficult to banish from his thoughts the sudden death of Beaumont and the manner of his parting; the repercussions were endless.

Bob, still in charge of the district, had, once again, gone back to being the only officer. Sandy couldn't help feeling sorry for him and, since he also felt responsible, gave him some sound advice before they parted. He reflected on his own words which echoed over and over in his mind.

'Bob ... there's been a spate of road ambushes just lately, a number of which have been a double-tap *... be aware of that fact. Stay alert at all times and if you are caught and manage to drive or fight your way out, don't ... under any circumstances ... then turn and attack if the situation looks like it hides another surprise party ... to attack in this instance would, without doubt, put you into a situation you would not come out of alive ...!'*

Bob's parting reply still rang in his ears.

'Don't worry, Sir ... I'll keep my head down, I won't let the bastards get me!'

'Well ... do that small thing and remember ... "He who fights and runs away may live to fight another day; but he who's in the battle slain will never live to fight again ...!"'

Sandy was not oblivious to the casualties that occurred in the field but so far they'd always been people he didn't know personally, so this thing about Beaumont had brought home to him the transient dividing line between life and death; so much more *real* when it was someone you had known! He'd been given a shock. Nor could he stop wondering who was going to be next and shuddered at the prospect of further casualties amongst his immediate comrades and friends.

'Didn't they come in threes ... or was it four ... like the Horsemen of the Apocalypse? It's started ... one down ...!'

132

The days dragged on and he was beginning to wish he was back in the field instead of at HQ waiting for something to happen. The proposed Saturday night in Singapore with Kay didn't materialise.

A signal came in saying that a man had gone missing, presumed dead after the capsize of one of the long boats shooting the rapids on the Sungai Terbang. The casualty was a member of Pat Kennedy's platoon returning after the change-over from the fort. A second signal told how the body had eventually been found down-river and taken to Segamat. So Sandy took the decision to go up there and get first-hand information about the incident, help with the identification and press on to the fort in the helicopter which had been forewarned to pick him up there.

His compatriots, duly alerted, stood in for him and with Ken Schofield's confirmation ringing in his ears to the effect that the helicopter was standing-by awaiting his signal he hurriedly put his jungle gear together and drove off to Segamat attired in civilian clothes.

On arrival he made his number with the OSPC who greeted him warmly. Sandy brought up the plight Bob was in (acting i/c district with no officers to help him!).

'I know, Sir, it's ...'

Sandy hesitated, trying to pick the right words.

'It's not for me to say ... Sutcliffe's in the difficult situation of having to do everything himself ... which puts him in a very dangerous position!'

Taking a deep breath he blurted,

'He needs help ... and needs it *now* ...!'

Red-faced, he looked intently at his superior who'd listened to him without interruption.

'Look, Sandy, I do know ... and I do understand how you feel about this ... I have applied for an ASP to take over – and I've asked also for another Lieutenant! KL informs me that replacements are in short supply due to home leave and casualties. I've spoken to Sutcliffe about this ... and I'm in the process of temporarily giving him a Lieutenant from here ...'

Sandy breathed a sigh of relief and changing his tone, replied,

'Sorry, Sir ... I had to strengthen the case for assistance ... he's too good a chap to be wasted and needs to be looked after ... thank you for letting me sound off!'

'Well, don't worry, old chap, we'll look after him. Now how about you? Going into the fort again?'

The OSPC inclined his head looking at him intently.

'You too will have to take care ...!' he declared.

'How long are you going in for ...?'

'Oh ... only four days ... approximately ... long enough to inspect everything. I'm looking forward to seeing what progress has been made and how the *Semelai* are settling down in their new *ladangs*. Well the best of luck to you ... I'll no doubt see you on your return ...'

With that Sandy departed making his way to see Mactavish. He found him beavering away at a pile of papers on his desk.

'Hello, laddie, how are you ...?'

'Fine, Mac, how are you?'

'Oh ...! weary, laddie, weary. Never seem to get on top of all this paperwork. Information comes in many guises! On your travels again, Sandy ...? Take care ... we can't have you go missing!'

'Don't worry, Mac – I'm just a tiddler ... there's bigger fish in the pond!'

'Aye ... famous last words ... Let's get out of here and I'll buy you a Tiger at the rest house ... you can then tell me the news from the big city.'

Later that evening after dinner Pat Kennedy arrived to see Sandy and discuss the visit to the mortuary the following morning.

'Hello, Pat!'

Sandy greeted him as he strode onto the veranda where he was sitting relaxing with Mac.

'How are you? Sorry about your chap – let's hope the family can find some comfort in that his body was recovered from the river – what went wrong?'

'W ... ell, it's the usual long story, one that could have happened before, but without a casualty!'

Pat was obviously cut up about it and Mac indicated with his hand the empty chair on the veranda.

'Take a pew, lad ... I'll get you a dram before you debrief ...!' With that he got up and sauntered into the dining-room.

Pat, his face drained, sighed and nodded to Sandy then sat down to await Mac's return. A stiff whisky was quickly produced – he took a gulp – appeared more at ease and they patiently waited for him to begin.

'It's quite simple, Abdullah wouldn't have drowned ... if he'd carried out my orders!'

His tone was uncompromising and looking towards Sandy he continued,

'You know, Sir, what they are ...! checks were made ... but as soon as my back was turned he just belted up and put his boots back on!'

He took another sip, smaller this time, and resumed.

'Before we started on the return river journey I gave orders that the boats were to pull into the riverbank downstream from the *kampong* – at the spot where we normally camp on the way in! On arrival we landed and two experienced watermen with paddles were detailed to each of the boats going over the rapids ...! their carbines, ammo and gear were given to the main party to carry ...

'The boats were not to take to the water until thirty minutes after the main party had left so as to let us get into position below the rapids. They were then to proceed independently at intervals of five minutes. This was normal procedure, to make sure if a boat engine packed up the paddlers could keep the prow head on in the rapids and control its passage ...!'

'It all went to plan until the last boat which got into difficulties halfway through, when the engine stopped and it hit a boulder and capsized! The fellas were thrown into the water and swept down to the pool below; two swam to one of the offshore boats – positioned to help if anything went wrong. Again, all normal procedure ... as you know!'

Pat now looked haggard.

'We all saw the boat turn over as it lost way and hit the boulder ... I couldn't believe it!'

His eyes looked glazed.

'Abdullah ... he just disappeared and sank! There's no doubt about it ... no doubt at all ... the weight of the ammo in his pouches and the jungle boots he was wearing ... which we found out later ...! Disaster! Bloody stupid man! The other man just waded ashore with the boatman and only lost his belt and pouches – he managed to catch his jungle boots which were ... as instructed, laced together!'

He paused to take another sip of whisky.

'The other three boats and myself set about searching for Abdullah and we managed to recover the upturned boat in the process ... we carried the search on till sunset and had to give up because of bad light ... we camped and continued searching again at daybreak ... at the same time the boatman stripped down the engine ...!'

The zip appeared to have gone out of Pat and his speech slowed markedly.

'We found Abdullah about midday further down the river ... caught up in some undergrowth on the other side – he was wearing his boots, belt and pouches ...! and that's the gist of it Sir ...!'

Without saying a word Mac took the empty whisky glass from Pat's clenched hand and returned it recharged. They fell silent, lost in thought. They had listened to Pat's explanation without comment; he was exhausted but was the first to speak, turning to Sandy saying,

'I'm grateful to you, Sir ... for your offer to accompany me tomorrow to the mortuary ... his father will be there ... it's only a formality, but it has to be done ... and ...' he sighed, 'it won't be pleasant – I can pick you up at 0900 hours ... it shouldn't take more than 20 minutes ... I can then give you a lift to the airstrip for the helicopter at 1100 hours – if that's OK ...?'

'Thanks Pat, that'll be fine. By the way, who's the Lieutenant at the fort now?'

'Tom Hardy ... a Geordie ... you'll like him ... comes from somewhere along the river Derwent in Durham!'

'Really?'

Sandy perked up.

'I'm sure I know the chap – met him when Sir Thomas and Lady Lloyd did the tour of Malaya. The tour started in Johore Baharu and the Field Force platoon commander was Hardy ...'

Kennedy turned to face Mac.

'I'll have to be on my way now, Sir, thanks for the whisky and your understanding ... I reckon I'm very lucky to have you to talk to. I know it goes with the job but in the field we're in the wrong position to get things off our chest and just have to bury it all in the hopes that it'll go away.'

Mac shook his hand vigorously and, as if to endorse his sincerity, clapped him heartily on the back.

'Well, lad, you know where I live ... you're welcome any time you feel you want to talk to someone – and I know I can vouch for Sandy here too.'

'Yes, Pat, you can depend on me ... and thanks for your offer tomorrow ... I'll take you up on all counts ... 0900 hours it is, I'll be standing by ...!'

The next morning Pat arrived and they completed their distressing task, together with Abdullah's father, who came dressed in his best sarong, complete with *sonkok* (hat). He worked in the office of the District Officer and facing them, he presented a picture of a small, very sad, middle-aged man. Arrangements were made for Abdullah's body to be taken back to his village where he would be accorded a ceremonial burial.

As promised, Pat took Sandy to the airstrip to board the helicopter for his journey to the fort. It was an exhilarating flight which took under an hour – quite a difference from the two and half days his first journey had taken!

They flew at a thousand feet and Sandy had a grandstand view in every direction atop the undulating, multicoloured carpet of trees which stretched for miles, broken only from time to time by small clearings in which *kampongs* could be identified by their gleaming tin roofs which flashed in the sunlight. Meandering rivers and streams carved their courses out of the solid mass as though a gigantic painting of the '*Tree of Life*'.

There was little that he could identify until they approached their destination, when he spotted a curling wisp of smoke as they descended on the flight path to the fort; the signal to home-in on the landing pad!

Memories flooded back as the fort came into view. It sat astride the knoll, now a haven of assurance to its little community of Aborigines. The pilot flew down the river clearing and circled the landing pad once; the arching green Very light was fired and he had clearance to land.

Tail up, the aircraft nosed down to the highlighted landing zone, which in the distance looked like a postage stamp on a envelope, the pilot feeling his way amidst the fallen trees which appeared from above like haphazardly scattered matchsticks. With a roar, man's 'bird' came to rest on the designated pad, the engine was cut and the long blades free-wheeled before coming to rest.

The pilot gave Sandy the thumbs-up and he jumped out of the open doorway, turning quickly to take his carbine and haversack from the outstretched hands of the wireless operator. Tom Hardy, the Fort Commander, greeted him with a smart salute.

'Hello, Sir ... great to see you again,' the Geordie beamed.

'You too, Hardy ...' Sandy answered returning the compliment.

'It's a fabulous sight coming in on the fort – it certainly has a commanding view ... I see that everyone's been busy, judging by the number of trees felled and cleared around to the river!'

'Yes, Sir ... Pat did a canny job of it, there wasn't much we could do to improve the clearing, mind, but we're still makin' improvements on the fort and billetin' for the men ...'

Sandy shouldered his carbine and bent down to pick up the haversack.

'I'll take that, Sir. You're to be quartered in the guest room in the fort ...' he said with an air of confidence.

Sandy laughed.

'Heavens, you have got cracking ... sounds marvellous, lead on Macduff! Can't wait to see it all.'

The pilot restarted the engine as soon as Sandy was clear of the pad, and with a gesture of thumbs-up to the two watching officers, took off with a roar and thrashing of blades. In a trice the helicopter, once airborne, seemed magically transformed from cumbersome machine to dancing hover-fly, spinning its way back to base.

It was a short walk to the fort on the knoll and Sandy took the opportunity to look about.

He observed there was little cover for an attacking force since the whole area was well protected and the base of the knoll had been encircled with a barrier of concertina barbed wire, many feet thick, which could only be entered by one gateway. He was aware of the sandbagged *sangar* (sentry post) covering the gate and, as he entered, the sentry came to attention.

They approached the fort up a winding path; it was a long, solitary building on the knoll, built behind a barricade of stout logs revetted together with sandbags to form a protective bullet-proof barrier.

Hardy led Sandy to the centre of the west wall of the barrier through which they passed, then on into a square hall containing a number of doors, three of which faced him, with another two on his left and the other to his right. Hardy explained,

'Here we have to your front, Sir, three small rooms, radio storeroom, fort commander's quarters and spare – which is yours, Sir! The fort garrison is divided half to the right and half to the left, each responsible for the north and south ends, east and west. The building and breast works are positioned north, south, east and west ... to make sure it's protected on all sides ... Bren guns are in all these sectors' ... he paused.

'Any questions, Sir?'

'Not at the moment ... carry on, Hardy!'

'All four sectors are manned at all times ... skeleton strength ... that is, a total of eight men ... each day at dawn we have full strength, sixteen men stand-to ... plus remainder, mobile reserve and HQ muster here ...!'

He hesitated, then resumed.

'The gate is only manned during daylight by one man on shifts ... two of the posts cover him and at night time the gate is closed and covered by two searchlights, the same as the other side of the hill!'

'Heavens, you have got it buttoned up ...' Sandy said, impressed. 'But how about the water point and latrines?' he questioned.

'Oh that's all taken care of, Sir, water from the well within the wire perimeter at the west base of the hill ... pumped up to three points ... cookhouse to the north ... latrine east, wash house south.'

'Well, Tom ... I won't ask any more questions until I'm settled in.'

The room Sandy entered was tiny, approximately eight feet square with a window looking out onto the breastworks. It was furnished with a camp bed, small table and a 'director's' collapsible, canvas chair; on the wall there were hooks to hang equipment and weapons – and that was it! The walls were of split bamboo fastened with wire to the aluminium frame of the building. It was adequate protection from the elements and as the whole structure nestled down on top of the hill was out of range of attackers' fire.

It took only a few minutes to stow away his kit and hang up his carbine ... the Browning automatic he kept on his waist. Tom Hardy was waiting for him to return and, cutting out preliminaries, said,

'Would you like to look about up here, Sir?'

'Yes, Tom, that would be a good idea ... I'm intrigued how everyone fits into this long house.'

'Right, Sir ... ah'll give you the *"Cooks Tour"*. Follow me!'

Sandy was taken first into the Radio Room which was identical to his except there wasn't a bed and, apart from the table on which the radio sat and chair for the operator, it was chock-a-block with boxes of ammunition and stores. It transpired that except in an emergency, the radio was only operated on a schedule to receive messages and transmit the Sitrep.

The next room was that of the Fort Commander; again it was identical except for the map board on the wall, indicating past and present patrols and contacts.

The rest of the building, left and right of the centre room, was the living and sleeping quarters of the contingent. Long, raised platforms on each of the outside walls had draped over them the mosquito nets of the men. A series of windows allowed light to filter through and a door at each end enabled them to muster quickly to action stations.

Next was the cook house and food store which were a hive of activity; the wash house contained a large galvanised tank of water with a dipper which allowed the men to scoop out water and pour it over themselves whilst standing on a bamboo floor acting as duck-boards.

Lastly, they came to the latrines which were divided, with a separate one for the Commander. Sandy was impressed! *'Robinson Crusoe'* couldn't have done better; a lot of thought and effort had been put into the project and he took note of it.

In the evening he joined Hardy in his room for a meal and was informed that a routine patrol was down-river and would be reporting back sometime in the morning.

He turned in early to make notes before the lights went out at 20.00 hrs. Apart from the water pump which was operated from its own engine, the searchlights and fort lights were generated from a small plant in a bunker behind the radio room, which Sandy found a nuisance until lights out!

Next morning he traversed the area with the platoon Sergeant and three men as escort, Tom Hardy having gone down with a mild bout of malaria. He found that the proposed programme of clearing trees had gone to plan, only leaving Mother Nature to dispose of the debris. He sighted Aborigines across the river working in their new *ladangs*, indicating that they had also been taken care of and were settling down.

On returning to the fort he inspected the cook house, wash house and latrines and found that their positioning and construction was in keeping with the hygiene and good health of the garrison. As he was returning to his quarters, the patrol reported in and Tom Hardy, despite feeling unwell, was debriefing the Corporal.

'Bit of bad news, Sir ... the patrol contacted CTs ... no casualties on our side but a man lost his carbine ... no kills or casualties inflicted as far as we know on the CTs!'

'Glad to hear we're all right ... but how on earth did a man lose his carbine?' Sandy enquired.

'They were crossing the river and came under fire from an unknown number – the Corporal ordered a tactical withdrawal to assess the situation and as they were getting out the man waded into a deep pool out of his depth,' Hardy explained. 'We'll have to recover it ...! I suppose the enemy don't realise it's there!'

'How far away was the contact?' Sandy questioned.

'About a day's march, Sir ...!'

He twitched, his face glistening with perspiration as he continued.

'Normally I'd take a fresh patrol out to investigate and retrieve the weapon, but ah don't feel up to it now ... am afraid this malaria has knocked the stuffin' out of me ...!'

Sandy registered how ill the man looked and asked,

'How long do these bouts last, Tom ...?'

'Two to three days at the most ... its been some time since ah had an attack ... this one just come on without warning and it's makin' me feel ah'ful ... am taking the tablets which keeps it down!'

'Well ... I'll take the patrol out myself in the morning, if that's all right with you ... and I'll need the Corporal to lead us to the spot where the weapon was dropped, so we don't waste time.'

'Ah'll right, Sir ... that's good of you to offer ... ah could send the platoon Sergeant ... you don't have to go, Sir ...' he protested.

'Think no more of it, Tom ... it won't do me any harm.' Hardy reflected a moment then spoke.

'If you don't mind, Sir ... it might be a good idea if you also took Batin Mat with you and two of his henchmen to act as scouts ...!'

'Oh I know Batin Mat from my first visit!', Sandy said. 'He's the horrific little man with a porcupine quill through his nose!'

'Aye, that's him all right ... and very useful he is ...!'

'Well, that's settled ... I'll leave at dawn so as to be back the day after tomorrow ... you'd better put that in your Sitrep ...!'

'Right ho, Sir ...! I'll brief the Sergeant to have the patrol ready ... what about your kit, Sir ...' he queried, 'for the trip ...?'

'Not to worry ... I've got all I'll need ... always come prepared.'
Sandy laughed.

'Including rubbers ... to put my watch and matches in, of course ...!!'

As always with a dawn start, Sandy turned in early in preparation; he realised that it could be a trying venture.

After a makeshift breakfast and just as the dawn was breaking over the horizon he met the patrol; the Corporal had them lined up for inspection. Each man was carrying two days' rations ... his provided the previous evening by Hardy.

'*Selamat pagi tuan!*

'*Selamat hari*, Corporal ... *Siapa nama anda?*' he queried.

'*Nama saya Ahmad, tuan ...*! he replied, barely controlling the corners of his mouth from twitching (no doubt at Sandy's attempt to speak Malay).

'Right, Ahmad ... we shall get on our way ... put out your point-man ... I'll come behind you with Batin Mat and his two men ... *Baik ...*!

'*Ya Tuan ...*!

And the little party started off down the hill towards the river, weaving their way through the fallen trees to join a track which took them down the left bank of the river. At first the going was easy, as they passed through the newly created *ladangs*. However, at this early hour there were no *Semelai* to be seen.

The terrain was similar to that which he'd encountered on his first approach to the river with Kennedy, passing through intermittent clearings and *belukar*.

The track became difficult to discern and strayed away from the river forcing them to bypass innumerable bluffs. The river took them on a winding course, at times stealing back on itself, which had a unsettling, disorientating effect. Gorges were encountered, bluffs climbed and Sandy perspired profusely finding the heat intolerable.

Eventually, in the middle of the afternoon the party reached the last bluff to be climbed, prior to attaining their goal, and so they halted to rest. The *Semelai* were sent ahead with two scouts to investigate the other side where the contact with CTs had been made.

Sandy was by now exhausted and uninterested – a bad sign! Reeling on his feet, his head ached and he longed for the end of the journey.

They waited half an hour before the scouting party returned to report that they could find no trace of the terrorists and so Sandy instructed the Corporal to proceed.

However, halfway up the bluff and after falling to his knees a number of times, head pounding, it slowly dawned on him that his condition was far from right.

His general state had become serious, the headache, dizziness and muscular cramp indicated he was succumbing to heat exhaustion. He felt weak and his breathing became fast and shallow with all the symptoms of *Tachycardia*, pulse fibrillation and nausea.

He realised he was in trouble and had to make a positive decision in order to survive.

It was important to get his body temperature down as fast as he could in case he lost consciousness, and the only way to do that was to get into the river and submerge his body in running water. As the position they were in was unsuitable to make camp he referred the matter to the Corporal.

'Corporal Ahmad ... what is the situation like to camp on the other side of this bluff ... is it safe ... once in ... from attack?'

'Yes, *tuan* ... under the hill on the river side ... safe to camp ... plenty cover, *tuan*!'

'*Baik* ...! *sekarang* ... can I get through the gorge down the river on a *rakit* [bamboo raft] ... I'll never get up this hill ...!'

Ahmad hesitated a moment and turned to Batin Mat, putting the question to him. Sandy saw him nod his head but couldn't catch what he said.

'*Tuan* ... he says it will be an honour to make you a *rakit* and take you through the gorge himself ...!'

Sandy then instructed the Corporal to take the patrol up and over the other side of the bluff and wait for him to come through on the raft.

He watched as two men left with him and the *Semelai* began to cut lengths of bamboo which they tied together with long creepers taken from nearby trees. This they quickly beat out on flat stones at the river side, twisting it into ropes adequate to tie the bamboo into a bundle.

Sandy then took off his jungle boots, tied the laces together, undid his belt with his automatic on and held it up to keep it dry, then climbed on board to sit straddle-legged behind Batin Mat who pushed the *rakit* into the river with a stout bamboo pole.

His haversack and carbine were already on their way over the bluff in the care of one of the section.

The current quickly caught the makeshift raft and they disappeared into the gorge out of sight of the launching party who were set to join the patrol again.

The pace of the craft was leisurely, the current not too strong; a mix of small rugged rapids interspersed with tranquil pools, allowing Sandy time to study the terrain along the side of the gorge. Batin Mat proved to be an expert waterman, keeping the raft away from periodic rocks and snags of undergrowth along the sides.

The journey was short and they passed through safely to come out into an open shallow basin where the patrol was waiting for them. Ahmad greeted Sandy.

'*Selamat datang, tuan* ...! we camp here, *tuan* ... carbine found ... down river ... we find when waiting!'

Sandy congratulated him.

'*Baik sekali,* Ahmad ... you have done well ...! I must now lie in the river to take the heat out of my blood ... understand?'

Ahmad, looking worried, nodded his head. Sandy wasn't quite sure if he understood so found a sheltered, shallow spot alongside the camp, stripped off and lay down, allowing the water to gently flow over him.

He lay there until dusk, taking small sips of water from time to time. He knew not to allow himself to be sick, which was important, since vomiting would cause the body an even greater fluid loss.

He dried himself thoroughly and put on his spare jungle green, enabling him to spend a comfortable night, then turned in with the knowledge that Ahmad had taken adequate precautions to ensure their safety should they have unexpected visitors.

He awoke feeling much better despite a restless night, and managed to drink several mugs of sweet coffee. He also decided his gear would be better carried by one of Batin Mat's men. The carbine, minus the magazine, he gave to Batin Mat himself, who became his constant companion on the trail. The little man was thrilled to be allowed to carry the fire stick of the *bomoh*!

The journey back was somewhat easier without the weight of the haversack and the carbine, but he felt weak and sick and it took all his willpower to keep going. He rested many times on the journey but struggled on eventually making the fort by sunset. It was a welcome sound when he heard the cheery greeting from Tom Hardy.

'H'way, Sir ... so y' managed to find the carbine ... great stuff ... but y' don't look so good, Sir ... if y' don't mind me saying, like!'

'No, I'm not ... heat exhaustion ... I feel rotten ... I'll have to get out as soon as possible ...!'

'Why aye, Sir ... there's a helicopter comin' in the mornin' with stores and a'll get them to casa-vac you out ...!'

'Great ... better get a signal off tonight to warn them ... thanks, Tom!'

Bang on time the delivery helicopter with the routine stores duly arrived. It shed its load and Sandy hauled himself on board. At the pilot's suggestion he sat up front taking the navigator's seat – the occupant having agreed to sit on the floor in the cabin of the empty machine. Tom Hardy stowed his gear and made sure he was comfortably installed before waving him off. Batin Mat stood by his side having been told of the evacuation of the *bomoh* and insisting on being present!

The helicopter climbed quickly and the group by the landing pad were soon out of sight; their paths didn't cross again during his tour of duty.

Once airborne, the pilot indicated to him to put on the navigator's headphones; subconsciously he did as he was bid.

For once, the rolling tops of the trees below and the winding water courses seemed to have lost their magic and Sandy's thoughts were confused, he was unaware what was going on around him.

'Come on, give us a hand, old chap ...!'.

Sandy came to with a jolt, a voice booming in his ear.

'It's stuck ... can't get the bloody thing free ...!

The helicopter was oscillating but Sandy had been oblivious of the fact. The pilot was flying the aircraft with the control column between his legs and was agitatedly pointing at a lever he was desperately trying to operate positioned between the seats.

Sandy realised with a shock that they were approaching the JB airstrip at approximately 1000 feet. The collective had jammed and the pilot couldn't release it. Sandy gave him thumbs up and took over the task; once again the voice in his ear roared above the noise of the engine and thrashing rotor blades.

'Whatever you do, don't turn it! ... carefully does it ...! Slowly ...! Slowly ...!'

Sandy took hold of the collective and the pilot, in control but unable to descend, circled around the airstrip. Eventually, he felt it fractionally move and the aircraft bucked, then did a little dance from side to side.

'Try again ... you're releasing it!' the pilot shouted grinning at him.

Sandy grappled again and the collective suddenly unlocked, slicing past his knuckles and skinning them on the seat frame! The pilot calmly took over and they came in to make a normal landing; however, the moment they touched down the engine stalled!

Nobody filled him in on what the trouble was, but he later mused on the fact that when something goes wrong you just get on with it, it's only in retrospect that the danger highlights itself.

Waiting for him was Mac.

'We ... ll, Sandy, you've done yourself in at last ... I'm here to take you straight to the hospital and have you checked over!'

'Mac ... am I glad to see you ... what are you doing down here?'

'Oh, I was called down by the great SB chief ... heard that you were in trouble, so volunteered to pick you up.'

'No-one I'd rather see ... hope it's not fouled-up your trip ... thanks!'

'Not at all, lad only too pleased to be of service!'

He hesitated, looking at Sandy intently.

'Quite honestly you don't look like your old self ...!'

'I'm not ... I'll be glad to get between clean sheets again ...!'

Sandy fell silent whilst Mac drove him to the hospital, dropping him off at reception.

Sometime later, tucked up in bed in a clean, quiet room with a nurse fussing over him, Sandy was examined and given the diagnosis.

'You're a lucky man, Mr MacIntyre ...!'

The Eurasian lady doctor explained,

'Fortunately for you, you diagnosed your condition correctly ... it was a mild attack, or things could have been much worse for you ... still, with a little rest in here we'll have you fighting fit again.'

The doctor chuckled.

'It's rest you really require – you've been overdoing it ... so don't think you'll get away with a quick about-turn ... you're to stay put!'

Smiling, she turned on her heel and left him to contemplate her words. He was to learn later that he'd had a brush with someone quite famous; the doctor was also an author and one of her books had been made into an international film!

The sleep that followed was long and uninterrupted.

He was having a late meal when Mac came in.

'Hello there ... came in earlier but didn't want to disturb you, so here I am again. Got a bit of news for you which should make you feel that Lady Luck's on your side ... that helicopter you came in on was almost out of fuel! It seems it was on an unscheduled flight ... it had to be filled up to return to base ... should really have taken you to Segamat ... not here!'

'Well, I'll be darned ... how did that come about? No wonder the engine conked out on landing ... the pilot never turned a hair or said a word!'

Indicating with his hand he said, 'Pull up that chair. Sorry I can't offer you a dram!'

Mac crossed the room, picked up the chair and placing it opposite Sandy sat astride.

'Not to worry, lad, I can do without the dram!'

'Heavens ...!' Sandy exclaimed. 'I've just remembered my car is up in Segamat! Will you look after it until I can collect it?'

'Och, of course, old chap ... I'll try and get it returned so you don't have to worry about it ... is there anything else you want me to do?'

'No ... but thanks, Mac.'

He hesitated.

'I'm not going to tell Kay where I am yet ... maybe tomorrow if I can get to a phone! When are you going back?'

'Tomorrow morning ... would have been tonight but I put it off to see you first,' his friend replied.

'Take care, Mac ... and thanks again ... you're the berries! By the way, pass on my salaams to everyone ... it's funny about the helicopter bringing me here to JB ... it wouldn't surprise me if Ken Schofield was behind the flight, but we'll say nothing because of the fuel!'

'Aye ... it might be so ... that fort of yours wasn't the only one visited that morning ...! I reckon mum's the word, no point in letting the cat out of the bag!'

He looked at his watch.

'You take care, lad – rest up while you can. I must get off now ... got some things to attend to before departing ... see you soon!'

They shook hands and Mac waved as he went out the door.

'So long, Mac ... thanks again!' Sandy called.

He felt much better the following morning and tested his still unsteady legs by taking – as he thought – a stealthy few steps down the corridor.

Too late! – the beady eye of 'the dragon' spotted him and ordered him straight back to bed! He should have known better than to have-a-go when Matron was doing her morning rounds! How he hated being cooped up! However, after he'd heaped apologies on 'the chief' she did agree that he could use the telephone, so he made his way down the corridor shortly after lunch and rang Kay.

'Hello, Kay ... sorry it's been so long, things got a bit hectic out there ... you know how it is! I've missed you ... hope you've been OK? Miss me?'

'Oh Sandy! how lovely to hear from you ... so glad you're safe. Of course I've missed you, in fact I've been worried sick about you – when the gap gets this long I don't know what to think.'

The sound of her voice sent a shiver down his spine and he felt a surge of longing to be with her.

'You sound so composed, Sandy, you're unbelievable ... where on earth are you?' she queried. 'I've been trying to contact you for days ... but kept being told you weren't available!'

'Sorry, Kay ... it's ... well, it's a long story!'

He pondered, hesitating to say exactly what had happened and where he was.

'Sandy ... what's up ... you sound ... are you all right?'

Her voice was edgy.

'Fine, Kay ... really!'

Wriggling out of the truth wasn't easy!

'Don't dodge the issue, Sandy MacIntyre ... something's happened and I want to know what ...! Come on, Sandy, tell me ... don't keep me in suspense, I can sense something's not right.'

She sounded worried ... and he felt guilty!

'OK, Sister Tutor ... you win, I'm in JB ... in the General, just having a check up! ...'

... 'No ... actually I'm a patient here ... just a bit of heat exhaustion though, nothing to worry about!'

'Oh no, Sandy, now I *am* worried – as soon as I've finished my turn of duty I'll be there ... wish I could look after you!'

'So do I! ... my own nurse!'

Beads of perspiration stood out on his brow!

'I'm dying to see you ... run all the way! Look Kay, must go now, someone wants to use the 'phone. Bye ...!'

'Bye darling – love you ...!'

Her voice trailed away.

Sandy stared at the 'phone.

'Darling ... love you!!'

A smile creased his face, his eyes twinkled and his pace was a little more jaunty as he made his way back to bed!

Kay arrived just as he was finishing his evening meal. Through the open doorway he caught sight of her as she stood talking to the Duty Sister. Her back was to him, auburn hair loosely draped over her shoulders; it swayed gently as she turned her head. She had never looked lovelier.

He knew he was a lucky man. Wonderful to have someone who cares whether you live or die!

He looked at her again ... as only a man can look at a woman!

'Lovely ... truly lovely!' he thought.

'Boy-oh-boy, am I a lucky man' ... and he felt warm inside!

She gave him a big smile, approached the bed and without hesitation put her arms gently around him kissing him on the forehead.

'Oh, it is so good to see you, how are you, tell me what happened to land you in here? You've had a rough time from what Sister tells me.'

She held his hand and gazed into his eyes without thought for restraint of feeling.

He was, quite simply, staggered!

'This girl – this woman ... this gorgeous creature ... is in love with me. Sandy-my-boy, you only get one chance like this!'

Yet ... when he spoke, it was with caution.

'Really, Kay, I'm fine now, it was just the conditions – you know? It's been damn hard out there and you have to keep going no matter what – but it *is* good to be missed – and thank you for coming.'

She's delightful ...! 'Darling ... love you' ... she did say it, I'm sure she did ... I know she did!

He gulped, then heard himself say in a voice no more than a whisper,

'Now, Sister Sutherland ... how about giving a chap a proper kiss ...
I love you too, you know!'

The colour flowed into her cheeks.

They looked into each other's eyes. He leaned forward, cupped her
face in his hands and their lips met; soft and gentle, caressing away the
cares of parting and bringing forth the need to be loved.

Ian Buchanan, the sawmill manager at Labis, was Sandy's next visitor.
He arrived just before lunch the following day. He sauntered into the
room wearing a battered bush hat that had seen better days, rumpled
khaki trousers and shirt and clutched in his left hand an old Army
haversack.

'Sandy ...! hallo there ... Bob gave me the news last night ... how
are you ...?'

His greeting was concerned, his dark face anxious.

'Well, I'll be darned ... *Ian*! You're the last person I'd have expected ...
not too bad ... in fact, much better! How are you my friend?'

'Oh, all the better for seeing you, Sandy. Things haven't been the same
since you left ... and that's no reflection on Bob ... I've just missed our
little chats about the old days.'

'Yes, me too. It seems a long time since I last saw you and a great
deal has happened ... pull up a chair.'

He indicated the hard, wooden visitors' seat on the opposite wall.

Pausing a moment, Ian fumbled in his haversack and – like a magician
pulling a rabbit out of a hat – he extricated a bottle of whisky. With a
flourish he handed it to Sandy.

'For you, my friend, thought this might cheer you up. I don't know
if it's allowed, but it's there when you are!'

He plonked himself down on the chair.

'Thanks, old chap ... very kind of you, I appreciate it, only it's not
on the menu yet. What about you breaking it open and having a dram?'

'No-can-do, thanks all the same, I'm riding the bike and I have to
make my way back this afternoon.'

They chatted easily, exchanging the latest news. Ian was genuinely
pleased to learn of Kay and riveted by Sandy's adventures since leaving
Labis. Only the arrival of lunch brought their conversation to an end
and Ian departed.

'Cheerio now ... great to see you ... take care. I'll keep in touch.'

He shook Sandy's hand.

'You too, Ian ... all the best ... I'll drop in next time I'm on my way
to Segamat ... take care, old friend ... thanks for the whisky!' ... and
he was gone.

148

A restless night followed; he was plagued by short, stabbing nightmares ...

... dense jungle ... the unseen silent enemy ... face to face confrontation ... gunfire; explosions; swamps; reptiles; leeches ... death! ...

... the flashbacks were relentless!

He picked at his breakfast, drank copious cups of hot, sweet tea and read the *Straits Times*. As he turned the pages a knock at the door startled him; looking over the top of the paper he called,

'Enter!'

In walked Bob Sutcliffe dressed in civilian clothes, the outfit looking incongruous with the Browning automatic at his waist and the carbine cradled under his arm.

'Hello, Sir ... hope you're feeling better. I've brought your car down for you!'

'Well I'll be darned ... *Bob*! By Jove, you're a sight for sore eyes ... I'm getting along just fine now ... thank you! How are you ...? Take a pew ... give me all the news.'

Bob did as he was instructed and sat down with a heavy sigh. His face was anxious and he hesitated, looking at Sandy with concern. The uneasy silence was broken by Sandy.

'What's the matter, Bob – the cat got your tongue?' he joked.

Bob swallowed visibly and when he spoke, his voice choked him.

'I've got some bad news for you, Sir! Ian ...'

He stumbled over the words.

'Ian Buchanan ... he's dead! ... He was killed ... yesterday afternoon!'

Sandy froze.

'Oh my God! No!' he cried in anguish.

'I knew, Sir, you'd be distressed at the news, I'm ...'

'But ... he only came to see me yester ... how ...?'

'I'm sorry! – I told him about you ... he said he would come and see you ...! It happened just south of Chaar on a corner just before you reach the palm oil estate ... he ran slap-bang into one of the Army's armoured cars ...! he was dead when they got to him ...!'

His chest heaved.

'The armoured car was in the middle of the bend and he hadn't a chance ... the driver's being charged.'

Sandy was stunned. Bob's explanation was difficult to take in.

'When's the funeral?'

'This afternoon in Labis –16.00 hrs. I'm going straight back on the train at 10.00 hrs. so that I can be there! I'll inform Ian's friends that I've seen you here today – in hospital ... not much else we can do for the poor blighter.'

'Yes! Thanks Bob. At least he wouldn't know what hit him ... I suppose that's something. Poor old Ian – he was so proud of serving in the Army ... and to be killed by one of their vehicles ... what the hell was the bloody thing doing in the middle of the bend? It's awful ... bloody awful! God, what a waste!' he cried.

They sat, silent, both visualising the grim scene.

'Bob! Thanks for coming in person to tell me, I do appreciate it. Now – the funeral, yes, watch your time – I should be there ... how are you getting to the station?'

'Oh, that's been taken care of – Mac's arranged for an SB chap here to stand by and take me. I've left your car at the Mess and given the keys to your Orderly.'

'Thanks again, Bob ... I owe you one. Now, take care ... for heavens sake don't take any chances ...!'

'Right-ho, Sir ... you get better ... I must be on my way, don't want to miss the train. Oh by the way ... Mac asked me to tell you that he'll stand in for you at Ian's funeral!'

'Give him my salaams and grateful thanks. And again, my thanks to you for the delivery of the car. Off you go!'

Bob departed with a wave of his hand and Sandy was left alone with his thoughts.

I need a break ...!

14

Malacca

Sandy pondered on the pressures closing in on him; the events of last month had been grim, the deaths of Beaumont and Ian haunting him throughout the day and night.

Back on duty, he'd put off the recommended convalescent leave thinking work was the best solution; now he felt desperate and a change of scene became vital. So far he'd taken little local leave – only the few days in Singapore when he met Kay again and the occasional long weekend and Saturday night out at the Swimming Club – and of course Dinger's.

He mused on the idea of spending a whole week in Kay's company and the thought fired him, spurring him on to request a week off. They would go to Malacca and get away from it all ... it was one of the old Straits Settlements and a back-water, so hardly touched by the emergency. However, he'd have to check with Kay, going on his own was not an option! At seven he rang her.

'Kay – hallo darling, marvellous to hear your voice. Kay, I've simply got to get away, life over here's bloody awful, all hell's let loose again!'

Controlling himself and introducing an altogether more persuasive tone, he continued before she could answer,

'Let's give ourselves a break and try and forget this ghastly emergency – I've got something to put to you ... something I hope you'll like!'

'Sandy! you OK ...? you don't sound too good ... sorry, you were saying ... what's this "thing" you hope I'll like?'

She sensed he was making an effort to tease her.

'How about coming with me to Malacca – for seven whole days?' he cajoled. 'We could stay at the Rest House – the food's good ... and the honour would be all mine ...!! Now with an invitation like that you can't turn me down.'

He chuckled and was astonished at how good it felt!

She sighed, inwardly tingling!

'Sandy MacIntyre, you are one hell of a guy and I just love you, what a wonderful surprise. Yes, yes, Y-E-S, of course I'll come! I've heard it's oldie worldy and full of charm. Ooooh, can't wait. I need to feel your arms around me – with no interruptions – I've missed you so much!'

Her laughter was music to his ears.

'I'd better arrange a number of dates with the hospital so I can fit in with you ... I'll get on to it first thing in the morning and then let you know.

'By the way, are you able to get away this weekend for dinner at the Swimming Club? Anita and Dinger have asked me to go with them and they would put us up for the night; then we could talk over the details of this heaven-sent break.'

She paused, breathless.

Sandy hesitated for only a moment, then spoke his thoughts aloud.

'That sounds just what the doctor ordered, yes, I think I can manage it ... of course it does depend on situations arising leading up to the weekend ... still ... I could have someone stand in for me and they'll always know where I am ... we can't move now without leaving a telephone number!'

For once, everything worked in his favour and on the Saturday Sandy collected Kay from the Sisters' Mess and took her to the Bell's home. They changed cars at the bungalow and the four of them piled into Dinger's Citroen and made their way to the Swimming Club for dinner.

Whilst the others were getting a table, Sandy strolled to the bar and ordered drinks, nipping in front of four other off-duty officers who arrived at the same time.

'Two gins, *terima kaseh* – one with orange and ice – the other lime – no ice ... and a couple of double malts.'

The steward placed the drinks on a tray as Sandy handed him vouchers to the value of the bill, then carried the drinks over to their table.

The club was a hive of activity as they settled down to pour over the menu. Selecting was fun and after much deliberation they chose a dish of succulent king prawns, large sirloin steaks and, on Sandy's recommendation, a bottle of Chablis '49 and a Nuit St George '47 to complement the meal.

Conversation flowed easily and Sandy could feel himself slowly relaxing, the cares of the past few, foul, weeks ebbing away. He dropped into the conversation that he was planning seven days in Malacca with Kay and was in the process of arranging leave.

'Malacca!' cried Anita, 'you lucky pair. Seven days, mmm ...!'

He couldn't be sure, but Sandy thought Kay blushed!

Dinger without turning a hair tossed off half his whisky and then, looking Sandy straight in the eye, said,

'Malacca ... one of the Straits Settlements?'

The topic was set and engrossed the group for the remainder of the evening.

'That's right, Dinger! ... since 1824 I believe, though in 1795 during the Napoleonic Wars we took peaceful possession of it from the Dutch and returned it back to them when the French threat was over ...'

'But I thought it belonged to the Portuguese?' Kay interjected.

'Yes ... clever you ... it did! At least, until the Dutch took it off them in 1641. The Portuguese held Malacca from 1511 until 1641 when the city was captured by the Dutch and, as I said, held their new possession until 1795.'

'Well ... how on earth did the Dutch beat the Portuguese after all that time?' queried Anita.

'Simple, my dear Watson.'

Dinger butted in pompously.

'The Dutch were traders ... which was in striking contrast to their predecessors who were crusaders ... I'm correct about that, aren't I, Sandy – you're the historian?'

Sandy cuffed Dinger's ear playfully.

'Actually, Dinger's right about that ... it's an historical and logistical fact that the Portuguese were badly supplied with reinforcements from the homeland, which was a contributory factor in their defeat ... all this despite their encouragement for soldiers to intermarry with the local women and thus enlist the sons of these unions in their armed forces. The Muslim Malays, of course, were also alienated because of compulsory conversions to Christianity ...!'

He paused, giving Dinger a steadying look, then smiled.

'Hence Dinger's pun ... the Dutch were traders not crusaders!'

Anita, Kay and Dinger groaned in unison at this remark just as an enormous dish, piled high with prawns, was brought to the table, followed by hot crusty bread enfolded in a crisp white napkin.

The Chablis followed and Dinger poured the chilled nectar as the others helped themselves to the food.

'Oh ... this smells delicious, I'm ravenous, let's eat! However, back to Malacca ... all velly in-ter-es-ting,' Kay mimicked, 'do tell us more, what happened before the Portuguese came?'

Dinger shook his head, helping himself to more prawns.

'Beats me ... before my time! ... d' you know Sandy?'

'Well ... it's a long story ... however, since we're going there and you seem pretty interested I'll tell you what I know ... but briefly!'

He paused a moment.

'What actually happened was that Malacca, ruled by Sultan Mahmud, was a "Malay Kingdom" which came to an end in 1511 after fierce fighting ... when it was captured by the Portuguese fleet under the command of the navigator and statesman Alfonso de Albuquerque ... the ruler fled to Johore where, in the course of time, he set up a new kingdom.

'Now please, don't ask me any more, it really is very complicated ... however ... I will add this ...'

He took a deep breath.

'The Straits of Malacca is one of the most important shipping lanes in the world and in the era of the sailing ship the port of Malacca was one of the busiest on the peninsula. Of course today shipping is confined to coastal trade because the harbour is inaccessible to the modern ocean-going vessels ...'

Kay said,

'Yes, but what neither of you has explained is why the British have possession of the state now ... how did they manage to get it back from the Dutch ...?'

'Carry on, Sandy, you have the chair ...!'

Sandy took a sip from his glass.

'OK ... but leave some prawns for me, you're all eating whilst I'm talking.

'History has it that in 1824 the British sphere of influence on the Malay peninsula was as strong as it is today ... we acquired the city and state in exchange for Benkulen, Sumatra, which was British at that time ... it geographically tied up the area into definite packets ... "Dutch East Indies and British Straits Settlements ..." however, as you all know ... the former doesn't exist any more ...! nevertheless, the town was left with a fabulous heritage of mixed Portuguese and Dutch architecture which is still in use today ...!'

Anita said, 'Sounds like you've been there, Sandy ...!'

'Yes, as a matter of fact I have ... but only on an operational visit. I was impressed with everything I saw ... they even have a sports and swimming club ... albeit the latter is out of town and a little up the coast – and to use it you have to be a member, I think.'

'Our trip sounds marvellous ...' Kay enthused, giving Sandy's hand a squeeze which she hoped the others wouldn't notice.

'I'm so looking forward to it ...!'

'Yes, so am I ... can't wait to show you the sights ...' and leaning forward, Sandy kissed her ear and whispered,

'It'll be great to be on our own.'

Kay looked up at him, eyes sparking, and in that moment they were alone.

The strains of 'Cocktails for Two' floated towards them. Sandy stood up, took her hand, kissed it and bowed in elaborate, mock formality.

'Miss Sutherland, this Fox-trot is mine I believe … come on, let's dance!'

Kay threw her head back with laughter.

'OK, Maestro … lead on, I thought you'd never ask!'

He pulled her gently, guiding her between the tables and onto the dance floor.

They danced together with ease and before long Sandy could feel Kay's lithe body against his own as second by second she relaxed. Leaning closer to him, she turned her head, their cheeks brushed … and they danced as one.

'Love you …' he whispered.

'Love you too …' she whispered back.

They danced many times that night, but those first joyous moments would live with them forever.

Sandy reported for duty on Monday morning and put in his application for leave; by midday an answer in the affirmative had been received.

Hoping to catch Kay in the mess at lunch time he telephoned her straight away; as he waited expectantly he drummed his fingers on the desk top to check his agitation. After a short wait she came to the phone.

'Hallo … Sister Sutherland speaking …?'

Sandy, playing the fool, answered in a broad Irish brogue.

'Well now, Sister Sutherland … I've been asked to relay a most important message to you …'

Kay giggled.

'Sandy … you idiot, I know it's you – what are you up to now?'

The sheer nonsense of the moment made them laugh till they ached.

Sandy, with tears running down his cheeks, recovered first.

'I've got it! I've got leave as from Friday night … and seven days as from the Monday … how's that?'

He was elated.

'Oh, darling, you must have read my mind … I put my first request in to start this Saturday … and Matron immediately said I could go anytime. I can't believe our luck!'

'Right, sweetie … I'll get cracking and book the Rest House from then until the following week Sunday – if that's OK by you?'

'Yes please … I'm in your hands! Oh, I'm so looking forward to our break!'

'Right … the preliminaries are … I'll collect you on Saturday morning at 0900 hours and we'll drive via Ayer Hitam, Batu Pahat, and Muar …'

'How far is it to Malacca …?' she interrupted.

'I should say about a hundred and twenty-seven miles from JB …

roughly four hours travelling ... however we'll have to take in the Singapore bit ... five should do it ... ETA ... late lunch at the Rest House!'

'As long as that ... it's further away than I imagined.'

'Yes ... there are two rivers with toll bridges we have to negotiate ... which, if we get held up, can be a time consumer; however we could get a clear run and be a little early!'

'Oh, I hope so ... then we can start sight-seeing after lunch ... as long as the driving doesn't prove too much! I've got to remember you're convalescing. Heavens, aren't you the lucky one – it's just struck me you got your wish ... here you are going on leave with your own private nurse ...! 'What's next ...?' she teased.

'For God's sake Barker don't rise to the bait, this line could be tapped!'

'Sandy ... are you there?'

'Of course, Kay ... yes, drifted off to Malacca ...!'

'Sandy, that's not fair ... you can't go without me ...!'

'That's what they all say!' he said playfully.

'I'll have to take you in hand ...!'

'Yes please ... anytime ... any place ...!'

'Well ... the weekend's the earliest I can make it, I'm, afraid! Must dash – got my lunch to finish – I'll be ready Saturday. Bye darling ... take care!'

She blew a kiss down the line and was gone.

Sandy passed the rest of the day light-headed, only just remembering to make the booking. He thought quickly about the selection of rooms the Rest House offered.

'I've been involved in some damnable situations out here, but none which involves more courage than this.'

And that said, he plumped for two single rooms with an adjoining door between!

Saturday morning dawned and he drew up outside the Sisters' Mess just as Kay walked out the door, her luggage already on the steps.

'Morning, Kay ... ready for the grand tour?'

'Hi Sandy ... lovely to see you, I'm glad you're on time ... I've been waiting since 6.00 a.m ... the longest three hours I've had to endure for a very long time!'

'Well, sweetie, that's how it should be, I've been looking forward to it since last Monday!'

Laughing light-heartedly he came round the front of the car. He put his arm round her shoulders, gave her a squeeze and kissed her on the cheek, then picked up her suitcase and lobbed it into the boot and put her soft bag on the back seat.

It was a beautiful morning and since there was little likelihood of rain he had removed the rear side windows, but kept the hood up to protect them from the sun and prying eyes.

She was lovely! Attired in mint green blouse and slacks, she looked cool, her long auburn hair drawn back at the nape of her neck by a silk, peach coloured, scarf. Sandy's heart leapt ...!

They were quickly on their way and crossing the causeway, passing the *Istana*, the Sultan's Palace, which overlooked the Straits. They continued through a varied landscape of rubber and palm-oil plantations interspersed with tracks of jungle. It was Kay's first visit into the heart of the mainland and she found the ever changing landscape a revelation.

They made good time to Ayer Hitam at which point they left the Kuala Lumpur main road heading for Batu Pahat through the coastal plain.

On approaching Parit Raja Sandy saw on the left-hand side of the road, a bus disgorging its passengers. They stood at its side, huddled together in an expectant manner, waiting for him to pass so they could cross over the road.

Accordingly he continued slowing down, and as he did so, he caught a fleeting glimpse of a figure emerging from the front of the bus ... right into his path!

There was a loud click on the inside wheel arch as he hit something hard. He slammed on the brakes, tussled with the steering and came to a screeching halt some yards further on. Glancing in his rear view mirror he saw to his horror an old Chinese lady, umbrella under her arm, spinning round and round across the road like a '*Whirling Dervish*' and finally coming to rest on the other side of the road, where she flopped over.

Sandy, with his Browning automatic under his right thigh, hurriedly handed it to Kay, saying,

'Hang on to this ... the safety catch is on ... I'm going back to see if she's all right ...!'

'What? Sandy ...!' she cried.

'No! ... listen ... I've got to ... but if I'm attacked you're to drive off and leave me ... that's an order ... and *that* ...' indicating the Browning ... 'is for your protection!'

With that he ran back to where the figure was lying surrounded by the other passengers.

They were a mixed bunch of Malays and a few Chinese; one, a young male, said,

'Velly silly woman ... she no look where she go ...'

'Is she all right ...? I didn't hit *her*, but *something* hit my radio aerial.'

Taking a closer look at the prostrate figure lying on the ground still clutching tightly the umbrella made of wood and tarred paper, he noted a graze mark about two inches from its end; without doubt it had connected with his aerial!

Mercifully he had missed her, she was only dazed, shocked and a little dizzy from the effect of spinning. The onlookers remonstrated with her, telling her what a foolish women she was and how lucky she was to be alive.

The young man introduced himself to Sandy as her nephew and said in Malay,

'*Tida' apa tuan* ... silly woman not hurt ... just dizzy ... you no blame ...'

Shoving Sandy in the direction of his car he said,

'Better you leave now ...!'

Sandy, taking the hint, walked slowly back, methodically checking the surrounding landscape as he did so.

'By Jove, that was a near thing ... but not to worry, darling ... she's all right, just a little confused and giddy ...!'

Looking at the aerial he saw that it was dented at the base where it had come into contact with the umbrella.

'Oh Sandy ... I was so worried, they might have turned on you ...!' she shuddered at the thought.

'We'll have to report the incident, I'm afraid, at the Police Station in Batu Pahat, in case of repercussions ... might have to change plans about lunch now, maybe have it at the Muar Rest House ... we'll see how we get on!'

And with that he drove off and for the next few miles they continued their journey in silence.

Suddenly, and without prior warning, Kay exploded.

'Sandy MacIntyre ...! I don't know what you expected me to do with that ... that ... "cannon" of yours ... I don't even know *how* to take the safety catch off ... never mind shoot the damn thing ...! and ... and to expect me to run off and leave you ...!'

Her voice trailed away into a sob and Sandy, throwing all caution to the wind, pulled over onto the side of the road and put his arms around her.

'Oh Kay ... darling, don't upset yourself ... it's all over now ... it's my fault, I should have taken more care and anticipated something like that happening!'

'Oh no! no darling ... I was worried sick that you might be hurt ...!'

She lifted her face to his and kissed his lips, her arms around his neck holding him tight.

'Oh Sandy, I love you ...!'

'My sweet Kay ... I love you too ...!'

They held each other for a moment then Sandy, lifting her arms from around his neck, wiped the tears from her flushed face.

They were parked overlooking some paddy fields and although still acutely aware they were a sitting target, he had grabbed this fleeting moment allowing himself – for once – the privilege of self indulgence; then they pushed on to Batu Pahat!

On arrival at the Police Station Sandy reported the incident, which was duly recorded in the day book, and soon they were once again on their way, this time heading for Muar.

The countryside, although picturesque, had become flat and interlaced with meandering streams which fed the paddy fields as far as the eye could see.

Little wooden houses on stilts, with roofs of palm atap or corrugated tin, were dotted about the landscape amidst swaying palms. The narrow road passed over innumerable wooden bridges and they began to encounter colourful bullock carts with pointed roofs in the shape of the horns of a bull and bedecked with varicoloured trappings, which are generally only to be found on the carts of Malacca.

Sandy explained,

'In by-gone days the noblemen used to travel in carts similar to these ... the roofs kept the weather – rain or sun – off the occupants ...'

'They are unusually colourful for carts.'

It was a question really, Kay looked expectantly at him.

'Yes, I don't know why ... to keep off evil spirits possibly ... or maybe just like us having different coloured cars ...!' he suggested. The magic of the countryside was infectious and their mood gradually changed as they progressed on their journey.

Sandy had made good time, the anticipated hold-ups at the two toll bridges hadn't materialised and soon they were entering Jalan Ujong Pasir and he was pointing out St John's Fort way up on the hill.

'Look, Kay ... that's an old Portuguese fort; it was rebuilt by the Dutch and there used to be a private chapel dedicated to St John the Baptist in it. The place is also known as *Bukit* St John!'

'Bucket, what does that mean?' she queried. 'What a funny name to give to a place ...!'

'Oh that's quite simple "*Bukit*" means hill,' Sandy answered with a smile. 'And ... it's not spelt ... b-u-c-k-e-t, but B-u-k-i-t ... nothing to do with Jack and Jill!'

By now they were entering Jalan Parameswara and approaching the Rest House overlooking the *padang*. The air was charged with excitement and Kay, trying to take it all in, could hardly contain herself.

'Oh Sandy ... it's lovely!'

The large wooden building, with a roof created by a series of curving, oriental structures, was certainly impressive and soon they were climbing the steep wooden steps leading up to its entrance. The porter followed them with their luggage as they entered the spacious hall and reception area, which doubled as a sitting room and had a bar at one end.

Formalities were quick and efficient and they were shown to their rooms in an extension at the back of the building.

Sandy, since he had omitted to tell Kay about the communicating door, was decidedly apprehensive!

Putting his case on the bed he strode towards the window and took in the view. Minutes elapsed and the silence was deafening.

There was a gentle tap on the inner door; he swallowed hard, opened it, and found Kay standing there grinning from ear to ear.

'What a clever boy, Sandy ...!' she exclaimed, giving him a flirtatious peck, then skirting deftly round him towards the window.

'This is bliss – and thank you for bringing me. Now, I'm absolutely ravenous, so I think we should have something to eat before we – unpack!' she trifled ... Don't you?'

'We-ell – OK, yes – yes if you say so. We should be able to have lunch, it's not yet two o'clock but ... hey ... don't I deserve a better kiss than that?'

She sashayed towards him, curled her arms around his neck and their lips met.

'Wow!' was all he could manage.

Disentangling themselves they locked up and made their way across the open courtyard to the dining room behind the reception.

The food was worth waiting for. The Rest House, famous for its seafood, produced a meal of succulent sea bass and local vegetables plus the ubiquitous 'Tiger beer'.

Once the meal was over Sandy began to feel the strain of the journey and so they retired, unpacked and changed before sallying forth into the town.

Five o'clock arrived and, walking hand in hand, their tour of exploration began with the prepossessing building of the Malacca Club at the corner of Jalan Kota. Overlooking the *padang*, the solid, square stoned, gothic looking building had a balconied central entrance which was flanked by two oriental domed structures. Across the road Sandy pointed out Malacca's hallmark.

'Look Kay ... that's Porta de Santiago, the old gateway; notice the belfry on top ... it's now all that remains of the Portuguese fortress built in 1511 ... the fort sustained severe structural damage during the Dutch invasion – they wanted to get rid of it at some time or other, but Stamford Raffles persuaded them to keep it. They made some repairs and over the entrance cut out in stone the coat of arms of the Chartered Company of the Dutch East Indies!'

'It's so old … and tragic … all so long ago! I'm glad they kept it!'

Looking through the gate she pointed to the hill behind.

'What's that big square building?'

Overshadowing the gate up on the hill behind loomed the chapel of 'Our Lady of the Hill' built by the Portuguese Captain, Duarte Coelho. It had been turned into a burial ground by the Dutch for their noble dead and here St Francis Xavier was briefly interned in 1553 before being shipped to the Portuguese possession Goa, in India. The grave was left open and has remained so throughout time.

'Can we go there?'

'Yes, but not today … maybe tomorrow, Sweetheart, when we've more time.'

They continued their walk and, turning left, proceeded past another Dutch cemetery in which a war memorial could be seen dedicated to the British soldiers who died in the Naning War of 1831–32.

'That's a war I've not heard of …!?' she said, looking up at him expectantly.

He laughed.

'Heavens … I've never known anyone ask so many questions … I'm not quite sure … I'm not a walking Encyclopaedia …!'

'Yes you are, Sandy …' she replied, eyes twinkling.

A little further on they entered the Jalan Gereja and, crossing the roundabout, they paused at the circular fountain in the centre which had an upright carved obelisk erected in memory of Queen Victoria.

Opposite and still in use, was Christ Church built by the Dutch in 1753, a testimony to the Dutch architectural ingenuity. The stucco, salmon-painted front (as were all the Dutch buildings) beckoned them to enter and they were entranced and amazed by the hand-carved pews and ceiling beams all constructed without joints.

'Oh Sandy, it's lovely … and look … look at this brass bound Bible … after all this time …!'

'Yes … and here, take a look at these tombstones in the floor … they're carved in Armenian … it must have been done by an artist, they're so beautiful …'

There was so much to see; the glazed tiles depicting 'The Last Supper' just one example. They were enthralled. Time seemed to fly and the sun was beginning to set as they came out past the old clock tower and the Stadthuys, which Sandy indicated, pointing.

'That's the old official residence of the Dutch Governors, it was also used as their offices.'

'Heavens, it doesn't look that old ...!

Kay was fascinated.

'Well it is ... built in 1650 it's the original structure and is still used as offices ...! Anyway ... enough's enough, don't you think we should get back and change for dinner?'

'Yes I do ... it's been a long hard day for you and it's not yet over – you mustn't over-do it. I must look after you ...!'

She smiled.

'We've got a whole week ... I can't believe it ...!'

They walked swinging their arms, hands entwined, it all felt so natural. Slowly they sauntered back to the Rest House passing again the Malacca Club.

To observe the protocol of the day Sandy and Kay made a pact, deciding it would be prudent at all times for them to enter and exit their bedrooms separately to eliminate unsavoury speculation from other residents. So it was that they each returned to their own rooms to prepare for dinner.

Saturday night was always a busy time in the restaurant and Sandy, anticipating this, had ensured they had a table to his liking reserved for their entire stay.

He soaked his aching limbs in a hot bath, changed into clean clothes and felt much better, the tension of the journey fading away. He began to wish they were together and not separated by a door. And yet ... his thoughts about Kay were confused.

He was in love with her, loved her, yet hadn't been with her more than a weekend, sometimes only one night – and always in the company of others.

This was going to be a testing time for them both, they'd never been so close and he was suddenly apprehensive.

He was sure of one thing, however ... he wanted to love her!

Waiting for her to knock on his door – as agreed – made him feel vulnerable and he reflected ...

'... *maybe she's unsure of me ... maybe it's all a mistake – infatuation even ... she might want to call it off ... damn ... damn, damn ...*'

A soft tap on the door, followed by ...

'Sandy!' broke into his thoughts.

It opened and there stood Kay – beautiful – her face radiant, looking at him with adoring eyes. Her hair, shining, was off her face and swept up in an elegant chignon.

In a voice barely above a whisper she said,

'Good evening, Sir … will I do …?

'*Oh Lordy I'm lost …!*' he thought.

'Oh darling, you look ravishing …!'

Striding across the room he took her in his arms and kissed her pouting lips, electrifying him. He stepped back to take in her entire presence and acknowledged with singular delight the lemon dress, silky, caressing her body, the low neckline.

'Flattery will get you nowhere, Sandy MacIntyre.'

She gave him a knowing wink.

'. . . and … if you carry on like this we'll never get to dinner!'

'Right … young lady!'

Turning, he offered her his arm and, without a clear thought between them, they left together from Sandy's room!

It was only a short walk to the restaurant and before dining they went into the lounge bar for an aperitif. It was filled with people; families, couples, parties, all chattering and buzzing with the delight of being free for a short while.

There was one exception, a man sitting on his own in the window, opposite two empty seats. He appeared to be relaxed, enjoying in solitude his whisky and soda and the view out on the *padang*.

Something about him – the back of his head – something – that Sandy recognised.

Silently he guided Kay towards the two empty seats, indicating to her to sit down; at the same time he turned to the man and addressed him, his voice booming'

'These seats are taken, old chap … haven't you anything better to do than idle your time here …?'

The contrasting reaction to his outburst couldn't have been greater and Sandy could hardly contain himself, not knowing who to look at first.

Kay thought he had taken leave of his senses, and the sitting figure leapt to life, turned, gave him a wide grin and thrust his hand forward in welcome.

'Well, laddie … I thought you'd never come … and me guarding these extra seats for you and your lovely lady …!'

He paused a moment then beamed at Kay.

'At last we meet … now I know why he's been keeping you under wraps!'

Sandy chuckled.

'Kay … take no notice of him! Come and meet my old buddy from Segamat … Tam Mactavish!'

'Mac! this is indeed the lady I told you about … Sister Kay Sutherland.'

Mac clasped both her hands in welcome, saying,

'I've been waiting for this day to meet you, Kay ... an may I tell you, bonny lass ... 'am not disappointed.'

Kay blushed.

'And I've been looking forward to meeting you ... Sandy holds you in high regard ... but ... how on earth did you know we were here?'

'Yes Mac ... how?' Sandy endorsed her astonishment.

'Well, that's simple ... I came here for a weekend break and saw that wee car at the front and put two and two together!'

'But the seats Mac ... are you on your own?'

'Aye, I am that ... and knowing that they get busy here before dinner, thought you would need a seat for the sundowner! So – what's it to be, Kay?'

'Thank you, Mac, a dry sherry would be nice.'

'And there's no need to ask what your tipple will be, laddie ...'

He summoned the waiter.

'Two double malts and a glass of the best dry sherry in the house, *terima kaseh*!'

Now comfortably seated Mac turned to Kay.

'What d'you think of our little watering hole? Have you settled in? I suppose this is your first visit?'

His questions sounded awkward.

Kay smiled, sensing the slight unease that virgin conversations often bring. She leant forward and put her hand on his.

'I think it's lovely ... just as I imagined it to be ... and you're right, it *is* my first visit, Mac!'

The ice was broken! Mac reverted to his jovial self and the conversation and laughter flowed like water over pebbles.

Sandy's table was called and, with a squeeze of Kay's hand, he asked for another place to be set so his friend could join them. Before Mactavish could say a word Kay added,

'Oh, please, Mac, we'd love you to join us.'

'Well now, that's very generous of you both. I'd love to, thank you – and – if you'll allow me to return the compliment, I'd like to invite you to join me at the Malacca Club after we've eaten. I've been a member for some time ... it's nice there, you'll like it!'

The night felt special; no rushing or being constantly alert; the service was efficient yet unobtrusive and Sandy was well pleased!

The evening was balmy and the air fragrant with blossoms as they descended the steps onto the road leading to the club.

Fireflies twinkled and danced in the warm air under the old flame trees bordering the road, momentarily casting an enchanted spell as they walked abreast; Kay, as though escorted on either side by medieval knights strolling down the moonlit road, minute fairies heralding their way.

The 'knights and their lady' entered the portals of the old club to the sound of dance music from a bygone era.

The place was a blaze of lights and the dance floor and bar a hive of activity. Planters, their families and other club members were evident and many waved in recognition as Mac entered.

There was an air of festivity about the place as though the morrow didn't matter. He led the way showing them into the library where, around a small table in the corner of the room, there were still a few empty chairs.

'I'm afraid this is all we're likely to get this evening ... Saturday night's very popular and the outside always gets filled up first ... never fear, it'll be quieter and we can get drinks in from the bar.'

Turning to Sandy and Kay,

'You two ... take a pew and keep the fort ... I'll get the drinks.'

With that he was off. However he only got as far as the door before turning, embarrassed, exclaiming,

'Sorry, Kay ... I should have asked what you'll have ... comes with the territory, lass, not enough female company!'

She flashed him a smile and teased,

'Och, dinna fash yourself, Mac ...! I'll have a gin and lime with a dash of soda ... please.'

Sandy could have sworn that Mac flushed a rosy hue before nodding and continuing on his errand.

At last on their own Sandy took Kay's hand and whispered,

'Sorry, darling ... I honestly didn't know Mac was coming here this weekend ...'

'Oh, not to worry, sweetheart, it's only tonight ... I think he's rather special ... you must be glad to count him as a friend.'

Mac was soon back, the music beckoned and they took to the dance floor. The strains of 'Body and Soul' was their excuse to put their arms around each other.

The world they had entered was so far removed from what had become the 'norm': terrorists, gunfire, mutilated bodies and the fear of always having to look over your shoulder ... that the magic of the evening became intoxicating.

They danced the evening in a dream, with chatter and laughter punctuating the air. Mac took his turn on the floor, twirling Kay off her feet and loving every minute of it.

Sandy watched him with interest and saw the tiredness fall away; saw Kay, the long hours of responsibility slip from her, and pondered the need of extremes between duty and play in strife-torn situations ... and realised it was the very essence of sanity!

Midnight came and they bade goodnight to Mac who, enjoying the ambience of the club, stayed on. They promised to see him in the morning before his departure for Segamat.

They retraced their steps to the Rest House, sauntering hand in hand and occasionally kissing as they strolled.

As they passed, once again, under the Flame trees the nearness of their presence to each other became irresistible and Sandy halted, pulling Kay firmly towards him.

He tilted her face upwards and kissed her with the longing of one who's found their soul mate. He kissed her forehead, her cheeks, her neck, and his hands moved from her face to deftly remove the combs from her hair allowing it to cascade.

His fingers ran gently through the auburn locks whilst his tongue, searching with instinct, made their kisses sweet as honey.

Kay's response was spontaneous and their passion equal. As his hands caressed the lemon silk she gently took them in hers and whispered,

'Love you too ...'

Without another word she smoothed the chignon back into place, and arms entwined they walked along the *padang*'s perimeter and up the steps of the Rest House, the intoxicating perfume of the blooms transfixed in their heady thoughts as they entered by the way they had left ...!

Kay walked towards the window, her silhouette caught in the first fingers of the dawn's rays. She breathed deeply, a smile playing at the corners of her mouth suggesting contentment. She turned her head slightly, the hairs on the back of her neck rising as she sensed a movement behind her. Sandy's arms enveloped her and he rested his chin on her bare shoulder. They stood, cuddled, rocking gently too and fro watching the morning sky awaken.

'Kay ...? Will you marry me?'

The whispered words made her turn within his embrace and her mouth found his in answer.

Mac was already seated when they made their way to breakfast.

'Morning, Mac,' they said in unison.

'Morning! you both look remarkably fresh after all that dancing, I hope you enjoyed the Club – I know I did. In fact, to be honest, I haven't had such a good time since ... och, I don't know when! You're a good dancer, Kay ... lucky man Sandy!'

'Don't I know it.'

Sandy winked at Kay, who lowered her eyes thereby avoiding his appraising gaze.

'Have you ordered, Mac?'

'No, thought I'd wait for you both, but let's order now you're here, I'm hungry.'

Kay murmured in agreement.

'Me, too ... I think I could eat a horse!'

'Well, I can't fulfil that order, but perhaps a little bacon, eggs, mushrooms and hot buttered toast would suffice for madam!'

Sandy felt on top of the world.

'Coffee or tea?'

'I think we should have that three times over – and I'll have tea, laddie, since you're asking,' Mac laughed. 'You know, Kay ... this young man has had a standing invitation to bring you up to Segamat for a weekend ... and he's never taken it up ...!'

Without blinking he looked Sandy straight in the eye.

'Isn't that right, Sandy lad! Now ... how about calling in for the night on your way back from here next Saturday?'

And without giving Sandy time to answer he turned his gaze to Kay.

'It would give this lassie a chance to see the countryside and break your journey.'

Kay's face lit up.

'Thank you, Mac ... that's a wonderful idea ... we'd love to ...'

Turning to Sandy she enthused,

'Please Sandy, I'd love to go ... one night less here won't matter ... will it?'

Sandy, caught in the crossfire, didn't know what to say. Not for a minute did he expect Mac to suggest a visit, now of all times!

He looked into her face, so earnestly appealing, and gave in with good grace. *Fait accompli*! There was after all the week ahead of them! Sandy looked at Kay, reached for her hand and turned to Mac, looking suitably serious.

'Well, Mactavish, we've shared many a secret in our time together, now Kay and I would like to share with you another, very special, secret.

'A short while ago I asked Kay to be my wife and ... lucky devil that I am ... she accepted me.'

Tam exploded, pushing his chair back and ringing Sandy by the hand.

'What ...! well I never! That's wonderful ... great news ... congratulations, we'll have to celebrate this!

'And Kay, what can I say ... you're a bonnie lass, he's a lucky man ... and I'm jealous as hell. Truly! I wish I could be as fortunate. My best wishes to you both. He's had a rough time and this is the best thing that could happen to him.'

In a stage whisper he added,

'I wouldn't let him know this, Kay, but he's a good catch!'

Mac kissed Kay on both cheeks before sitting down again.

'Well now ... what I've got to say will be just the ticket for you. Sandy! I've made you a temporary member of the Malacca Club while you're here ... there'll be nothing to pay, apart from your drinks ... my treat!'

'Oh Mac, that's wonderful ... it will make our holiday complete ... thank you so much!'

Kay moved from the table and gave him a hug. Mac preened himself with delight, then recovering, asked,

'Now, what are you doing this morning? I could take you out to the Club's pool up the coast and introduce you there before I depart after lunch, you'll be set-up then.'

'Mac, you're the berries ...', Sandy answered glancing sideways at Kay, her face reassuring him she approved.

They piled into Sandy's car, the roof down and left the Rest House making for the bridge crossing the Malacca river and down Jalan Hang Jabat with its decorative Baba Nyonya Chinese houses, resplendent with carved wooden doorways.

The Swimming Club was located only a short drive away, its pool fed by seawater which changed with the rise and fall of the tide.

The Club House appeared through the palm trees, cottage loafed, atap roofed and crowned by a smaller structure, allowing ventilation. It was still early and the club not yet filled with members, thus giving them a chance to look around. Kay was thrilled.

'Sandy! What a heavenly location ... it's all just part of the land-scape ...'

She hugged him, her eyes lingering finally on the clear, cool water of the pool.

Mac butted in.

'The sun's coming overhead and it's getting hot, anyone for a dip? I can't wait to get in ... The changing rooms are over there!'

He pointed to a smaller, oblong structure, also roofed in atap. They followed him.

Sandy was already lying by the pool when Kay emerged resplendent in a scarlet, strapless one-piece which curved over her body, showing to advantage her slender arms and long legs and exposing a hint of cleavage; just enough to take Sandy's breath away!

She smiled as she walked over to him.

'Hallo tiger,' she growled as she bent over, gently nibbling his ear. 'This is lovely ... we could come here every day and have a swim.'

'That's a jolly good idea, can't think of a better way to relax. Like the costume!'

As she passed to sit on the bamboo chair his outstretched hand caressed her long limbs, his heart missing a beat!

She giggled.

'Weren't we lucky to find each other, Sandy?'

'We sure were, lady ... we sure were! Kiss me!' he teased.

'What do you think of the place, Sandy ... nice, isn't it?' Mac interrupted, his eyes resting on Kay and interpreting the scenario.

'Mac, it's great – a perfect place to come in the evening, relax with a sundowner, look out across the sea and watch that giant ball of orange flame sinking on the horizon, the sky changing with every second into a blaze of colour!'

'Poetic, but true, Sandy, I couldn't have put it better myself ... now, how about some beers?'

He sat down at the wooden table and beckoned the steward.

'Mac ... it's lovely' Kay said. 'This is going to make such a difference to our holiday ... I don't suppose there will be many people here during the week?'

'No ... it's the weekends which are busy ... Sunday morning's OK ... but avoid the afternoon ... it's generally packed.'

They swam in the pool, lazed in the sun and slipped back into the pool, times without number. Drinks were replenished, the chatter minimal as the sun rose high in the heavens.

Then, before they knew it, it was time to return to the Rest House for lunch and see Mac on his way to Segamat.

'See you two next Saturday afternoon ... don't be late! Kay can have a look round our one-horse town. Look after yourselves ... and enjoy your week! Again, my heartiest congratulations.'

They stood side by side until his car disappeared out of sight, their arms flailing as they waved him off in salute.

At last they were on their own!

15

The Reaper Takes his Toll

They hugged each other. 'Free at last!' he breathed. Kay nodded in agreement.

It was decided that each morning they would explore a little of Malacca's history, and on their travels they came across the 1459 Well of Hang Li Poh, a Chinese princess who married the Sultan of Malacca. According to the records it was the only source of water during droughts and never dried up.

Sandy also took Kay exploring down Jonker Street, famous for its antiques; he had an innate gift for bartering and, more often than not, came out with a 'prize'.

It was an idyllic time for them and they ended up each midday by the Club's pool, where they swam and lazed in the sun, staying until they could see each day's glorious sunset, its beauty etched in their memories.

At the Rest House they showered, changed and relaxed over dinner, enjoying the good, freshly cooked food, especially the fish; and the wine, although by any standards run-of-the-mill, flowed freely. Each evening they walked down to the Malacca Club in the moonlight, arms tightly about each other, marvelling at how lucky they were. During those days they loved each other with a passion, a caring, an intense depth of feeling which few are destined to experience.

They decided to leave until their last day the visit to the Gothic-towered church dedicated to St Francis Xavier (known as the Apostle of the East), which was built in 1849 by the Reverend Farve, a Frenchman.

As they stood there on that Saturday morning before departing for Segamat, the breeze on the crest of the hill catching and billowing Kay's skirt, Sandy turned to her and, taking her in his arms, cradled her.

'My pretty Kay, I think we should be married as soon as possible, what d'you say?'

'That would be wonderful, darling! How soon could we arrange it? I'd have to get permission to terminate my contract with the hospital authorities ... it could take ages, couldn't it?'

'Well, let's move as quickly as we can. I want you with me as my wife, I love you so very much … my precious Kay!'

They departed the Rest House with a pang of nostalgia, but in high spirits took to the road for Segamat via Jasin. Sandy drove briskly once clear of Malacca and pushed the little car hard to make up as much time as possible; he knew the going would be slow when climbing through the jungle clad hillside. Conversation was animated as they drew further and further away from habitation.

The long hot fingers of tropical sunlight shafted through the lush, dank undergrowth on the cutback jungle along the foot of Gunung Ledang (Mt. Ophir), causing misty spirals of air to crown its peak. High above, a kite hawk circled lazily on the noonday thermals and in the still oppressive air the bird at first appeared to hang motionless. After a while it began to soar in ever increasing circles, higher and higher, until it was directly over the last bend on the road to the summit of the pass.

The rain forest's elaborate, undulating pattern of thousands of crowns made a multicoloured carpet of green and blue, stretching unbroken into the distance, except for short glimpses of the road twisting beneath. The intense silence over the hillside was punctuated momentarily by the cooing of doves and screams of monkeys from high in the branches, orchestrated by the insistent noise of cicadas and chirping of crickets.

The kite hawk high above suddenly changed the pattern of its flight and with wings tipped it began a slow glide following the curves of the road. The bird's piercing eyes had spotted movement, the unfamiliar shape of humans.

Furtive figures clad in dingy green and khaki flitted to and fro across the road's dusty surface to disappear within the mantle of the secondary growth of the forest's perimeter. Communist terrorists were setting an ambush!

The bird soon lost interest, and drawn by a rapid thermal began to climb again, disappearing over the top of the pass.

Meanwhile, down in the valley a minute cloud appeared above the trees, its size increasing with every second. The lone car, enveloped in swirling red laterite dust, eventually emerged, carefully taking the winding curves of the road.

Sandy cautiously negotiated the narrow, tight bends, aware that vehicles often hogged the centre of the road; anticipation he knew was the bedfellow of safety!

Climbing now on the final steep gradient the engine began to labour in the hot, humid air as they slowly cleared the last bend to the top of the pass.

Gently Kay touched his arm and turning her face to him said,

'I'm so glad, darling, we had this week in Malacca ... it was heaven being on our own!'

'Yes it was, sweetheart, we'll do it again, I promise.'

Sandy smiled, trying hard not to look at her pretty face but keep his eyes firmly ahead.

'I've always had a soft spot for the place ... now I have good reason!'

He reached across and took her hand in his, giving it a squeeze.

'Love you, sweetheart ... I've never been so happy, I can't wait to tell everyone we're engaged.'

Kay smiled happily as the car began to huff and puff on the sharp ascent causing it to slow down.

In that split second, fate grasped her moment!

Suddenly all around them the air was rent with a long, rattling burst of Bren gun fire, followed by sporadic cracks of rifle.

Kay's face changed from one of happiness to that of abject horror ... she cried out,

'No! ... Sandy! ... darling!' ... and threw her arms around him, causing the car to swerve to the left.

'Quick ... *down* ...!' he commanded.

Lines of dust kicked up by the machine-gun bullets ran across the road in the direction of the vehicle, ricocheting on stones, whining and screaming about them like banshees. Some ripped into the car's canvas roof and blew out the windscreen, others burst the front inside tyre causing the car to continue on its erratic course, and overturn with a crunch into the ditch.

Sandy was thrown over Kay's body as she lay, now silent, across the door. Bullets thudded into the underside of the upturned vehicle – a searing pain shot through him as something hit him in the back!

Grimacing he leaned over her, struggling with the door latch. Suddenly it gave way, spilling them into the deep, overgrown, monsoon drain, just as the radiator burst in erupting torrents of steam.

The smell of petrol fumes focused Sandy's subconscious to get clear before it blew up! Instinctively he dragged her senseless body uphill, struggling beneath the tangled canopy of undergrowth covering the drain. He prayed he would find a culvert under the road to hide in out of sight and danger!

Shots echoed and rebounded across the hills and jungle edge awakening its inhabitants and causing flights of birds to rocket into the air. Guttural commands in Chinese echoed across the road controlling the attackers' fire towards the crashed vehicle.

Sandy battled on, determined to find the culvert which he knew must be there; they were needed at intervals to channel monsoon water off the road, reducing the erosion of its surface.

Oblivious to the inherent danger of the drain's inhabitants he harnessed his diminishing strength, dragging Kay inch by inch over the rough ground until he found his goal. He pushed her unconscious form into the culvert and collapsed at the entrance. At that same moment the car burst into flames and the firing ceased, the assailants holding back, gloating over the spectacle.

A minute or two later, fire from the engine compartment ran along the ground, sniffing its way towards the petrol leaking from the tank. It ignited, erupting like a furnace, black plumes of smoke billowing into the sky.

The onlookers waited, like vultures, for the eventual explosion which reverberated across the hills making small monkeys on the jungle perimeter scream with fright.

Fragments of the car were strewn about the area so the perpetrators made no effort to hunt for their quarry or look for booty, assuming there would be none!

On a bugle note they quickly regrouped, and in single file slunk back out of sight under cover of the jungle, with self congratulations on the achievement of their plan, without casualties to themselves.

Just over the summit of the pass the sound of heavy gunfire and the accompanying explosion had been heard by an Army convoy proceeding to Malacca. The Commander halted, quickly despatching the Scout car with a Sergeant to forge ahead and investigate.

Arriving on the scene he found the still burning remnants of a vehicle and nearby undergrowth, and radioed back to the convoy which continued its approach.

The Sergeant instructed one of his crew to climb into the drain and investigate further; traces of blood were found. The soldier followed the bright red trail and discovered a short distance away, slumped over the entrance of a culvert, the body of a man with a bullet in his back, and on searching further within, a woman covered in leeches.

They were both unconscious and in a critical condition. The woman had been hit a number of times and was bleeding profusely. The man also had lost a lot of blood from the gunshot wound in his badly burnt back. With great care they were extricated from the drain and given emergency treatment by the medical orderlies who'd arrived in an ambulance with the convoy.

The Commander reported the incident to Joint Operations, Police HQ Malacca who, in turn, alerted the hospital to receive the casualties.

Meanwhile in Segamat, Tam Mactavish was eagerly awaiting the arrival of his weekend guests when the telephone rang. It was Clive Thurgood, the weekend Duty Officer, with some disturbing news.

'Mac – I've got some bad news for you, old chap.'

'Damn! What now?'

'Gurkhas on a routine patrol in the Labis area came across a burnt out Police Land Rover on the Buket Kepong plantation road ... casualties were ... a Police Lieutenant ... a driver and three escorts ... no survivers ... the Lieutenant's body was recovered from the bonnet of the burnt out vehicle.

'The bodies are now on their way to the Segamat Hospital mortuary ... a follow-up operation has been instigated ... investigations are being carried out ...'

'Bloody hell! Clive, this is dreadful. The Lieutenant? There's two down there now ...!'

'Bob Sutcliffe ...!' Clive answered tersely.

'Oh my God ...! not Bob ... no! How the hell did it happen ...?'

'Not sure yet ... except it looked like a double ambush ...'

Mac closed his eyes and murmured,

'Dear God ... hope the poor blighter was dead when they put him on the bonnet ...'

'Mac! you there ...?' Clive's insistent voice broke into his thoughts.

'Yes, Clive ... just wondering how I'm going to break the news to Sandy this afternoon ... he's been on leave in Malacca with his lady friend and they're coming here overnight on their way back ...'

'Rather you than me, old chap ... I'll keep you informed ... must dash ...!'

With a mounting feeling of doom Mac put down the receiver. His weekend with Sandy and Kay had briefly pivoted him away from the action and now he began to feel apprehensive about their safety in coming to Segamat.

Rising from his chair he paced up and down the veranda in agitation. He went into the double room he'd had prepared for them to check again that the amah had everything ready ...

Brr ... brr ... brr ... brrrr ... the insistent, strident, ring of the telephone brought him back to reality and he raced back to the living room.

'Yes! ... oh ... Clive, it's you again ...'

'Yes, look ... old chap ... got ... some dreadful news for you ... there's been another ambush ...'

'Merciful God ... who?'

'Not in our parish ... in Muar's ... it's ... Eh ... it's Sandy ... and a lady passenger!'

'Oh dear Lord ... Clive ... are they alive?'

'Yes ... but critically wounded ... the woman's not expected to survive. Mac, I'm in the process of being relieved. I'll come over to you and give you all the details ... OK ...?'

'Yes, I need to know everything ... don't for heaven's sake be long, Clive ...!'

'Right ho ... hang in there!'

Mac stumbled in a daze, his world collapsing around him. He staggered blindly across the room to the sideboard and poured himself a stiff whisky. He tossed it off, poured another and took it out to the veranda where he sat down to wait for Clive.

Within minutes and true to his promise Clive arrived. Preoccupied with the day's major incidents his entry was heralded by a squeal of brakes.

'Bad business Mac ... Sandy of *all* people ... and the girl ...!'

'Aye and ... ah blame m'self ...! ah should never have asked them to break their journey an' come here!'

He sat hunched up, a sad figure, his hands covering his striken face. As he spoke the tears ran down his cheeks.

'The pair of them ... Sandy and his lass ... have just got engaged!'

'Get yourself a whisky, lad, and tell me all you know ...'

'Thanks, old chap ... I could certainly do with one ... it's been a bloody awful day.'

He returned with a half tumbler of Scotch clenched in his fist and plonked himself down in a chair next to Tam.

'They're both in the Malacca hospital ... Sandy came to and identified himself and the girl; she's a nursing sister from the Singapore General ...'

'Aye ...!'

Mac, desperate, nodded his head.

'Ah knew that ... ah met her last weekend in Malacca ... lovely girl ... and they were so *happy* ... y'know just before ah left they told me they were engaged ...'.

He paused picked up his whisky and swallowed long and hard. Clive waited patiently, feeling there was more to come.

'D'you know, Clive ...'

His speech was beginning to slur.

'Sandy asked me to be his besh man ... ah felt honoured ... honoured! ... ah'll have to go and see if there's anything ah can do! Now ... fill this up for me, there'sh a good lad, an' get another for y'self and fill me in!'

Clive took the glasses and called from the other room.

'Don't know all the details of the ambush but apparently the Army came on the scene from over the pass and found the burnt-out wreck of Sandy's car ... a thorough investigation of a monsoon drain found Sandy lying unconscious over a culvert ... and the woman was found further in ... at that point they'd not been identified ... and as the convoy was *en route* to Malacca and it was the nearest hospital, they carried on ...'

Mac stared ahead.

'It was a little later, after the Army had left, that Sandy regained consciousness and identified himself and his passenger ... that's all I know ... except they're both critical!'

Suddenly Mac changed gear, his operational experience taking over.

'Now listen ... what action have you taken, Clive?'

'Well ... I've passed the information on to the Duty Officer, HQ Johore Baharu; he'll notify the Singapore General Hospital with regards the Sister ... there's nothing for us to do here – other than make personal contact with the Malacca Hospital to let Sandy know we're there for him!'

'Aye ...! ah'll speak to the Gaffer and ask for some time off an' go to Malacca an' see what ah can do ...!'

'Well, Mac, I'd advise you to do it now and get it over with ... and I'll arrange an escort to take you there in the morning ... the Gaffer's in the picture so there should be no difficulty in you going for as long as it takes.'

'Right ... ah'll do that ... by the way any more info on the other ambush?'

'Yes, the first report was correct, it was a double! Evidence indicates that Bob drove through, dismounted, then attacked the position that had fired on him first ... he and his escort were killed in the crossfire from a second position ... the bastards then picked up his body and put it onto the Land Rover which they set on fire!'

The last words he spat with venom, his face flushed.

Mac was ashen faced.

'I'll never be able to tell Sandy ... it'd kill him ... he's got enough on his plate ... I just can't, I couldn't do that to him, and ... you must promise, Clive ... say nothing ...!'

'Wouldn't dream of it, I agree with you Mac ... now pick up that 'phone and speak to the Gaffer, before I leave!'

John Thwaites the OSPC Segamat had anticipated the call from Mac and was deeply sympathetic, immediately agreeing that he should go, and giving him *carte blanche* as to his return.

Finishing his call Mac turned to Clive.

'It's on! I can go in the morning ... hell's teeth, I've forgotten about *Bob's* funeral ...!'

'Don't worry, Mac, he's being taken to JB tomorrow and it's all arranged for Kranji Monday morning ... the Gaffer will be representing us there!'

'Good ... I'll accept that offer of an escort ... I'll need my car to get about ... 07.00 hrs. all right?'

'Yes, Mac – and I advise you to have no more to drink and have an early night!'

'Ach, you're a good lad, Clive, ah'll just do that ...! my thanks.'

Mac's night was fretful and he woke early the next morning.

The escort arrived and *en route* they came upon the scene of the ambush. A sward of blackened ground and burnt undergrowth, with scattered pieces of twisted metal strewn around, was all that remained of Sandy's Morris tourer.

Mac stopped, the escort dismounted and took up strategic positions whilst he rummaged around, searching.

He marvelled that Sandy and Kay hadn't perished in the attack! There was absolutely no doubt in his mind that the car had careered in the right direction, away from the attackers and towards the monsoon drain, which only now was visible because of the burnt-out undergrowth.

Mac held his breath, then with an involuntary gush expelled it in sheer despair.

'Sandy, laddie, you've had Lady Luck on your side ending up here ...'

He noticed the dark patches of congealed blood at the bottom of the drain and shook his head in wonder at how they ended up at the entrance to the culvert. He shuddered, scanned the landscape, imagining the positions the terrorists had fired from.

'You must have kept your head, laddie, to get out of this ... dear Lord, let them get through this ordeal ...!'

He brought himself back to reality and the waiting escort. The journey must be resumed.

On arrival at the outskirts of Malacca he pulled up, thanked the men for their protection then dismissed them, and drove to the hospital with a feeling of trepidation growing within him.

At reception he identified himself as a fellow officer and friend of the injured DSP, and asked about his condition and that of his fiancée Sister Sutherland. He was told his colleague was comfortable, but heavily sedated and not in a condition to receive visitors just yet.

Kay was another matter! She had not recovered consciousness and was in the hospital's Intensive Care Unit. The duty Sister advised him to return in the evening, when he could perhaps see Sandy for a short while, but said that because Kay's condition was critical it would be inadvisable for her to receive visitors.

'We are extremely concerned about Sister Sutherland's condition, Mr Mactavish; I'm sorry – she may not pull through, we must be patient ... and pray!'

Tam left with a heavy heart. Of all the times for things to go wrong! Sandy would be devastated about Kay.

He prayed.

'Ah hope the good Lord helps her make it.'

Mactavish then returned to the Rest House where only a short time ago he'd had such fun with Sandy and Kay. Out here life was certainly no bowl of cherries!

At 5 o'clock, restless, he took his leave and on arrival at the hospital was requested to provided the Registrar with details of Sandy and give what little information he knew about Kay.

'Mr Mactavish, please take a seat.

'I am so sorry about your colleague and his fiancée; the news is not all good, I'm afraid. It is extremely doubtful that Sister Sutherland will survive the night. Her injuries are savage to say the least ... and to be honest with you ... it would be a good idea if you could have ready funeral arrangements, with interment in Malacca ... as a precautionary measure! I appreciate how difficult this will be for you.

'Your friend, Mr MacIntyre will however be OK – eventually that is – but please, when you see him, don't mention the implications of Sister Sutherland's condition – it won't do him any good to learn of this at this stage.'

Mac, his feet like lead, walked along the corridor to Sandy's room, mumbling to himself.

'This is a nightmare, a terrifying, bloody nightmare!'

Sandy, drifting in and out of sleep, only just recognised Mac. He was unable to follow a conversation, which suited the big man's disposition, allowing him to talk a load of drivel, thus avoiding Malacca, their holiday ... and Kay!

Mac drew on his reserves of inner strength. He rang the Singapore General and told the administration what had happened to Kay and of her acute condition. Then he contacted Dinger and Anita through the Singapore Police and informed them of the situation and the likelihood of Kay not surviving ... and made arrangements for her funeral!

Whisky was again his solace that evening!

Numb, he returned to the hospital the following morning to be told that Kay had died in the night, without regaining consciousness.

He choked back tears. Sandy mustn't be told ... yet! He swallowed hard and walked along the corridor to see him.

Kay's funeral was attended by a fellow Sister from Singapore General,

Dinger and Anita and himself. Small consolation though it was, they all knew that it would have been Sandy's wish that she be buried in the place where they had found such happiness. Sandy's wounds did recover, of course ... all except one!

He departed for the UK on convalescent leave travelling on the *Chusan* and didn't return. Mac and Dinger saw him off, promising to keep in touch, but Dinger's appointment with the Singapore Police was not renewed and Sandy lost all contact with him and Anita.

Sandy was later offered an appointment with the Nigerian Police, which he accepted, and Mactavish did catch up with him when they served again in another area of conflict.

The End

Glossary

ada baik, Malay	all right
ahlan wa sahlan! eiltak sa'ida! a fandi! Arabic	welcome, good evening, Sir!
al-hamdu lillahi, Hausa, Nigeria	the praise (be) to God
amah, Malay	a female servant
apa, Malay	what?
apa nama, Malay	your name?
ayer panas, Malay	hot water
bature, Hausa, Nigeria	white man / Sir / form of address
baik, Malay	good
bandits, English	colloquial for terrorist
belukar, Malay	brushwood, secondary growth
CT, Cts, English	communist terrorist(s)
dhobi, Urdu	washing, laundry, laundry man
dua stengah, Malay	two whiskies and soda
duba, Hausa, Nigeria	look
giwa, Hausa, Nigeria	elephant
GSO	General Staff Officer, 3, 2, 1, (Captain, Major, Lieutenant Colonel)
haji, Arabic	made the pilgrimage to Mecca
kampong, Malay	village
Konsi, Chinese	Business (house) (work force)
kamu darimana datang, Malay	where do you come from?
lalang, Malay	long grass
madala, Hausa, Nigeria	splendid
makan sudah siap, Malay	the meal is ready
Ma Hla Shwe, Burmese	*literally* – Miss Pretty Gold (en)
memsahib, Urdu	title of address to European lady
Mimosa pudica, Latin	Humble plant – low growing, touch sensitive tropical plant

181

motokar ada dimuka rumah, Malay	the car is in the front of the house
Nama saya ... Malay	My name is ...
padang, Malay	open space, village green
rakit, Malay	raft made of bundled bamboo
sahib, Urdu	Sir, title of address to European
sangar, Indian	fortification, pillbox, sentry post
selamat hari, Malay	good day
selamat malam, Malay	good night
selamat pagi, Malay	good morning
selamat pertang, Malay	good evening
selamat tingah-hari, Malay	good afternoon
selamat tuan, Malay	greetings, Sir
selamat jalan, Malay	greetings on passing (on the way)
selamat datang tuan! Malay	greetings Sir (on arriving)
selamat tinggal! Malay	goodbye
siapa nama anda? Malay	What is your name?
Sitrep	*literally short for Situation Report*
sungai, Malay	river
tabek, Malay	greeting
terima kaseh, Malay	thank you
tida'apa, Malay	it doesn't matter
towkay, Chinese	Chinese shopkeeper, boss
tuan, Malay	Sir, title for a European gentleman
tuan besar, Malay	great, large, big
tuan mau makan seka-rang? Malay	do you want to eat now?
U Aung Bo, Burmese	Mr Successful Leader
ulu = hulu, Malay	up river, upper course of river
walla, wallah, Anglo-Indian	colloquial term, man, person
ya, Allah, Tuhan!, Malay	O God! = yes
yum sing! Hong Kong Chinese	lit: bottoms up, cheers (Renamed)